FA CONFIDENTIAL

Riko Radojcic

The Bout of the Century

t-0 = November of an Election Year, Washington DC

As they say, big things often do have small beginnings.

Aside from choosing to sit indoors rather than occupying one of the tables on the sidewalk, neither participant at this meeting was particularly notable; both appeared to be polished professionals—the type who ran government bureaucracy and who were ubiquitous in this town.

One was a middle-aged woman, neither tall nor short. She was neither fat nor skinny. She was neither particularly attractive nor unattractive. Her brown hair featured the usual professional bob but showed no attempt to hide emerging streaks of gray. She was dressed in a typical business suit: light-colored blouse, navy blazer, gray skirt and sensible pumps. At first glance something about her conveyed a sense of quiet competence. Perhaps it was her stern expression, or her erect posture, or the lack of any jewelry other than a practical wristwatch. Juxtaposed to her unassuming persona were her striking, dark green eyes; they shone with intelligence and vigor, or perhaps amusement at the world around her, and conveyed the impression that there was a lot more going on inside her head than one might first suppose.

The man, somewhat older, had a bit of a pot belly and long white hair. He wore faded jeans and a pullover under his corduroy jacket. An overcoat was tossed in a heap on the chair beside him.

At the time of the meeting, the Quill Bar and Grill—one of hundreds of 'watering holes' within walking distance from the principle seats of power in Washington DC—was still fairly deserted. A couple of lonely drinkers perched on the bar stools indoors, and a few hardier souls sitting outside. In normal times, government offices would still be open and buzzing with activity at this early afternoon hour, and the bar would be relatively quiet; but by sunset, the offices would be spewing worker bees who would then congregate at such establishments. These days, however, now nine months into the Covid-19 pandemic, and with all the disruptions and lockdowns, the tavern might remain deserted even past standard government working hours—this despite the implementation of the so-called Phase 2 restrictions which allowed up to fifty percent indoor occupancy.

Obviously, a tavern like The Quill was not a venue for top-secret meetings that would be required for the kind of leaks that made it to the front page of *New York Times* or *Washington Post*, but it was sufficiently discrete for run-of-the-mill informal meetings and other off-the-grid exchanges. 'Officials who wished to remain anonymous', or even 'unnamed but well-placed senior sources' could meet trusted contacts over a drink or two and provide 'authorized' and/or 'unauthorized' leaks and gossip that fueled the media and the political machine of the United States of America.

After the waitress had brought their drinks—a glass of red wine and a steaming mug of bourbon-spiked hot cider—the woman cleared her throat and repeated, "Professor, thank you for agreeing to meet me. I appreciate it."

In spite of numerous invitations to do so, she had never felt comfortable addressing the older gentlemen by his first name, and preferred using titles such as: 'Mr. Consul' or 'Mr. Ambassador' or 'Mr. Under Secretary', or 'Mr. Deputy Secretary', or, lately, 'Professor'...

"Oh Jane, when someone rumored to be on the short list for appointment as the next National Security Adviser calls, of course you come running, pandemic or not," he responded. "Congratulations! The first woman National Security Adviser. What a fantastic achievement, Jane! I am very proud of you. *This* President has picked the right...*man*." He smirked at his own joke.

"No comment," she muttered with a satisfied smile that seemed to confirm the rumor.

Now that the election results have been called, the town was a veritable hive of whispers about postings and assignments with the new administration. Who was in and who was out, in which department and in what position. The ever-present professional civil servants and career government officials, as opposed to the ephemeral political creatures, were agog with excitement. They were confident that the chaos and lunacy of the previous administration had come to a close, and that a sense of normalcy would soon return. Hopeful that many among their ranks would be re-instated to their old positions, or even assigned to some better higher-level posts, they felt vindicated and eager to settle the score.

"Are you sure that you do not want to join us? You mentioned on the phone…"

"Definitely not," said the older man, holding up his hands in a defensive gesture. "I am lucky; I can afford to remain an academic. These days I prefer teaching, and don't miss Foggy Bottom at all. Maybe in a year or two I will retire and write a book. No, this old horse is done with the wars of Washington. I just don't have the energy, or the will, for another tour of duty."

"That is a pity. We need people like you—now more than ever—to clean up the mess that the last administration has left behind all over the world, but especially with China. Your area, Professor…"

They fell silent and turned to their drinks. Professor Bartholomew Harriman, a distant relative of the more famous Averell Harriman, tentatively drew a sip from his mug to make sure that he would not burn his lips, while Jane Mary Stewart, the woman, inhaled deeply the rich aroma of her Petite Syrah.

"I always valued your wise words and will miss you not only on a personal level," Jane conveyed, "but I also feel that it is a loss to the country. I really appreciate and admire all your contributions. In fact, I believe that the white paper you did on China back in the early 80s was a seminal position paper. In my opinion, in terms of its historic significance, it is right up there with George Keenan's X-Article."

"Oh Jane, thank you. That means a lot to me, regardless if it is deserved or not. But objectively speaking, 'Using the Open Door Policy to Co-Opt the Communist Party of China'—the white paper to which I think you are referring—was never published and was therefore not nearly as influential as the X Article," Bartholomew—Bart to his friends—protested.

"Maybe so," Jane continued, "but enough of us have read it, and truth-be-told, with your ever-so-subtle prodding, the country has consistently followed its recommendations through five presidencies. More than thirty years—nearly as long as it followed the Containment Policy against USSR. That is, of course, until our previous president came into office, and, well, fucked it all up, pardon my language. And that in spite of the fact that everything that your paper predicted was coming true…"

Well, yeah, I guess," Bart squirmed a bit, somewhat embarrassed by his protégé's overt compliments, "but it was obvious, I think."

"Only with 20:20 hindsight," Jane retorted. "Proposing that we follow a two-pronged approach with China—open borders and trade on one hand and tight control on the technology exports on the other—to eventually co-opt the CPC was downright farsighted back in 1982. It was a profound policy for converting China into just another trading nation and avoiding military conflict. And, dammit, it was working." Jane emphatically slapped the table to emphasize her point, and a flash in her green eyes betrayed how strongly she felt about it. "Over the last few decades western trade and investments encouraged by the successive US governments lifted its population out of abject poverty. Its middle class exploded and was developing a taste for further economic and political freedoms. Unlike the previous generation that was brought up to believe that Imperialist America was the enemy, the new generation looked favorably on us and adopted many of our ways. People were travelling abroad and sending their kids to be educated in the West. Many of their companies raised capital by listing on western exchanges. The Chinese economy, even including State-Owned Enterprises, was increasingly intertwined with the rest of the world. The CPC had its wings clipped, and it was gradually becoming more liberal. They allowed—even embraced—market economy and became accustomed to routinely changing the Chairman every ten years. Altogether, China had joined the world order and was becoming a normal country…" Jane elaborated, as if to convince Bart that she really did get it. "Your policy was working!"

Bart shrugged and lamented, "Too late now."

"You think so?" Jane asked, earnestly leaning forward. "In fact, which is exactly what I wanted to talk to you about. Do you—the author of the original policy—really believe that it is beyond salvaging?"

Bart considered the question. Partially to project an impression that he was giving it serious thought despite having a ready answer—a habit he has acquired long ago in the diplomatic service, partially to ensure that he phrased the answer in a way that filtered out, or at least muted, his anger and disappointments with the developments over the last few years, and partially to enjoy another warming swig of his spiked cider. "Yes, I am afraid that I do. I believe that the last president's jingoism has unwittingly, but perhaps not surprisingly, provoked a lot of nationalistic feelings in China. The Chinese, and especially the mainland Han Chinese, have a strong sense of cultural heritage. As it was, they were prone to a feeling that the rest of the world did not give them the respect that they were due—the kind of respect that they always felt that the largest ethnic group on the planet with more than 5,000 years of continuous history deserved... Arguably, rightly so given the indignity of how they were treated by westerners over the last few hundred years, and the suffering that foreigners, or foreign-inspired ideas, brought to them during the twentieth century."

He paused there and conducted an internal audit of his emotions, a habit from his days as a diplomat, and then carried on in the same measured tone. "The Chinese do not take kindly to losing face."

Professor Harriman, fluent in Mandarin and Cantonese since his student days, was demonstrating the kinds of deep insights that he had accumulated through a life-long habit of spending a few hours every day tracking events in China; reading newspapers, magazines and books when he started, and nowadays following the legal, and maybe not-so-legal web sites and blogs.

Knowing the professor, Jane remained quiet to allow him to finish his exposition.

"And I believe that Chairman Xi and the CPC have been very clever in exploiting that surge of nationalism. The CPC is riding a wave of resurgence, and the government is pursuing all sorts of

5

policies which would have been unlikely before that nationalism was provoked. They have 'clipped the wings'—to use your phrase—of their capitalist and billionaire class, and are re-instituting party control over much of the so-called free-market sector. They are reining in many of the companies that have become overly visible. The critics of the party and the government are pursued and silenced with renewed vigor. Xi will stay on for at least one more term and is championing a renewed drive for ideological purity. These are insidious changes, but they are readily accepted by a population whose national pride has been hurt. And most alarming, the government's investments in a modernized military are popular. Guns-before-Butter politics always resonates well with hurt national pride. The stuff going on in Hong Kong and the South China Sea and to some extent in Xinjiang and Tibet are all quite illustrative of that resurgence. Tips of the proverbial iceberg…"

"Exactly," Jane interjected, nodding emphatically, "but do you think that there is anything we can do to turn back the tide?"

"No, I don't think so. Rolling back some of the western values—personal and corporate liberties—were the low hanging fruit for the party. These moves were popular with the masses, particularly when couched in terms of anti-corruption drives. And the CPC really did play its cards very well. Especially now, given how well the government is perceived to have handled the pandemic. Very much in contrast to the epic failures that our own president managed… At this stage there is nothing that we can do to affect the perceptions of the general populace, or the way CPC manages their challenges. Our president played the role of 'the ugly American' very well, and blew all the 'political capital' that we had accumulated over the last few decades."

"So you really don't think that there is anything constructive that we can do?"

"I did not say that. There is a lot that we can and must do. There is nothing that we can do to prevent further decoupling between the US and China. Thanks to the last president's boorishness it is too late for that—but there is a lot we can do to give future presidents some options."

"What options?"

"Well, the Chinese government and the CPC do face some

formidable challenges: demographic issues, climate change, the difficulty in maintaining the economic growth rate... So, I believe that when they face a snag of some kind—as they inevitably will—the leadership will play the nationalism card. If I were the CPC and facing internal issues, I too would fan the nationalistic flames. Truth be told, that is quite an old trick that has been used by many. And in China the easiest way to do that is Taiwan. The people of China generally do believe that Taiwan is theirs, and genuinely do support a policy of unification. I suppose they would call it 'liberation'. So, if I were the CPC facing popular discontent, or God forbid, if I were some kind of a firebrand ultranationalist zealot who had ambitions to lead the party, I would stir up the Taiwanese independence issue. The people would all line up behind me and forget about whatever was bothering them. If – or when – that happens, the way things are today, any US president would have absolutely no other choice but to order the Seventh fleet into the Straits of Taiwan, and boom! We could very well have a shooting war."

Without realizing how prophetic his words would be, Bart stopped there. But then, probably in reaction to Jane's stolid facial expression, he decided that further elaboration was merited to drive home his point. "The way things are now, we do have vital interest in Taiwan, and all national security considerations—not to mention harsh economic realities—would dictate that we must keep it independent and away from China. I would say that as things stand now the probability of some kind of armed conflict with China is increasing. Two out of three game theory studies modeling various what-if-scenarios for the next thirty to forty years end up in a confrontation. And if and when there is a conflict, the probability of it being fought over Taiwan is more like ninety percent!"

"So, you think that we are heading towards a war with China and that there is nothing that we can do to avoid it?" Jane pressed.

"No, I did not say that either. The Chinese care about kitchen table issues as much as anybody else and have no more wish to fight a war with their best customer than any sane businessman would. Normally, I would say that the way to avoid a war is to increase mutual interdependence. More trade. If your objective is to avoid a war, then trade-killing tariffs is the worst possible thing to do. But that monumental mistake has already been made... And now, I believe that reversing those tariffs is politically unpalatable to our new president, and hence that possibility is low to nonexistent. On the other hand, to be fair, the probability of China allowing itself to again become economically dependent on the US, or to again permit western liberalism to creep into their society, is equally nonexistent... So, tariffs or no tariffs, economic barriers and a drive for technological and ideological independence are inevitable on both sides."

"What do you think we should do?"

"The one thing that we can and absolutely must do is give the Commander in Chief some latitude. Once you do take that job and move into the West Wing, that should be your primary, and probably the most urgent, task. It does not take a rocket scientist to figure out that US vital interests in Taiwan are all about semiconductors. There is no doubt that if the supply of chips from Taiwan were to be cut off, then our economy would grind to a halt. Imagine our world with no new phones, new TVs, new cars, new games or computers—on your lap or in the cloud! Our digital way of life would collapse and overnight we would be forced back to a 1950s-type of economy. All electronic gizmos built today have chips that are manufactured in Taiwan. Designed here in the US but manufactured in Taiwan. The recent shortages of cars caused by restrictions in the supply of chips only serve to illustrate that point. Semiconductor supply chains all lead to Taiwan first, and Korea second, which leaves the US quite vulnerable. Even if the military did have an ample store of the chips, they need for modern weaponry squirreled away somewhere, our national security would be extremely compromised. So, the best thing that we can do now that globalization is dead or dying is to ensure our independence from Taiwan. The only way that POTUS—any responsible POTUS—would have any degree of freedom in deciding whether to engage China in a shooting war over Taiwan is to on-shore the semiconductor supply chain and to repatriate the most advanced manufacturing facilities. Otherwise, he or she would have no choice."

Jane fell silent.

"So, the way I see it," the professor concluded, "today there are just two realistic options. Either we invest in onshoring semiconductor manufacturing to loosen our dependence on Taiwan, or we invest even more money in a lot more weapons to make sure that we win the coming confrontation over Taiwan. No third way..."

Somber faced, Jane nodded.

"In my opinion doing nothing is like sitting on the proverbial speeding train heading toward an abyss," Bart added, to amplify the urgency.

"Not a pretty picture..."

They retreated into their drinks as Jane internalized the lecture and Bart considered whether there were additional points he should make.

"You know, Professor, I was thinking much along the same lines. Perhaps that might not be surprising, since I am supposed to be your *disciple*," Jane said, sarcastically alluding to the label that some in the press had given her. "But these are not exactly what you could call *happy thoughts*."

Bart's eyes were concerned and maybe filled with sympathy because he knew how difficult was the job that she was about to take on. "Good luck talking your new boss, and Congress, into spending money on this—especially now that the government is bleeding liquidity into our pandemic-stricken economy! You will need something like one hundred billion in tax breaks and direct incentives, preferably to be allocated over the next couple of fiscal years. I understand that those advanced semiconductor facilities cost something like ten or twenty billion dollars a pop, and to achieve that independence from Taiwan, you will need more than one. Plus funding to bootstrap Engineering and Technology R&D. So..." Bart trailed off and drained his mug. "And in the subsequent years you will need not just perseverance and executive orders, or even fear mongering or moral high ground," he hurriedly added to make sure that Jane understood the magnitude, "but more cash. The semiconductor industry has got religion now, so to speak. This soon after the disruptions of the pandemic they are all very supportive of on-shoring chip manufacturing. But give them a year or two and they will revert to their base instincts: pursuit of high profits and low risks. You will need to make sure that the home-grown facilities are competitive and at least as good as those in Taiwan… A tall order, I am told."

"Thanks for the encouraging words," Jane said sarcastically.

"Well," Bart was on a roll now, past trying to be politically correct, "you know how Corporate America is. Any snag or hiccup and they will revert to their old ways—back to the suppliers and the relationships that they trust to bring them the maximum profits. It will not be easy to keep them on track just for so-called 'greater good' reasons. You will need some sweeteners down the road to convince the industry to retool and then to stick with a new all-American supply chain through the inevitable bumps. And to convince their lobbyists to keep those whores in Senate on your side…"

Jane perked up a bit and asked, "May I tap your brain some more on topics like this? Like now? I hope that would be okay…"

"Sure…of course," Bart acquiesced slowly, but looked hesitant. "Especially if you are buying the drinks," he added to lighten the mood that was turning somber.

"Maybe I can share some of the recent CIA reports. Quite illustrative, I thought. You have the clearance, of course?"

"Actually, no… I let mine lapse and am now just under standard non-disclosure orders. So please do not tell me anything that is too sensitive."

"Hmm, I think I should be able to fix that."

"No, no, no. That is a slippery slope," Bart protested. "Please, Jane, understand: I do not want security clearance. If I got it I would soon get sucked – or suckered – into the Foggy Bottom whirlwind. No thanks!"

Jane looked a bit sullen and just nodded her understanding. "So, I am on my own?" She threw a couple of twenties on the table and reached for her overcoat. "On that depressing note, I am afraid I must go."

"Thanks, Jane," Bart nodded toward the cash. "And good luck! Happy to help as much as I can—but on an informal basis only— just as a tired old prof…" He repeated, "Good luck!"

t-0 + 7 months, Washington DC

"Congratulations, Jane! Job well done! Now, I suggest a day or two off to celebrate and to catch your breath. Take it from an old man, don't ask for permission and just do it!"

Jane listened to the message that the professor had left with a smug smile. Yes, it had been quite a slog, but now it was done. The funding for those on-shore semiconductor manufacturing facilities had just been approved by the Senate. Fingers crossed, the House would not be a problem. As for a day off: no way! There was a new government in Israel, a new president in Peru, and the mess in Afghanistan was ongoing. Jane Stewart was not one who permitted herself to rest upon her laurels.

"*Janet Marion Stewart, do not brag. It is unbecoming.*" Her mother's stern voice still rang in her ears. For some reason, her mother often used the longer version of her names whenever she was chastising her, even though her Birth Certificate identified her just as 'Jane' and 'Mary'.

Her father had been killed in a car accident when she was very young, so Jane was brought up by a single mom who coped with the challenges of bringing up three girls on a teacher's salary mostly by becoming a taskmaster who was never quite satisfied. Recalling some of the events from that time in her life still brought up a familiar knot-in-the-belly anxiety to Jane. Like the time when she told her mom—perhaps boasted—that she finished her sophomore year with second highest score in school history. She was amped up and excited, feeling proud and even elated. Mom's response, with a slight tilt of her head away from her work: 'Who was first'? That incident had burrowed deep into Jane's psyche, and she never could quite shake the feeling that she was a

11

disappointment. Perhaps some of those memories were amplified by the passage of time. Or perhaps her mom was right, and she was just feeling sorry for herself. Still, she had no fond memories of a cozy home life when she was growing up and consequently felt no nostalgia for her youth.

Early in her teen years she realized that for her the only way out of that dismal sense of being a 'disappointment'—as well as the gray New England working class neighborhood where they lived—was through education, not through daydreams of Prince Charming, or the miracle of being discovered as a special talent, or whatever other fantasies girls of her age might entertain. No, she knew that for her the ticket to freedom was through a good job, which only came after a good education. She knew that she had to stand on her own two feet, and that she could achieve her independence only through hard work.

She aced her high school grades and scored exemplary SAT results, which won her a full scholarship at Boston University. The scholarship, augmented by income from part-time hostess jobs plus summertime jobs in Nantucket, put her through school. She earned a BA in Political Science and followed that up with a JD degree, supplementing further scholarships with income from intern positions. Instead of embarking on a career in law, she'd decided that she wanted even more academic experience, and pursued an MA degree in Global, International, and Comparative History from Georgetown. As a part of that course of study she'd secured a position at the State Department, which set her on the path that she'd pursued as her career. The Internship became a full-time position, and she rose through the ranks and even attained a series of foreign postings: Bangladesh, India, Uganda, New Zealand…

And it was there that she'd met Dr. Bartholomew Harriman, who became her mentor and helped to shape not only her career, but also her world view. Even in young middle age she had achieved a lofty status in her professional life through hard work and competence, and the tagline that the media always seemed to attach to her name: 'the first female National Security Adviser', was her crowning achievement to date.

In her personal life, however, Jane was not so fortunate. Of course, she had relationships and even proposals, but for her these always came second to her career. During her thirties she had come to realize that the best solution for her were long-distance relationships. Those seemed to fulfill her emotional needs and gave her romance and occasional sex, but they never got in the way of her work life. With that type of arrangement she was able to travel and experience many of the positive aspects of a relationship, but it was always transitory, and when those long weekends were over she returned, satisfied, to her everyday life. The way she saw it, the only real reason to have a more intimate and permanent relationship—both in fact as well as in form—was to provide a stable home for a child. But she worried that she might ultimately be her mother's daughter and that she did not have it in her to give the kind of nurturing that every child deserved to have. Besides, she was busy—ever more so as she climbed the organizational ladder in the State Department. Nowadays, with her White House position, even the little time that those remote affairs required was unaffordable.

As she matured, she also tried to build an adult-to-adult relationship with her mother and made an effort to visit on a regular basis and even to spend the holidays with her. She came to appreciate that her mother had had a tough time bringing her and her two sisters up alone, and made an honest attempt to view her childhood through her mother's eyes, with more sympathy and understanding. However, sometime around then—around the time when she was visiting her then man-friend in London—an ad 'on the telly' for *Irn-Bru* soda caught her attention. Probably because of its tagline: *Made in Scotland from girders.* She was intrigued—perhaps amused—by the concept of people attracted to a soda that advertised itself as being made of scrap iron. But she also thought that it was a very apt description for her mother. Not just because mother was of Scottish origins, but because the tagline really suited her: tough, inflexible, cold, covered in rust; *made of girders*. So, in her mind she came to refer to her mother as 'Iron Brew' and had lately even started using it to mother's face, making sure to roll the 'r' in a proper Scottish accent.

Jane Stewart, the twenty-eighth National Security Adviser to the President of the United States, shook her head and forced herself to stop staring out of the window and to return to the

13

here-and-now—which at that point in time meant the pile of papers in her in basket. She hung up the phone, deleted the message from the professor, and proceeded to scan the daily papers and the prominent news sites. But she did admire the headline in the *Washington Post* that announced the passage of the CHIPS (Creating Helpful Incentives to Produce Semiconductors) Act by the Senate. She—and the professor—knew this to be *her* accomplishment.

In the Red Corner: Argon Zhi

t-0 + 8 months, Hsinchu, Taiwan

After spending a major part of his weekend trudging through the forest looking for a snake—a relatively distasteful step in an otherwise exciting side project—Argon was tired and did not feel like going out to dinner. Not even with Cliff, his best friend since childhood.

These days they were both busy and rarely had an opportunity to meet and spend time together—especially the kind of personal time that they used to share when they were children. In those days they could while away the hours daydreaming about the great things that they would accomplish in their lives. Even back then Argon looked up to Cliff, who always liked to play the leader— Cliff was a king and Argon his wise counsel; Cliff was a powerful general and Argon his able adjutant; Cliff was a titan of the industry and Argon his brilliant Nobel-prize winning scientist... Argon recalled fondly their secret hiding hole in the rarely used attic of the apartment building tucked away in a crowded neighborhood of Taipei, where the Lingdao's—Cliff's parents and two siblings— lived. They were safe there from nagging adults, and they could make all their plans to take over the world. They were inseparable all the way through middle and high school, when one had chosen to study Economics while the other chose Engineering and they had gradually grown apart...

"The price of success that they never tell you about," Argon thought ruefully while getting dressed. "I think the gray suit tonight. No tie though... And maybe just the Scholls rather than the Fukudas. Much more comfortable despite the obscene price difference..."

He was not the type of a man who paid much attention to things like clothes, but after his last promotion, Akemi, his wife, had ordered him to come with her to Tokyo, took him to an exclusive tailor in *Ginza* district—comparable to Savile Row in London—and presided over selection of not only his custom made suits but also the off-the-shelf clothes and accessories that now filled his walk-in closet. As if he were a child rather than a sixty-year-old man. But, in matters like these there was no arguing with his '*tai-tai*': a colloquial term for powerful wives of prominent men that he sometimes applied to Akemi, usually with some satisfaction. That shopping spree had cost an eye-watering amount of money, but he had to admit that he did feel good in his new suits. And, as she observed, they could afford it now.

And she was probably also right that Cliff, and the other men in the group, would be wearing equally expensive suits. Not that any of them gave an impression that they noticed such things, since they needed to appear as if it were normal for them. But to people who surrounded them it was like a uniform which was recognized. Akemi understood that the right outfit helped to gain respect and to command authority from the underlings.

The group of men he was meeting with included four others in addition to Cliff and himself. They were people that he knew well—and who knew him equally well. Some, like Cliff, since his childhood; others from university days; still others from when he was at ITRI; some from work. To all appearances it was simply six old friends getting together at a restaurant to have a private dinner. But, although it was never overtly stated, and certainly never talked about, it was known by those within the group that these meetings were about much more than good food and wine and a friendly chat.

Invariably they would begin with polite superficialities—how was the family, health, business, but after a while—usually by the time the soup course was cleared—they would migrate to a more serious topic, which they would then examine and discuss for the rest of the evening. Usually, it was a significant current event, but other times they talked about their perspectives on the future, or circumstances that worried them.

The topic would normally be selected by Cliff, who not only

tended to be the organizer of these events but seemed to have assumed the mantle of a senior member. It had happened without anything formal such as an election or even a conversation. When he chose, Cliff could be one of those affable, back-slapping types that everybody liked—perhaps a skill that he had honed in his position with the government. Without appearing to be doing so, he was masterful at manipulating conversations toward the subjects that he wanted explored, and the group had simply and naturally drifted into a pattern of following his lead. They did not have a formal agenda, or a formal role, or even a name (Argon just thought of them as 'The Group') but it was clear that they had an impact. Truth be told, Argon valued the opportunity to affect strategies and events that were so much larger than himself.

Their dinner conversations would often result in a plan of action—usually by agreement between all six—with tacit but clearly understood action items and target deadlines. Sometimes, when appropriate, their discussion topics would appear a few days later in the form of an op-ed piece in the national newspapers, or as a topic of discussion on a current affairs TV show, or as a press release announcing a new initiative by a notable company or an industry group, or even as a policy statement described by a government spokesman. Usually, but not always, their discussions and the ensuing plans of action would come to fruition in one way or another.

People who espoused conspiracy theories would probably liken The Group to The Illuminati or the Free Masons or some other similar secret society or perhaps a sinister cabal of some kind. The British would maybe compare it to old-boy network of Etonians gathering in a private Gentlemen's Club. Americans might be tempted to think of it as some kind of a blue-ribbon Advisory Panel of Experts, and the Russians could compare it to the *Siloviki* who ran that country. In fact, The Group was a bit of all of those—in the sense that it consisted of a few very well-connected men with influence, who happened to have similar values and thus tended to agree on topics of importance, and who helped to put ideas into practice.

In fact, in Taiwan—a small country that grew up in the shadow of ever-present and ever-threatening Mainland China—informal discussions amongst a select group of men who had personal connections with each other was just how things were done. In Taiwan some things were not written down on paper or formally defined or even talked about. In Taiwan people were trusted because they were known over a lifetime, not because some bureaucratic security check indicated that they were trustworthy.

So, a system based on a network of independent 'cells', where the individuals within a cell were tightly connected by personal bonds of trust, and the cells were loosely connected through a hierarchy that ultimately fed the 'center', made a lot of sense for Taiwan. At least, that is what Argon thought. In truth, he did not know for sure that there was such a system, or if there was, how these cells interacted with each other, and who really controlled it. His suspicions were mostly based on empirical observations of how things happened in Taiwan. He suspected that Cliff may be that link between The Group and the rest of the system, but he never asked directly. He knew that similar systems were used by many underground movements because they tend to be resilient and infiltration-proof. Such a system could never work in communist China, because Mainland China was too big, and because it had a history of party purges that destroyed interpersonal trust; which was precisely why it worked so well for Taiwan, a small country where there were no more than two degrees of separation between people who mattered. And such a system was especially useful in Taiwan because it was difficult for Mainland China and its numerous agents to penetrate. It had worked quite well since the time of Chiang Kai-shek.

Argon did not know, and did not ask, whether his membership in The Group had led to the successes in his professional and business life, or contrarily, whether it was his success that had led to the membership in the group. Whichever was the case, the two went together like hand in glove.

Argon was a Senior Vice President at FSMC—the top semiconductor manufacturer in Taiwan, and lately, in the world. He was in charge of 'Strategic Planning' and had a small team of world-class analysts reporting to him. This position, he suspected, also happened to be convenient for his role with The Group because it did not saddle him with onerous daily deliverables while legitimizing his access to whatever information he wanted without causing undue raising of proverbial eyebrows. Not to mention that it paid very well and carried significant stock option and bonus benefits.

The other members of The Group were all graduates from National Taiwan University, or other prestigious educational establishments, were a part of the Taiwanese upper-middle class and held similarly select positions, but with Foxconn, Asus, ASE, and MediaTech. And Cliff was with the government. When asked he normally described his position as that of a 'technical adviser' to various Ministries, but Argon suspected that in reality Cliff held some high-level position with the National Security Bureau (NSB). He knew better than to ask and believed that Cliff's official title 'Senior Permanent Consultant' was just euphemism intended to hide his real role and that it was probably custom made to bypass the government's salary caps. But he knew that Cliff used to be with the Ministry of Science and Technology and had moved to Defense a while back.

Argon got into his current position only after working for the company for more than twenty years. With his engineering degree from NTU and a PhD from Berkeley in the US, and after a few years at ITRI—the national research institute, he started at FSMC just as an engineer on the production line. But then he worked his way up to group leader, then department manager, and finally product and customer manager until he'd received his current assignment. A few more years and he would be able to retire in comfort, secure in the knowledge that he had accrued sufficient wealth to ensure that he and Akemi, as well as their two children and their families, would be safe and well off. Then he intended to focus on his true passion—music!

"Have you seen that the American Senate has finally managed to agree on something?" Cliff asked almost as in passing.

The main course was served Chinese style at the center of the table, and they all shared the various dishes. After serving the wine, the mute waiters closed the doors to the side room that ensured privacy—obviously critical for their purposes.

"You mean theInnovation and Competition Act? The 52-billion pot of cash that they actually got sixty-eight senators to approve?" someone said.

"Meaning that thirty-two disapproved..."

"Actually, I understand it was a total of 110 billion, with fifty-two for semiconductors and the rest for biotech and quantum computing."

"Hopefully some of us will be able to tap into that pot of gold when—or if—it ever becomes available."

"Do we know the next steps? Presumably, the House will pass it, but the question remains what riders will be tacked on."

"You mean, maybe something like building a fab in West Virginia? Even Conroy Jr. could not refuse that kind of pork and would end up toeing the party line," one of the group inserted sarcastically, referring to a conservative senator who was well-known for blocking many bills that involved government spending.

"Well, aside from being a politically attractive site, West Virginia does have the water and the energy, though finding high-tech workers might be a bit of a challenge," retorted another.

"True. But on the other hand, converting Appalachian coal miners to semiconductor fab operators in a single step might be a stretch."

"A lot better for their health than coal mining, though."

"But a disaster for their Country Music. You just cannot wail about pushing wafers like you can about going down in the pits."

"Or trucking…"

"So, you think it could be a bridge to nowhere?"

The serious topic of the evening has landed, and everybody added an opinion or a comment or even just a wise crack. But deeper examination would show that each and every contribution was insightful regardless of the conversational style. Having spent some time in the US for graduate studies or at various jobs, each member of The Group was quite familiar with American culture. They were also all very conversant in world affairs—after all, each of the members had been hand-picked!

After about thirty minutes of general discussion about American politics and its implications for the funding of semiconductor initiatives, Argon piped in seriously, "However you turn it, this initiative and the talk that goes with it is not good for us. I do not mean just for FSMC; I mean for Taiwan."

"Really?" someone asked. "Usually, any infusion of government money into technology is good for technology. And what is good for technology is good for Taiwan. Not to mention for tai-chip." The speaker used a familiar local name for FSMC, that made a clever play-on-word 'tai', as in Taiwan, or as in meaning 'main' or 'big'.

"That's true," Argon opined thoughtfully. "But this time the sentiments behind the cash cow are different. There is serious talk about on-shoring and re-patriating the entire supply chain. At first we all thought it was just president's bluster. But now I think it must be taken seriously. When top *American* chip makers are talking about copying our business model and becoming a found-ry to *American* design houses, then we must take it seriously."

After another half hour of discussion, there was a consensus in the room that if the current US administration did manage to do what they said they wanted to do, then it would indeed be bad for Taiwan. Not just in economic terms and what it might mean for their respective companies, but in strategic terms and what it might mean for Taiwan's defense.

There was no need to discuss whether defending Taiwan against a possible invasion from the Mainland was worth considering. Not in that room. All six of the men were second generation descendants of families that came with Chiang Kai-shek from the Mainland in 1949 to escape Mao's rebels. They were brought up with the conviction that as long as the communists were ruling the country across the straits, unification with Mainland China was unthinkable. Regardless of the depth of their roots in Taiwan, if public opinion polls were to be taken seriously, then the men in that room felt their conviction much more strongly than the rest of the population.

"I believe that we must not underestimate the importance of this," Argon argued in earnest. "This could be an existential issue for us. If the Americans ever reach a point where they have on-shored enough of the supply chain for them to feel that they do not need Taiwan, then the Mainland could invade. Without the American umbrella we would be quite vulnerable. And let's face it, regardless how much money we spend on armaments, China certainly has the means to overrun our island."

Cliff chose this as an opportune time to ring the bell for service and to have the dishes cleared and the next course served. A selection of fruits, nuts, French cheeses and Swiss and Belgian

chocolates, plus the after dinner drinks: port, brandy, spirits…
"The question is, what, if anything, can we do about it?" he said,
passing a bottle of Yamazaki-18 whiskey around.

"Clearly we cannot be seen to be wishing our American pro-
tectors to be unsuccessful…"

"It might be wise to reach out to Korea and Japan. These initiatives in America must be making them nervous too. Maybe not
as much as us, but…"

"True. But again, it is not like we can publicly get together
with our neighbors and talk about derailing American efforts…"

"So we must work quietly to align our strategies."

"*If* our neighbors can be trusted… I'm not so sure that some
of them would not think that the Mainland taking over Taiwan
would be such a bad thing."

"But Taiwan, Korea and Japan are all in the same boat. Some
more exposed than others, but it is still the same boat."

"Others might also want to join us. Southeast Asia must be
feeling the heat from China, and they must want an isolationist
America as little as we do. India, too. Australia…?"

"So, a quiet, low-key approach to other Asian nations," Cliff
summed up, "especially those along the Pacific Rim might be
merited. We should feel them out to see if we could craft a common strategic response to these American semiconductor initiatives. Agreed?" He looked around the table and concluded, "I will
see if that can be arranged."

"I believe," Argon pressed on to emphasize his point, "that the
best thing for us would be if the fabs built in America were not
competitive. For us, a fab in West Virginia that cannot be staffed
up would be ideal."

"Really? Why? Would it not be better if America opened up that
fund to some of their friends…like us? Would it not be better if we
were good little allies who helped America to have their on-shore
fabs? An act of a true friend that would presumably not be forgotten?"

"I agree. I think the proverbial pie is big enough for all of us.
Americans building a fab or two should make no difference to the
overall trends of digitization."

The two-thousand-dollar bottle of Japanese whiskey made another round.

"Let's face it," Argon took a tender sip of the whiskey and continued, "politically, and maybe morally, it is very hard for the American president to put American boys and girls in harm's way. In a polarized America, he could do that only if he really had to. Mainland knows this… It is vital," he pressed on emphatically, "that the Americans feel that they *need* Taiwan. I think that the best scenario for Taiwan would be if their fabs were not as good or as advanced as ours. We want them to spend the money regardless of whether we manage to catch some of it or not. That way the next time they worry about budget deficits they will stop funding this 'nationalistic' initiative and let the markets do what the markets do best. But, if their fabs are sub-standard and not on the bleading edge," Argon concluded, using the usual lingo portmanteau of 'lead' and 'bleed' to emphasize how difficult and costly modern fabs really were, "then their industry would sooner or later have to follow the natural laws of economy and come back to us, at least for the most advanced chips. And then the current status quo—and the balance of power that is protecting us—would be restored."

Half an hour later, the consensus around the table was that Argon was right and that the best outcome for Taiwan would be that American fabs were expensive and less efficient than Taiwanese fabs. They also agreed that given the political realities, respecting—or appearing to respect—America's sensitivities was of paramount importance, and that they could not possibly say in public what they had just said in private.

So, even as the evening was winding down, they had to recognize that there was no obvious solution to their conundrum. Very unusually for The Group, they departed without agreeing on a clear plan of action.

t-0 + 8 months, Hsinchu, Taiwan

Four days later Cliff called him on his private number—the one that he used only with Akemi and the family. It did not occur to Argon to ask how Cliff had acquired it.

"Argon, can we meet? This evening? Hsinchu Park?" Something in Cliff's voice conveyed that this was not a simple request for two old friends to get together and pass the time.

They met at 6:15 pm. It was still daylight, but the shadows were growing long, and the temperature was down to the high-70s—much more tolerable than the low 90s typical of midday in July on this tropical island. It was still quite humid, so even though they walked at a slow pace both men took off their jackets, slung them over their shoulders and rolled up their sleeves. The park was not crowded; it was a weekday and most moms with their preschoolers were probably at home keeping cool and perhaps fixing dinner. Just a few kids played on the playground. A couple of pensioners sat on the benches that hugged the cool shadows. Several people walked by purposefully, probably using the park as a shortcut to wherever they were going.

"Look," Cliff started, "what I'm about to say must stay between the two of us. Not even the rest of our dinner friends should know." He waited until Argon acknowledged the request.

"Okay," Argon prompted, "what's up?" This had never happened before, and even though he was somewhat flattered that Cliff was about to trust him with something special, he was wary.

"I have talked with friends," Cliff began. Then, as if he had to force himself not to follow his life-long habit of saying as little as possible about his work, he clarified, "People from National Security Bureau—the NSB—and the government. Even Minister

Chiu. They agree with you."

Argon acknowledged this with a silent nod.

"However," Cliff started, getting to the point, "whereas they agree with your assessment that the situation could be something very serious for Taiwan—what did you call it, 'existential'?—they are also extremely worried about pissing off the Americans."

"Of course," Argon acknowledged.

"The United States *is* our principal ally, our protector and our benefactor. So whereas we all agree that it would be better for us if this initiative of their current administration was not a success, it is absolutely critical that we must not be *seen* to be doing anything about it." Cliff's emphases on 'seen' was not lost on Argon. Clearly there was more to come.

Cliff hesitated, as if at a loss for the right words. He then blurted out, "The problem is that the government—or certain elements within the government—could be tempted to take action to ensure that these new fabs in America do not replace our fabs. Some people might be tempted to engage in things like misinformation campaigns, or blocking access to our technologies, or asking our companies and individuals not to help, or even outright sabotage—all of which would of course be stupid and rash, and would probably do us far more harm than good. We do not want to piss off the Americans. So, the Minister and everybody at NSB agrees that whatever happens, the Americans must not be made to feel like we are an impediment."

Argon nodded.

"On the other hand, just sitting on our hands and letting events unfold as they will, also seems wrong. Potentially, the fate of our independent island might hang in the balance. So, it would be foolish, if not irresponsible, for us to do nothing.

"They believe that some reaction may be prudent, but that crafting it is a technical problem," Cliff continued, "They feel that our response must be defined by someone who sees the big picture; someone who understands the fabs and the technology and the situation. This is not a case where you want old soldiers or spies or political hacks involved. That would be clumsy. And their response would probably be all wrong. This is the kind of situation where our reaction needs to be crafted by someone who has the technical as well as a political understanding.

"So Argon, in the name of the Minister, and few others, I am here to ask you to take on a new project. We need a proposal for a suitable plan of action—something which would handicap American fabs, but without the Americans being aware of it. Something that the ROC could do to ensure that our protective umbrella is not endangered by this new Initiative."

After a pregnant pause, Cliff also added a warning. "Obviously, the government cannot possibly do what it normally does and form a committee to discuss and explore options. The risk of a leak and the Americans finding out is too great. Hence, anything we do—including talking about it—must be done away from the usual channels."

The two old friends stopped at a bench, sat down, and looked directly at each other as if to read the others mind.

"So if you do take on the assignment it would have to be entirely off the grid," Cliff emphasized. "If anyone were to find out—especially the Americans—our government would have to deny all knowledge and responsibility, and would possibly prosecute you for promoting terrorism or working for the communists or who knows what? You'd be entirely on your own—entirely!"

Cliff nodded somberly to confirm the risks. They stood and walked on.

"Of course, you and I are old friends, and we can meet like this. Just a walk in the park… A cup of tea… A dinner here or there… Maybe even family get-togethers… And I could talk privately to other friends in the government or the industry. But only you and I can have the full picture. No one else can know what we are up to."

"I understand," Argon finally affirmed. "That would be the right thing to do. For us. For the government and for the country…"

Then, after two or three minutes, he added, "I need to think about this. Not so much the 'if' part, but much more the 'how' part. I am not sure that it can be done. Let me think about it."

"Of course," Cliff agreed. "Give me a call when you feel like getting together. But I must let the Minister know that you have accepted the challenge. He needs to inform the PM and the President that he is on top of it, so that they would actively extinguish any other efforts that may or may not be pursued."

"Yes, OK," Argon responded. But he was already absorbed in his thoughts.

It was only later—much later—that Argon actually questioned the wisdom of accepting this assignment. Maybe the sense of a conspiratorial adventure with Cliff had excited him; or maybe the engineer in him was intrigued by the challenge. Maybe he was flattered by the fact that the powers-that-be had considered him. Maybe it was because he agreed with the assessment that this was the kind of a project that only an insider—a semiconductor technologist—should undertake. Or maybe he felt that this was his duty toward The Group, toward his class and his country. Maybe he thought it was the best way to insure the safety of his family's future. Whichever the case, at that juncture in time he did not consider the risks and the seriousness, or even the rights or wrongs, of what he was contemplating – for himself, for Taiwan and for the globe.

Yes, he needed to think. Perhaps he would go to the mountains this weekend... to carry on his search for a Greater Green Snake.

t-0 + 13 months, Austin, TX

Cedric had called Lakshmi earlier in the day to tell her that he would not be home until after bedtime and not to wait up for him. She, as always, responded by letting him know what would be waiting for him in the oven. No questions or recriminations. After all, his working late was not unusual—especially now that the kids were grown and it was just the two of them. Funny how even after thirty years of marriage, and despite all his protestations, she still insisted on preparing dinner every night. It was not like she had time to kill what with her own job at the hospital (she was the chief administrator) and all the other activities with which she was involved. But every night she had a freshly made, home-cooked meal ready at 7:00 o'clock, unless, of course, they had arranged to go to a restaurant. Cedric rationalized that her attention to duty was cultural and that she could not change it. No Indian woman, not even the lowest of the Dalit, would dream of not having a home-cooked meal for her family. This habit was so strong with Lakshmi that he sometimes wondered if it might be somehow genetically hard-wired rather than simply ingrained through upbringing.

On the other hand, no one ever accused Cedric of being bound by tradition. If he had been, he would probably still be living in his father's two-up-two-down Victorian row house in Salford, England. Funny enough, just a few blocks away from the real *Coronation Street*, both physically and in terms of his cultural roots. No, for him phrases like 'that is how things are always done', or 'that is how normal men behave', or 'that is what is expected', or whatever people evoked when trying to talk him into being conventional, had little meaning. He was always analytical, thoughtful and deliberate. Everything had to be broken down and understood. That was probably why he found that he was so much more comfortable around things rather than around people. At first it was toys, then home appliances, then motorcars, and eventually electronic gizmos like radios and TVs. Machines—mechanical or electrical—were understandable. He knew that if he just took them apart, eventually they made all the sense in the world. People, not so much.

As a boy he'd had such horrible rows with his father over that. His parents had simply wanted a regular son, and his father—the domineering enforcer in the family—had tried to talk, or to order, or to shame, or sometimes even to beat him into behaving like one.

"Why are you such a loner? Go out and play with your mates!"

"Why are you reading instead of kicking the ball around with the lads in the park?"

"Why are you m-m-m-mumbling and s-s-s-stuttering, boy? Speak up!"

"What's wrong with you, and why are you always underfoot?"

"Why don't' you…"

By the time Cedric became a teenager those rows often blossomed into shouting matches, and even occasional punches. His poor mother found those so embarrassing, and possibly even frightening, that she would usually scurry out of their house and take refuge with some neighbor until it was over. Until one of them left the house in a huff, making sure to slam the door behind him, and went off to his safe-place—typically the local pub for his father, or the local garage for him.

Cedric left home when he was just seventeen. He wanted to go to the University and study electronics, because he knew that this was the only way he could possibly come to understand his newly discovered passion: integrated circuits. His father, on the other hand, thought that going to the university was uppity—something for pompous, upper-class *poofters*—not for his son. He took it as a slap in the face, feeling like his son was ashamed of him. A personal betrayal. For as long as anyone could remember, the Dyson men were good, honest, hardworking people who were always either factory workers or 'navvys', men who provided for their families

29

by working with their hands and their backs, and did not pretend to be any smarter or any better than anyone else of their class. Real men did not waste their time going to university. Real men did not cross the line and become *management.*

In the end, twenty years later, they managed to patch things up. Cedric had come to understand, and maybe even to accept, that the old man was a product of his time and place: depression era English Midlands; grimy cotton-mill cities like Manchester, Birmingham, Liverpool; places that were the heart of the industrial might of the British Empire, and the home of its abused working-class proletariat. And of course the world wars that shaped two generations of men: his 'Da' had served in WWII as his own father had done in WWI. In time, Cedric came to understand that whatever the old man did was probably done out of love. In fact, as he himself matured, Cedric even came to feel somewhat sorry for the old man. He probably would have liked to kick the ball around with his son, or take him to a football match, or to the pub, or do whatever normal fathers and sons did. But what was he supposed to do with the introverted 'Poindexter' that Cedric had turned out to be.

Fortunately, they mended bridges before the old man died. He went relatively young, probably due to the two packs of *Woodbines* that he had smoked every day since he was fourteen, along with the diet of beer and greasy *Chip Butties.*

And Mum went soon after. Possibly because the world had changed too much too fast, and that after Da was gone there was no place for her anymore. They had talked about her coming to live with them in New Mexico, but she dismissed the notion, mumbling something about a fish out of water.

These days, all that—his parents and his childhood in England—was far away from the realities of Cedric's life, centered on work in the semiconductor industry, a field so abstract that he could never have even begun to explain it to his old man. And he'd married a wonderful Indian woman with whom he'd had a couple of brown-skinned kids that his racist parents, brought up in imperial Britain, were embarrassed to acknowledge. But living in America and enjoying a lifestyle akin to the absurd people shown on the Yank series that Mum and Da used to watch on the

telly in the 70s and 80s—like *Dallas* or *Dynasty* or *Knots Landing*—wholly agreed with him. With two, and for a time even three
cars, and a 4,000-square-foot home that included a bathroom for
each and every one of the five bedrooms—a far cry from the 500
square-foot terraced house with a single loo (and thank god it
was indoors!) where he'd grown up, living on the edge of a new
development with spectacular view of the desert (as opposed to
centuries – old, sooty smokestacks), and with eternal summers and
maybe all of ten rainy days a year (compared to two hundred sixty
drizzly, cold and damp days in his native Salford). San Jose, Albu-
querque, Phoenix, Austin; talk about places that were so exotic to
his parents, whose wildest dreams were making it for a full one-
week holiday on the Costa del Sol in Spain. He might as well have
been talking about the moon, or Mars…

Cedric relished his life in America and would jokingly say that
he had served his time in the rain and now deserved his turn in the
sunshine regardless of how pink and freckly he turned whenever
he, a classic ginger Brit, went outside for more than a few hours.
Cedric Dyson, now a *Doctor* Cedric Dyson, had not only gone to
the university, but had completed graduate studies as well. He had
moved to America—the cradle of electronic and semiconductor
technology. He'd travelled the world and even lived in Singapore
for a few years, where he'd met and married his wonderful Indian–Singaporean wife. And he'd become one of the most respected
failure analysis experts in the semiconductor industry; a field so
specialized that there were possibly another ten or twenty people
on the entire planet who could do what he did as well as he did
it. There were even several analytical procedures now named 'the
Dyson method' and 'the Dyson etch' that were in common use
throughout the industry, a lasting legacy from his early days in the
business when he was still keen and wrote technical papers and attended conferences. Nowadays he let his juniors take care of those
chores and could barely be bothered to even read the numerous
papers and conference presentations that they wrote, of course,
always naming him as a co-author.

He was a 'Distinguished Failure Analysis Engineer'—an exalt-
ed title that was prominently displayed on his business card. In
public he scoffed at this and made fun of it in a self-depreciating

31

way typical of his dry British humor. "Distinguished by the many cock-ups I have managed so far," or "distinguished failure," or... But in his private moments he had to admit that he in fact did derive some satisfaction from the knowledge that he'd made it to the top of the engineering ladder, a rank equivalent in prestige, albeit probably not equivalent in pay, to a Senior Vice President on the management side.

And he chuckled to himself whenever his official *manager-de-jour* fretted or fawned over him—typically during the annual review cycle, trying to make sure that he would not retire on his watch, even though Cedric was already well over sixty. Lately it was this poor thirtysomething pup that was willing to put up with the incessant corporate paperwork, the office politics and all the other management chores, on which Cedric himself refused to waste his time.

"Not yet, please! The company needs you. You are irreplaceable..."

One thing that Cedric was especially proud of was that he had the attention of the most senior members of the company. The credibility that he commanded was important to him. He knew and reveled in the fact that when Cedric Dyson spoke, everyone listened.

Of course, when you have ten billion dollars invested in a fab that manufactures chips, and when that fab is shut down because it is producing chips that do not work the way they are supposed to work, then you should bloody well listen to the guy who can find the reason for the failure. And you should buy him all the tools and toys that he asks for, because finding the root cause a month, or a week, or even a day sooner, rather than later, can be worth millions. Do the math.

But Cedric understood that the real reason that he had this kind of a pull was because he spoke only when he had something important to say. And also because of the career choices that he had made: he moved when his boss or his boss's boss moved, in order to maintain a position in a network of professionals. In an industry characterized by a lot of job-hopping, he followed people who believed in him and trusted his skills, and who, after decades-long track record, did not treat him like he was just another techie tasked with a simple engineering job—which was an attitude not that unusual amongst a younger, un-informed MBA-driven management.

And also because he really was very good at teasing out the root cause that made semiconductor chips fail...

Earlier in his career he had tried all kinds of different roles: chip design, manufacturing process development, product management... But when one of his designs did not work as expected, he became involved with chip debug, and then absolutely fell in love with Failure Analysis—*FA* in the lingo. A separate niche specialty—some would say a dark art—that involved...well...*everything*. And he'd found that even after more than twenty years working at it, nothing turned him on as much as ferreting out the cause of a failure in one of those magnificent chips. Just the sheer physics of the failure mechanisms were mind-blowing and fascinating. Imagine something like a particle no more than a few atoms in size that created an obstruction in a tiny copper wire that resulted in electrical current densities of the order of tens of millions of amperes per square centimeter, producing enough heat to cause a local explosion! Literally like a microscopic volcano. Like something out of sci-fi. And then identifying that one single culprit feature among the few billion other ones on the chip that was responsible for a given failure, and proving that it was so, was absolutely the best adventure ever. Far better than anything Sherlock Holmes, or even 007—Bond girls notwithstanding—could ever dream of! He still got a charge out of it—the thrill of the chase—to the point that he was amazed that they paid him to do what he did. He would have done it for free—and maybe even paid them for the privilege. He of course kept that part to himself.

Even though the Company had given him the headcount, and he had a handful of engineers working in the lab—all very good and bright young men and women whom he'd selected, hired and trained—he still liked to do some of the analyses himself. Hands on, just him, the failing sample, and some of his amazing FA tools. Every now and then, when faced with a real puzzle, Cedric needed to feel the control knobs of his instruments at his fingertips. He needed to scan the chip and inspect whatever features caught his attention in whichever fancy microscope he chose—by himself—without having to explain why and how to anyone. He needed to do the deconstruction, either chemically peeling back layers of conductors and insulators that made up a chip or making microscopic peepholes using a laser or an ion beam cutter—an atomic version of something like a sand blaster—all by himself. He found that doing things directly, hands-on, somehow fueled his imagination and allowed him to make those subliminal leaps that might have seemed illogical but often made all the difference. Working hands-on honed his intuition, which made him good at what he did. That was what made coming to work, and on occasion even working through the night, worthwhile for him. That was what made him tick…

That night, Cedric had a sample like that on his hands and was excited to get into the analysis.

Somewhere in the back of his mind he also knew that he was delving into this particular failure, at least partially, just to avoid thinking about an unpleasant problem. Or at least to postpone thinking about it. It was the kind of problem that he did not like; unlike this little failing sample that was teasing him…taunting him…daring him… One of his 'patrons'—which was the term he used to describe the technically astute higher-level managers who appreciated his talents—had recently accepted a position with ElInt in Phoenix. Apparently, ElInt had decided to become a foundry—again—and they were looking to hire senior people from outside the company to participate in planning of, and ultimately the running of, their new mega-fab that they were building in Arizona. It was all over the news, with the federal government and even the president pushing for bringing chip manufacturing back to the US, and the new CEO of ElInt staking the reputation of the company on becoming a leading foundry. Just before he left, Matt Nowak, a guy he'd worked with for the last decade or so, pinged Cedric and asked directly if he would be willing to relocate as well, promising the best state of the art FA lab that money could buy. Wow! Tempting…

But moving? Ugh! And asking Lakshmi to relocate? Again? Not fair. She was happy living in Austin.

On the other hand, a brand-new, state-of-the-art FA Lab, attached to a brand new state-of-the-art fab, for a brand new state of the art foundry business sounded like a dream job.

Matt, his patron, had called again the day before and renewed the invitation, saying that he had to fill the role within a month. So Cedric had to seriously consider the offer and everything that it meant.

"C'mon, Sherlock," he urged himself, "back to the failing sample!"

Round 1: The Plan

t-0 + 9 months, Beipu, Taiwan

When he was a child he was given a book of short biographies of various American presidents. It was an assignment for his English class, and the book was one of those simplified versions for young adults with hard covers and big print and many illustrations. For some reason the biography of Theodor Roosevelt really caught his imagination, perhaps because Teddy seemed to be such a larger-than-life action man likely to appeal to a boy. Argon—although back then his assigned English name was RG—was especially intrigued by Roosevelt's strange pastime of 'Straight-Line walks' that involved climbing over obstacles that he encountered along the way. He resolved to emulate the practice. Unfortunately, it turned out that point-to-point walks were more easily done in the undeveloped Rock Creek Park of 1900s Washington DC, than in the densely urbanized Taipei of 1960s, and trying to climb over or walk through people's houses seemed to be a problem. After many calls from upset or concerned neighbors his parents absolutely forbade him to practice his newfound pastime – apparently not even caring that Teddy Roosevelt had originated it. He, of course, obeyed, but he resolved to practice the motto: 'over, under or through but never around' in other ways.

As he matured this resolution boiled down to him never cutting corners, to the extent of even avoiding the use of short cuts commonly practiced by his fellow students including the use of the back-of-the-book answers, the Taiwanese equivalent of Cliff's Notes, and other such harmless time-saving tricks. Instead he slogged through all aspects of a given topic until he felt that he thoroughly understood it.

Later, at the university, at Berkeley, and at work, he tried to apply this approach in his professional life but was instead encouraged to specialize. He was told that his chosen topic, semiconductor technology, was far too complicated for a single mind to grasp all aspects of the field. His professors told him that he was spending too much time 'bird walking' instead of learning a specific subject. His managers told him that he 'should stay in his lane' and not step on the toes of those in other departments. Argon had to accept the constraints and specialized in the physics of semiconductor devices. But, whenever the circumstances permitted, he delved into topics ranging from system architecture, to chip design, to process technology and material science, and over the years he evolved into a generalist rather than a specialist. Perhaps that was why his Strategic Planning role at FSMC suited him so well: he knew a little bit about many different, and technically diverse and distant, aspects of the semiconductor technology.

However, in his private life—concerning his hobbies and pastimes—he was merciless in adherence to his motto. His interest in classical music evolved well past normal pursuits, such as acquisition and assembly of a world class sound system, or collecting rare recordings, or even learning the mathematics behind the theory of music. No, for him, the interest evolved into a hobby of building musical instruments. And of course this meant doing everything hands on. Not just woodworking—he did have a well-equipped workshop—but also learning the tricks of wood joinery and the art of varnishing, and eventually cooking up his own recipes for special lacquers and glues that produced the right sound quality. After a while he mastered making standard violins and guitars and even the traditional Chinese instruments such as *Guqin*, *Se* and *Zheng*, and he moved on to inventing his own musical instruments. Most recently he was working on a kind of a lute that used the combination of a wood body and a resonant membrane. He thought that he would use leather for the membrane and decided that a reptilian skin rather than mammalian hide would give him the timbre he was looking for. Snake skin was supposed to be quite elastic and would presumably produce good resonances at lower frequencies; hence, his quest for the Greater Green snake, a harmless and common snake found in the hills of Taiwan.

Akemi had long ago given up trying to confine his interests to something more normal or respectable, like collecting art, or books, or even stamps. She had instead settled for an agreement that he would contain his strange hobbies, including the mess and the stench that those produced, solely to his workshop that was conveniently tucked away in a shed attached to the back of their house, and that he would never bring any of it into their home. So she thought nothing of it when one Saturday morning he announced over breakfast that he would be spending the day inland in the hills behind Hsinchu to look for a snake that he needed for a new instrument that he was building,

"Would you like to take a lunch with you?" she asked. "Also, wear your boots and bring a rain jacket. This time of the year it is sure to rain up there." She might have added that she was going to Taipei to meet with her sister for lunch and that they were planning to check out the exhibit at the new Asia Art Center. She might have even described what the exhibit was—something about Transgression—or where they were meeting for lunch. She probably suggested that this was likely to be far more pleasant and appropriate activity for a sixty-year-old *laoshi* than traipsing through the jungle. Her use of the title—something like 'Wise Old Man'—was flattering but made no difference. She might have said any number of other things…

But Argon did not hear any of that; in his mind he was already on his way. Not thinking so much about the Greater Green snake—that was a superficial quest—but rather about the problem that Cliff had parked at his door, so he focused first on clearly articulating the objective.

"What do we really want to achieve?"

The drive to Beipu, a small town in the foothills that he had selected as a starting point for his hike, should have taken around half an hour; instead it turned out to be more like an hour due to the congestion on the back country roads, caused by tractors and overloaded small trucks.

"Damned *nitui,*" he muttered under his breath, using a generic and a fairly derogatory term for peasants, literally meaning 'mud legs'.

Actually, he did not mind. His head was busy, and he was listening to a custom recording of a Tchaikovsky collection by the Vienna Symphony conducted by Herbert Von Karajan. It featured one of his favorites: Piano Concerto Number 1, with Svjatoslav Richter as the piano soloist.

It also took him a while to find a suitable parking area in Beipu, which turned out to be a usual chaotic Taiwanese township with what appeared to lack any semblance of urban planning. Crooked, crammed streets—all three of them!—lined by various shops, eateries and businesses. There was a log jam even at the one single traffic light. There were small, family-owned rice paddies and vegetable patches here and there. Messy overhead wiring supported by unevenly distributed old wooden utility posts marred the skyline. Houses seemingly placed at random and oriented everywhich-way made up the town center; some with tiled walls, some with red or blue roofs and painted all sorts of bright colors, some made of concrete blocks, some not much more than shacks covered with corrugated metal sheets.

By the time he locked his car and started his walk toward the trailhead he thought he had an outline of an approach. He began by listing all the attributes that made FSMC such a successful pure-play foundry: technology leadership, customer engineering support, competitive cost structure, capacity, a rich menu of technology offerings, reliable partnering, and so forth. Words like 'sub-par', 'handicapped', 'uncompetitive', 'inconsistent' also came to mind—impressions from conversations he'd had with Cliff and The Group. In the end, he decided to focus on 'inconsistent', primarily because it was a diametric opposite to one of FSMC's known positive attributes.

He knew that through the ups and downs that the industry had experienced over the past few decades, reliability in sourcing was an attribute that FSMC's clients valued most. Because when one was in a business where billions of dollars were at stake, consistency counted. There were times in the past when others had a technological edge over FSMC—ElInt or IBM or Samsung—but clients always returned to FSMC. FSMC always delivered on its commitments, on schedule and on budget!

So he decided that the objective of the enterprise should be to make the new American fabs inconsistent: maybe in terms of pricing, or in terms of service, or in terms of technological performance, but definitely inconsistent and unreliable. That was bound to turn real businessmen away and to bring them back to *ever consistent* FSMC…

He located the trailhead just a short walk up the road and used the picturesque historical footbridge to cross the river and start his hike into the mountains. He brought the equipment that he thought would be needed: a snake hook and a bag-on-a-stick, which was actually just a pillowcase that he'd tied to a long pole, and then set off. He basically followed the Shuilian Bridge Trail which was well marked and nicely cleared with steppingstones and wooden stairs for very steep ascents. But he kept his eyes on the underbrush, and often ventured off the beaten path, thinking that doing so might increase his chance of encountering a snake. The trail was pretty steep, and the bush was quite dense. It was hot and humid.

As it turned out, Akemi had been right…as always. He was glad for his boots and rain slicker, not so much to keep the rain away—even though there were a couple of tropical downpours that made the path into a muddy, slippery, mire—but mostly to keep the bugs away. The waterproof plastic material of the raincoat clung to his skin and made him hot and sweaty, but he preferred that to the incessant attacks from swarms of insects, some of which were the size of small birds! Certainly, an art exhibition would have been more pleasant. Still, he was there, so he might as well press on to the top of the trail.

This was clearly not the best time for hiking in the mountains, and he encountered absolutely no one. In Taiwan, such outdoor activities were popular in autumn and winter when it was cooler and dryer. However, for his purpose the conditions were perfect. There were no distractions so he was free to focus on his task, not having to address the banality of exchanging pleasantries with other hikers, or having to worry about what they might think if he started to talk to himself; a habit that he found helpful when he needed to prevent his mind from leapfrogging. He knew that for the task at hand he had to follow a disciplined and logical process, and he suspected that he would end up having quite a debate with himself—out loud!

"So, how does one make a modern fab *inconsistent?*"

He started at the top of a list he constructed in his head, and first focused on the 'fab' itself. He knew that semiconductor fabrication facilities were far more than just a building, they were marvels of modern technology in their own right, and once the sheer complexity of a fab was comprehended, a price tag on the order of a few billion dollars, excluding the processing equipment, seemed justifiable.

Fab facilities included infrastructure for handling clean room air, pure water, many different gasses, fumes of all sorts of noxious chemicals, anti-vibration cushions, power distribution and conditioning and… Miles of high grade stainless steel piping, plumbing and conduits for delivering various gasses, deionized water, vacuum and clean air—all ultra clean and guaranteed to be leakproof… Miles of electrical wiring housed in grounded and isolated conduits to prevent noise coupling… Clean rooms with laminar air flow and elevated floors… Cryogenic facilities for storage of liquid nitrogen…

But fairly quickly he decided that any issues with the fab infrastructure itself would be easily detectable. Any problems with the infrastructure would necessarily stop the entire fab; and hence the problem would have to be quickly fixed, and presumably quickly traced back to the root cause. Therefore, messing with the fab infrastructure did not meet Cliff's first constraint: that the Americans must not know or even suspect that anything was amiss.

He was now higher on the mountain where he was less likely to encounter his Greater Green snake which supposedly preferred lower elevations, but he carried on because he wanted to get to the end of the trail.

"Easily detectable?" For some reason the word 'detectable' stuck in his mind.

Which made him think of *yield*, the ultimate metric in the semiconductor industry—the ratio of 'good' chips that could be sold to paying clients, as opposed to the total number of chips started at the beginning of the manufacturing line. Yield was something that was not easily detectable, and certainly not easily fixable; because, yield was never one hundred percent, and identifying the reason why some chips did not work the way they were supposed to, was a very difficult process. And yet, yield was a parameter that companies lived and died by. Rule number one in chip business was that you had to have good yields. Good yields meant that you made money. Poor yields meant that your costs were out of control.

He knew only too well that when an IC failed to operate to spec, then the failing chip would first have to be electrically characterized, the fault would have to be isolated to some sub-section of the circuitry, and then physical Failure Analysis would have to be done to pinpoint the root cause of the problem. Then—and only then—could the problem be fixed.

"That is how chip debug works," he assured the nearest tree. "That is how you get products to meet their yield targets."

Fault Isolation and Failure Analysis of ICs were not necessarily realms of pure science or even of engineering. Since failures were mostly random events they were frequently difficult or even impossible to replicate. In addition, Failure Analysis not only took a lot of time, but was frequently never completed. FA was often inconclusive and produced fuzzy data points: the gaps were filled by judgment, conjecture and hand waving, which was at best debatable. It was like having to describe a picture in a jigsaw puzzle based on just a few tiles. FA required intuition and experience and modeling and analyses and…a lot of luck. The skills involved were virtually art forms that were difficult to replicate or automate. It was impossible to hire good FA engineers straight from school. They had to be molded and grown and nurtured, and it often took entire careers to make good Failure Analysts.

"Very difficult," he announced to the bushes. "Especially in a situation faced by a pure play foundry where you have only half the puzzle."

He knew that a foundry business such as FSMC had ready access only to partial information—the portion that pertained to the manufacturing process. The rest was with the designers who knew how a given chip was supposed to function, but who were employed by separate companies, which were usually suspicious and often sixteen time zones away!

All the difficult, and often contentious, conversations that he'd had with the customers when he was a product manager came to mind. Explaining why yield of a product may not have been what was expected, and then negotiating whose responsibility was it to fix it, was always difficult. Because a lot of money revolved around that question. In pure-play foundry business this always led to a lot of finger-pointing. And getting some of the fabless users to actively collaborate, and to share some of their proprietary data in the effort to isolate faults and analyze problems was always hard.

"That is one area where the vertically integrated companies—the so-called IDM's (Integrated Device Manufacturers)—have an intrinsic advantage over our pure-play foundry business model," he mumbled at the bugs hovering around him. "Having all the information, and presumably uniform motivation to debug a yield problem under a single roof is a definitive edge."

He also knew what every seasoned semiconductor technologist knew: that getting good product yield required going up a yield learning curve. When a new technology or a new IC product came along it always started with poor yields. Until the process recipes, the chip designs, the equipment and the fab were all fully debugged and tuned and optimized and all the interactions were rectified.

Furthermore, he knew that the race to go up the yield learning curve was repeated for each new technology node which came along every couple of years or so, as proscribed by Moore's Law. A competitor who could ramp up his yield the fastest, won. If you were late to market with a given technology, or had poor yields, then you lost.

That was one of the reasons for FSMC's success: best yield learning rate in the industry!

Yes! That was it. Focus on yield and Failure Analysis. That would meet Cliff's requirement that the Americans never know—or at least not know for sure—that there was a problem with their fabs.

By this time he had made it to the end of the trail, a ledge that was cleared of trees with a couple of damp benches facing the vista. Hills covered by a lush green carpet, poked out of the valleys. After a short breather he started his descent.

He went back to pondering his problem: "If we could some-how make their yields inconsistent, sporadic and unpredictable, then their fab would be sub-competitive. Expensive and generating lousy and inconsistent revenues... And if they had a slow yield learning curve—due to, say, poor FA—then their fab would get a reputation… All product managers would shy away from that fab… Yes!" He realized that he'd said all that out loud, but of course no one was there to hear him.

"Yes! Make their yield inconsistent and their learning curve slow, and all the business would eventually come back to Taiwan. Our objective would be met!"

Obviously, there was still a long way to go to get to a plan—if there was ever to be a definitive plan. "A journey of a thousand miles starts beneath one's feet," he encouraged himself, quoting a Chinese proverb. He knew he was on the right track. He knew. So he decided to move on to the next part of the puzzle.

"*How* can we impact the yield of a new fab? Or their learning curve in a way that is undetectable—and unstoppable?"

The way down was much faster because he did not dawdle and walked straight down the slippery path, partially because he was tired and thirsty and eager to sit down, cool off and rest, and partially because he was impatient to share his ideas with Cliff.

He stopped at a little teahouse that he'd noticed on the way up, close to the bridge at the bottom of the trail. A small tidy building next to a soggy campground, entirely deserted at this time of the year. Fortunately, the teahouse was open, and a tiny old woman welcomed him politely and invited him to sit anywhere he wished, pointing to any of the six unoccupied tables that filled a kind of a covered porch next to the building. Argon was delighted when she informed him that they had some hot Sishen Soup, and of course, tea or ice cold water, soda or beer. He happily sat down and stretched his tired legs.

Only then did he notice a couple of kids, around ten years old, examining him curiously. They must be the old woman's grandchildren, he thought to himself. After a while of eyeing him suspiciously and whispering between themselves, their curiosity got the better of them and the two boys cautiously approached him, pointed to the equipment that he'd carelessly leaned against the wall, and asked if he was a snake hunter. When the old lady came out bearing a tray with his beer and a bowl of soup, she yelled at them for disturbing the guest and apologized profusely. But he assured her that it was no imposition and engaged the kids in a lively conversation about snake hunting.

The two boys thought of themselves as wildlife trappers. They must have seen too many American frontier movies or some of the modern survivor reality shows. After ten minutes of conversation he'd struck a deal to buy, not one but two, Greater Green snakes that they had caught in the camp ground only a few days ago. Apparently, there were a lot of green snakes in local fields and farms, as well as all kinds of other critters: giant bugs and beetles, various rodents, lizards... For all of a thousand NT they delivered the goods, neatly wrapped in two double layered plastic bags. Clearly, a princely sum for the two boys... They were so proud of themselves—real professional hunters now!

And a great deal for Argon, too. No more trudging through the mud looking for a damned Greater Green snake—easily worth the sum he paid, equivalent to about thirty US dollars. So, he gladly threw in his hunting equipment as part of the deal as well.

He finished his beer and soup and parted from the boys as best friends, promising to return and look for them if he ever needed more snakes.

t-0 + 13 months, Taipei, Taiwan

They met in Snake Alley, which had become a bit of a tradition for them. Initially Argon wanted to meet there because he was hoping to pick up some tips about the tanning of snake skins from the handlers who worked the stands in the alley. Back in the 1990s he'd brought his best western customers there and he remembered witnessing some impressive displays of snake handling and butchery. Back then, taking foreigners on a tour of Snake Alley was a way of leaving them with a lasting impression—good for business.

But times had changed, and apparently the last of the snake meat restaurants, and the shows that went with them, had closed in 2018. The name Snake Alley had stuck, but the place had become a market of cheap knick-knacks and a food court.

Nevertheless, Cliff and Argon had continued to meet in Snake Alley, partially because the street food there was some of the best in Taipei, and partially because the place was always teeming with people, and hence anonymous. And the street food was a nice break from the fancy restaurants that they tended to frequent nowadays; the crowded, noisy, steamy, street-side stands were more reminiscent of the time when they were young and somehow felt more genuine.

For this meeting YouWen Zhao was to join them to discuss the 'arrangement'. They met at the agreed stand, confirmed each other's identity, ordered and took one of the three tiny tables squeezed along the sidewalk behind the stall.

"All right, YouWen, do we understand each other?" Cliff opened, clearly continuing from some prior conversation they'd had.

YouWen Zhao was a somewhat typical software nerd—at least

in appearance—twenty-something and wearing the obligatory uniform of software geeks: t-shirt, dark hoodie, baggy jeans, sneakers and sporting tattoos up his arms and others on the side of his neck. Based solely upon his appearance Argon was inclined to distrust him, but Cliff had assured him ahead of time that YouWen was very talented and could be relied on. Apparently, people at the NSB had used him for special jobs and were quite impressed. Of course, they'd had him thoroughly vetted and had found him to be clean and politically correct for their purposes and had recommended him to Cliff. YouWen was a recent immigrant from Hong Kong—one of the young people who'd become involved with the democracy movement and who was active enough during the protests to feel that he'd had to flee the country once the Mainland police moved in. He had a Computer Science graduate degree with some impressive credentials from Chinese University Hong Kong and was well known within hacker circles.

"Yeah, man, I think so," YouWen responded with a Cantonese overtone creeping into his Mandarin. "You pay me fifty thousand US, and I make you a custom worm. No questions; no leaks."

Cliff and Argon had spent months on the plan, refining it and looking for loopholes. In the end they'd agreed that it was reasonable, and that it may even work, but that they could not possibly carry it out by themselves. It was clear that they would need to bring in outsiders, but they agreed that they would have to keep this to a bare minimum—only for pieces that required critical skills which they did not have.

Cliff confirmed that he would take care of that, and for the software part of the plan he had enlisted this YouWen Zhao. This was the first meeting with the three of them.

"You understand that discretion is vital, and what the consequences would be if we find that you have compromised our project?" Cliff pressed.

"You sling my butt off this island and deliver me back to the Hong Kong authorities," YouWen confirmed. "Probably rough me up along the way, too…"

Cliff gave him a hard stare, which YouWen returned. After a while Cliff nodded and the tension eased.

"Okay," Argon stepped in, "this is what we need." He handed

YouWen a spec that outlined the behavioral constraints for the piece of software that they needed. Not in code; just a spec in words. A few pages of prose describing the required functionality and constraints. He and Cliff had gone over it a hundred times to make sure that they were not missing some weakness or not accounting for possible unintended consequences.

YouWen glanced through the spec quickly, muttering unintelligibly to himself. He finally looked up and said, "Looks like you need something like the Stuxnet worm, but more focused."

Argon had heard of the Stuxnet virus; it was all over the news a few years back, when the Israelis and the Americans were outed in their use of a cyber weapon that supposedly disrupted the Iranian nuclear enrichment program. But he'd never thought of this project in those terms. He was building malware? "Well, maybe. I guess you could describe it that way," he rambled, clearly uncomfortable.

"Fifteen years ago that would have been a very difficult thing to do," YouWen clarified, ignoring Argon's reluctance. "Stuxnet was a real piece of art that would have been impossible for a lone wolf like me. But today, I think I can do this." He nodded with a grin and a glint in his eyes. He clearly felt nothing but admiration for Stuxnet. "How do you want it tested and delivered?"

"We will do the validation," Cliff cut in. "You give us the code on a USB stick. You get ten thousand now and ten thousand then. When we have ensured that it works, we will pay you the remaining thirty thousand."

"How do I know that you will honor the agreement after I deliver the goods?" YouWen challenged.

"C'mon, YouWen. I'm sure that a smart hacker like you will build in the usual secondary secret keys and time locks, just in case we don't pay," Cliff replied, implying that he had done this kind of a thing before.

Of course, Cliff and Argon worried about YouWen knowing too much—or deducing too much from his piece of the puzzle—and they agreed that it would be best if YouWen believed that the worm was intended to target facilities in China; firstly, to cover the tracks of the real purpose, and secondly, as a way of further motivating YouWen, who was known to be passionately anti-communist. So, during the preliminary discussions Cliff had dropped hints asking questions about getting past the Great Firewall and avoiding detection by the usual Chinese government Internet snoops. This was apparently one of YouWen's special competencies. In addition, along with the spec for the software Argon included a list of targeted machines, which carelessly left the serial numbers that could be traced back to CMIC, HHGrace and HLMC, the three top Chinese foundries.

The ruse was probably not necessary, as it would not take very long for a smart guy like YouWen to ferret out the links between Cliff and the Taiwanese government. Given that, it would be natural for him to assume that the target would be something in Mainland China, known enemy number one for Taiwan security services.

"Are the requirements clear?" Argon asked. After months of thinking about it, it was very clear to him, but he was not sure if it would make sense to someone looking at it for the first time, especially as the overall objective was obviously missing. Besides, he did not want to have to meet with YouWen frequently and needed to get all the questions out of the way now.

YouWen looked over the spec again. "Yeah, I think so. You are looking for three behavioral modes. Do nothing or go into 'mode-A' when in type-one environment, or go into 'mode-'B' when in type-two environment... Sort of like Stuxnet, except that you have the specifics for the environments that you are looking for, so that the conditionalities can be pre-coded. Easier than dealing with general purpose industrial controls."

"Exactly," Argon confirmed, relieved that YouWen seemed to pick it up so quickly.

"That is the easy part. The hard part is finding the right digital certificates to get past the firewalls, and then taking over control of the host without being noticed," YouWen explained.

They fell silent as a boisterous group of tourists squeezed in at the table next to them. Judging from their dress and behavior, they were probably from the Mainland.

"All right," YouWen finally said. "I will study this and get going. I will contact you through the e-mail address you gave me if I have any questions. If I can find something on the dark web and re-use existing code, I expect I should have something for you in about a month. Maybe six weeks. Something like *Duqu*. If not, it will take me longer. I will let you know."

Cliff placed an envelope on the table. YouWen picked it up, glanced at its contents, nodded and stashed it in his backpack. He then got up, pulled on his hoodie, and disappeared into the crowd.

That meeting had marked the start of the execution phase of their plan. They were not yet past the point of no return, but they were definitely past the point of simply thinking and talking about it. They agreed that the execution phase was relevant to Cliff's expertise, and that he would take the lead. In fact, with the exception of this meeting with YouWen, Cliff not only took the lead but did virtually everything toward execution of the plan, and kept Argon informed only of the highlights. No details. Argon suspected that Cliff's links to NSB came in handy, and he trusted his friend to be careful and that no one would become aware of the overall scheme, and especially not the intended target!

Indeed, Cliff has been busy and had spent time screening, and then meeting and vetting, a variety of very carefully selected 'recruits' for their ploy. Phone calls and discrete face-to-face meetings. Anonymized and ephemeral text messages and e-mails. Nothing on paper, of course. He made sure that only someone who happened to be monitoring *all* of his communications—on *all* of his different phones and covering *all* the various identities that he used—would have any chance of piecing the whole story together. Otherwise, even if one of his conversation channels was compromised and he was overheard or even bugged, it would be unlikely that the ploy would be uncovered. All that would be picked up would be random snippets of random disconnected conversations.

Argon's only part in this phase of the project was to make up a story about possible M&A targets and to leverage his position in the company to request an analysis of the Mass Flow Controller market. This identified Fine-Flow, Inc., a prominent Taiwanese maker, as one of the top suppliers of semiconductor grade Mass Flow Controllers—even used by FSMC in their fabs.

Cliff then dug up a suitable collaborator who worked at Fine-Flow and satisfied himself that they would get the cooperation that they needed from him. This man, apparently quite high in the Fine-Flow organization, agreed to keep Cliff informed—informally, of course—about the sales, orders and shipments that the company was making.

Argon did not know—or want to know—what Cliff told this man or what he gave him in return.

Cliff had apparently also lined up a 'crew' who would carry out the only physical, and clearly illegal, step in their plan. When the time was right, they would clandestinely substitute their devices for the ones intended for the specific end buyers. No one would be any the wiser. Cliff said that he had made the arrangements and would need only forty-eight hours lead time to deploy the team. He said that his team was composed of real professionals from abroad with no connections to the Taiwanese government or to the secret service, and no prior history that would be known to Taiwanese police. They would be nothing but shadows, especially since, for all intents and purposes, nothing would be stolen, nothing would be missing.

He did not share the details with Argon.

And Cliff has also made arrangements with someone working at the Industrial Technology Research Institute—ITRI—to fill the miniature Teflon ampules with the specific chemicals that were needed. That was easy. A total of no more than two hundred ampules, adding up to no more than five hundred cubic centimeters of the stuff would be needed—an amount that no one would ever notice or miss. Apparently, the story that Cliff made up, about a startup that was in stealth mode and experimenting with some novel idea for printing quantum dots, had worked. Evidently the man at ITRI thought that building something like industrial printers that would deposit quantum dots was a good idea and he was more than prepared to cooperate, probably hoping for a lucrative position with the company, or maybe expecting that his help would be remembered in the friends-and-family stock option plans once the startup went public.

Again, Argon did not ask, and Cliff did not volunteer information.

Finally, Cliff found a machine shop somewhere in Tainan that was able to build the 'cartridges' and to implement the alterations to the Mass Flow Controllers. In fact, both Cliff and Argon thought that, with the skins on, the couple of demo units that this machine shop made were entirely and totally indistinguishable from the originals. Cliff was apparently confident that once they were paid, the people involved could be trusted to forget everything.

Again, Argon did not ask questions about the details.

Yes, now they were in the execution phase. All the pieces were moving into place, slowly and carefully, everything according to the plan.

t-0 + 13 months, Beijing, China

As always, by 8:30 am sharp, Houxi Wusheng was at his desk, in his office, at the Ministry of State Security—aka the MSS—building on Zhong Zhi Road in Haidian District of Beijing. At first glance, he appeared to be just another government employee, working in a soulless building that was typical of many government institutions. Seemingly, just one more minor party apparatchik. In fact, Houxi Wusheng was a foreign affairs analyst who spoke Tagalog, Korean and Hokkien languages, and specialized in the near-abroad Pacific Rim countries. He had been working at the MSS in various positions and on different assignments ever since he graduated from the university.

He'd always felt that he was lucky to have landed a job with the Ministry. It was an excellent job—sometimes maybe a bit dull, but with a very good salary even by the standards of the capital, with job security that guaranteed him full employment for his entire working life, to be followed by a generous pension, and with working conditions that were so much better than the so called 996 culture that was prevalent in the industry. Besides, it offered perks that came with working for the ministry such as access to special medical services, or his ability to arrange the *hukou* for his wife's family, thus ensuring that his son had two sets of doting grandparents nearby.

As always, he started his workday by pouring himself a cup of tea from the thermos he'd brought from home and then turned on his computer. The computer logged directly onto the daily briefs site that displayed updates that the system had allocated for his attention—a modern-day equivalent of an in-basket.

The computer system used by MSS had always been quite

efficient and with recent updates it automatically parsed the intelligence gathered over the last twenty-four hours and allocated appropriate portions for the attention of the few hundred analysts who worked in that particular branch of the ministry. Houxi Wusheng was one of the people who had been tasked with reviewing the data collected by the system. At this stage of development, the system was not fully autonomous yet, and human analysts were required to review the data and authorize suggested follow-up activity, if any. Houxi was one of the people selected for the task, partially because of his knowledge of foreign languages, and partially because of his familiarity with the territory that was assigned to him.

The system was a derivative—an extension—of the *Sharp Eyes* system used for domestic surveillance inside the People's Republic of China. Except that it was now being scaled up for use outside the country through a project code named '*All-Seeing-Eyes*'. Many application such as facial recognition, or seamless access to an individual's background data pulled from Social Credit System data bases that were readily available within the country were still quite poor when applied to foreigners. So, human interference was still very much required. The *All-Seeing-Eyes* system often produced total garbage and its Artificial Intelligence processor frequently reached conclusions and made recommendations that just did not make sense.

Houxi Wusheng did not know or care how the system worked. His job was to ensure that the auto-translation was reasonable and to review the items identified as noteworthy, and to decide what should be done about them. That morning, the system—or '*the Oracle*' as he liked to call it—offered a summary of various news items. Some were continuing stories that had already been reviewed and cleared for mass circulation (like the news on the radio that he listened to that morning during his commute to work). Nothing special. A bomb explosion in Mindanao, ongoing corruption case in South Korea, another wave of COVID infections in North Korea, snowstorm in Japan, protest rally in Jakarta, municipal elections in Taipei... He approved some of the items to be included in the daily brief for the higher-ups and nixed the ones that he thought were repetitive or obvious or just uninteresting.

The item that caught his attention that particular morning was an annotated photograph of three men sitting at a table and seemingly chatting over a meal. The banner read: Possible un-friendly activity. He clicked on the image of one of the men and a bubble with name and a few details of the individual popped up. 'YouWen Zhao. Male. Age twenty-seven. Person of Interest. Suspected of anti-social activities in Hong Kong 2018, 2019. Cur-rently resident of Taipei, Taiwan province.'

He clicked on the image of the second individual and a similar bubble popped up. 'Cliff Lingdao. Male. Age 61. Suspected high ranking officer, possibly commander, of the security bureau of the renegade Taipei regime.

He clicked on the third man but nothing came up, indicating that the system had failed to ID this individual or that it had no background information for him, which was not all that odd for foreigners who had never been to China,

The text at the bottom of the photograph, automatically gen-erated by the AI System, read:

- What: known illegal hacker and an enemy of the people from Hong Kong meeting with a suspected high-ranking member of the ROC secret service.

- Where: Huaxi Street Night Market, Taipei.

- When: 20:38 Taipei Standard Time (20:38 China Standard Time), December 8.

Houxi did not know where the photograph had originated, or why the system had picked it up. He suspected that the sys-tem may routinely scan images posted on social media and might rely on facial recognition to highlight those that included 'peo-ple of interest'. In this particular case it was likely triggered by the image of YouWen Zhao, a known protester from Hong Kong. And then it had flagged the picture because he was meeting with known member of Taipei secret services—probably one of the in-teractions that the system was programmed to identify. Clearly, the question that *the Oracle* was raising was why would a young refugee from Hong Kong be meeting with a senior member of the Taipei secret services?

He clicked on the available links and the dossiers for YouWen Zhao and Cliff Lingdao came up. He scanned through them and noticed that there were quite a few pages in Cliff Lingdao's file that were blanked out indicating that Houxi did not have sufficient security clearance to access that information.

Interesting, he thought. Cliff Lingdao must be some big fish.

He re-read the files for both men, this time carefully going through the information he was allowed to access and paying a lot more attention to the details. He knew that it was quite possible – perhaps even probable – that the meeting displayed in the photograph was totally innocuous. Maybe it was nothing more than a chance encounter of strangers sharing a table in a crowded restaurant. Maybe YouWen Zhao was a friend of Cliff's son, or courting Cliff's daughter. Maybe Cliff wanted to hire YouWen to wire his house. Maybe Cliff was interviewing him for a job. Or maybe they had some side hustle going. Who knew...

On the other hand, his training told him that a high-ranking big fish with NSB meeting with a hacker from Hong Kong was something that merited monitoring.

He scrolled down the menu of options and clicked on the 'machine track and monitor' box instead of a number of other options that the system offered, such as 'ignore and forget' or 'human track and monitor-level 1', or 'human agent disrupt'. He was fully empowered to authorize any one of these options, but according to the training that he'd received, he was encouraged to be mindful of the high cost of human assets abroad. So, he thought that given the scant hard data, the option he'd selected would be the most appropriate choice.

He knew that this meant that the system would elevate the priority on monitoring either of the two tagged individuals in all sources of the surveillance information to which it had access. Social media, tapped audio and video streams, on-line media, some mobile network data, and so on. If the system identified further contacts between them, it would alert him, and he would then elevate the response to 'human track and monitor level-1', which would put the suspects under casual observation by a human asset., or maybe even to 'human track and monitor level-2', which would direct a team of operatives to initiate twenty-four-hour surveillance of the suspects and possibly to bug their homes and offices.

He also typed in a few sentences that summarized his thinking into the 'comments' section, which he knew would flag his superiors' attention. He knew he would need their support to elevate the response level, and it was not a good idea to surprise them in such circumstances. Better to keep them in the loop.

Herding Cats

t-0 + 13 months, Chandler, AZ

She was bored and wished that she did not have to be in that stereotypical air-conditioned conference room with its polished wood table and high back leather chairs, and crammed with people who were competing to be heard. Yet she knew that she had to be there to maintain the momentum behind the initiative that she had championed. It had been hard enough to get POTUS to prioritize it, and the damn Congress to agree to fund it, and to goad the various federal agencies and state governments, as well as all kinds of companies, to pony up the rest of the money that was needed to build semiconductor factories.

"When you are in the business of herding cats, then maintaining momentum is your primary job," she reminded herself. "And it has to be you, personally; it's not something that can be delegated."

In addition to all that government money, she had personal political capital invested in this enterprise, and she would be damned if she was going to allow things to take their natural course just because the news cycle had moved on. She would not sit idly by while the schedule of her project stalled because everybody had lost interest and shifted to some other *crisis-de-jour*. Currently it was the Hong Kong LegCo elections that occupied the media, which, in the bigger scheme of things, was rather meaningless now that the CPC had enacted its new National Security Law. Still, it was a good opportunity to exert pressure on China and to score some publicity points so that commenting on it was one of the dozen or so items on her to-do list.

She knew that a good way of getting the needed media

attention back on her project was for the National Security Adviser to tour the construction sites. Not her deputy or some random assistant-something-or-other. It had to be her. Especially since POTUS had approved the trip and even made sure that it would be included in the Daily Briefing to the press. So, she had to sit there and listen, nod politely and look like she was paying attention, while the various geeks mansplained to her their stupid 'fabs' and what it took to build them. They were right in that she really did not understand most of it. She also did not care. *Her* job was to make sure that the media was there and to give them photo-ops. *Their* job was to pay attention and catch any slips in committed budgets and schedules. That was why she'd made sure that all the plans of these publicly supported construction projects were leaked to the press. *Their* job—whether they knew it or not—was to make sure that any delays or overruns would get all kinds of publicity, which would make it embarrassing for the parties involved, and therefore politically unacceptable.

In fact, the tour that they'd just completed had gone off very well. Women in hard hats made for good photo-ops, especially when they wore brightly colored silk scarves. Now that this was done, her job was to be a wallflower at this meeting.

The intermittent vibrations in the breast pocket of her blazer were a reminder that things were happening in the world beyond this conference room. And since it was her official phone that was buzzing, not her personal one, she was anxious to check those incoming messages. But instead of excusing herself to scroll through texts, she leaned forward and asked a simple question: "Why?"

The presenter, Miguel something-or-other, stopped in the mid-sentence, seemed to blush, and then spluttered, "Madam Adviser, Ms. Stewart, why what?"

Jane scrambled to rewind the tape in her head. What was it that Miguel was saying? Something about removing items from the budget to cover the cost of the overruns... He'd said that the schedule slip was unavoidable, but that they would stay within the budget constraints by covering the cost overruns through cuts in the 'auxiliary functions'—something about a 'Test Center' and 'Failure Analysis Labs'—whatever the hell those were!

"Why did you choose to eliminate those specific line items?

Only a few months ago you assured us that they were necessary?"

One of many pearls of wisdom that she'd picked up from the professor was that asking a question in such meetings was not only the best way of giving an impression that she was following the presentation, but also of making sure that the presenters were not glossing over things that should not be missed. Her job was to make sure that the experts in the room were not too inhibited to do their part.

Miguel Beuhler-Garcia was the Program Manager in charge of the construction of the first of the facilities. They had barely broken ground and he was already talking about running late and over budget. Jane understood that the budgets and schedules for projects of this complexity could move only one way: up and out! But that did not mean that she should blindly accept it. She hoped that asking a few leading questions would generally light a fire under everyone's feet.

"To be honest, ma'am, we underestimated the cost of making the facility earthquake proof." He was clearly quite flustered. It seemed like Jane had touched a nerve with her question.

"We thought that since this is Arizona—not California or Taiwan—and given the extremely tight schedule that the government has allowed for this tender—our original plan comprehended only the cost for making the facility compliant with the standard earthquake specifications, including FEMA P-749 and FEMA P-1050 regulations..."

Miguel took a hurried sip from his bottle of water, pulled his shoulders back and soldiered on in a shaky voice. "But just to be sure, we hired a consultant from Taiwan. After all, the Taiwanese have a lot of practice in building fabs in earthquake prone areas. She told us that the major problem for manufacturing facilities of this kind had turned out to be low intensity tremors, which did no damage to normal structures and often even went unnoticed, but which disrupted some of the more sensitive manufacturing processes. So we chased down the data for this area and were surprised to find out that such low intensity quakes were quite frequent here. Hundreds of occurrences per year below 3.0 on the Richter scale, and thousands below 2.0. Who knew? And the factory guys assured us that even if the equipment was mounted on suitable shock absorbers, there was no way that a semiconductor factory could run with daily disruptions of that kind. Hence we had to change the plans. The manufacturing equipment that is sensitive to vibrations will be confined to specially insulated zones within the facility. We actually have to make a section of the building float on a set of cushions, and we have to ensure that all the connections between these sensitive areas and the rest of the site are buffered, including the walls, floors, walkways and utility conduits. Springs, cushions and shock absorbers on everything!"

He seemed quite proud of what they had done and droned on for several minutes explaining why it would add time to the schedule and cost to the budget.

"Thank you," Jane interrupted, partially just to put the poor man out of his misery, "but my question was about eliminating the auxiliary functions, not what you needed the money for."

"Ah yes," Miguel caught himself. "As you may recall, the original proposal included three types of specifications which were lumped into the Fundamental, the Must-Have, and the Nice-to-Have buckets, so to speak. All the Nice-to-Have features were grouped under the 'Support Functions' section of the budget. We are reallocating funds from this Support Function section to the Fundamental section to cover the revised costs so that the bottom line—"

"No," Jane interrupted again, probably somewhat testily, "I do not recall the original proposal. But I certainly hope that someone here does." She looked around the room.

Most people started leafing frantically through the three-hundred-page proposal.

Then someone cleared his throat and offered, "Ma'am, the original thinking was that each of the three new fabs covered by the CHIPS Act would have its own test center and failure analysis facility. These were funded in order to meet *your* requirement for world class performance. We all agreed back then that if we are to guarantee rapid feedback loops and top-notch learning curves, then we needed these facilities to be local—on site. The thinking now is that we could consolidate these functions from the three projects and have a shared test center and failure analysis facility. This should save enough money from each project to cover the cost of the more expensive construction, and is expected to have only a relatively minor impact on operational efficiency..."

Jane eyed the volunteer and ascertained that it was not one of *her* people. His name badge identified him as Matt Nowak, and she recalled that he was the ElInt manager who was slated to run this site once it was done. She thanked him. Then she got up and paced about the room, mostly for show.

"Lady and gentlemen," she started, refraining from saying 'well boys' which would have been more accurate but not PC, "please forgive me, but I am only a Poly-Sci major, with a JD and a Masters in history. I do not understand anything you just told me. But I do not need to, because someone here does. So, please tell me: Is this the right thing to do?"

She once more scanned the faces in the room. She could tell from the way that most were avoiding eye contact that she was making them nervous. Good. There was a nerve here somewhere, she thought to herself. She sat down and folded her hands in an expectant gesture, making it obvious that hers was not a rhetorical question and that she was waiting for an answer.

A discussion ensued. It started off in quiet, almost fearful tones, but eventually blossomed into a lively debate. Not a shouting match but a good debate.

Good, Jane thought again, even though she was following only fragments of the discussion.

Somebody was saying that having a local failure analysis lab was essential for the foundry business, apparently because external customers tended to be a bit paranoid about protecting their proprietary data and hated to send the necessary information to a shared site where their competitors might see it. She then pointed out that a foundry business model placed different constraints on management of the Yield Learning Curve than those required by the simple IDM business model, and asked if perhaps most of the people in the room were familiar only with the second one.

The name tag identified the speaker simply as 'M. Teacher', leaving Jane to wonder if that was her name or her role. Very apt if it is her role, Jane thought to herself. She sounds snarky enough to be a school teacher. But then she caught herself and wondered if she, herself, was being somewhat sexist toward the only other woman in the room.

And someone else was pointing out that if the technology roadmap veered in the direction of 2.5D and 3D integration, then Test would become an integral part of the manufacturing process rather than a step at the end of the production line, and that having a remote test center would then be a serious logistical handicap for foundry operations.

"2.5D? What the hell? These geeks are inventing a half of a dimension?"

She deliberately opened her notebook and made a note of it, not so much because she wanted to follow up on it, but because she knew that taking notes—or even just appearing to be taking notes—made 'the room' extra vigilant. Another one of the professor's tricks...

It was all Greek to Jane. Nevertheless, she was glad that she precipitated the discussion. After ten or fifteen minutes, she rapped the table and cleared her throat. The room fell silent, and everyone turned to face her.

Jane spoke slowly, hopefully with sufficient gravitas. "You are the experts, and I need you to come to a consensus. The point that I need everyone in this room to fully understand is that our objective is to build a manufacturing facility that will be a commercial success." She underscored *commercial success* by lowering her voice and tapping the table. "If you believe that having these...what did you call them...*test center* and *failure analysis* facility on site is likely to increase the odds of the project being a commercial success, then we must find other ways to fund the cost overruns." She paused for dramatic effect. "Don't get me wrong," she continued, "fiscal responsibility is important. The government is not a bottomless pit. If these auxiliary functions are just window dressing that will not have an impact on the commercial viability of this factory, then I applaud your fiscal restraints." Again, she scanned the stony faces staring at her. "But, let me be clear. Everyone here will have failed if we spend all this money and end up with a white elephant. With something that is *not* commercially competitive."

"I do not want another fiasco like Solyndra. Or to have some smart-ass republican telling me a year or two down the road how the federal government has yet again shown itself to be unable to pick industrial winners." She might have imagined it, but she thought that some of the faces paled a bit. So she drove home the point.

"Commercial success," she repeated. "We must end up with a commercially successful facility!" She rapped the table. "A factory—fab as you call it—that will be churning out chips in three years and in six years and in ten years, whichever way the technology goes; a factory that will have American customers lining up for its services without subsidies from the government. A factory that will build the chips used in the next iPhone, or in whatever the next latest and greatest thing our brilliant American engineers might dream up…"

It felt like the temperature in the room had dropped a few degrees.

"As I said, I am a historian," she repeated, deciding to personalize her closing point. "Make no mistake, in a few years, I *will* write a book about this project. I *will* document all the facts and name all the names. *Your* names." She patted her notebook for effect. "It is up to you whether you go into history as people who brought semiconductor manufacturing back to our shores, and have therefore rekindled American technological leadership, or whether you will be remembered as the bunch of buffoons who have wasted a lot of taxpayers' money on an ivory tower that just sucks cash, or, worse, on a pile of rubble in the middle of the Arizona desert."

She then looked pointedly at Miguel and concluded, "I want a recommendation—and a rationalization that even I can understand—on my desk within forty-eight hours, with all of your signatures on it, as well as a press-release with new schedules. The president wants this project open and in the public eye."

Jane then got up, thanked everybody, put on her photo-op smile and walked out,. She had done her job well, and she even allowed herself to feel that the professor would have approved of her performance.

Maybe even *Iron Brew*…

Opportunity Knocks

t-0 + 16 months, Scottsdale, AZ

Cedric fretted about how Lakshmi would react, and whether it was even fair of him to ask her to move, again…

"What would you say if I were to suggest moving to Arizona. There is a job opportunity…"

"Sure," she interrupted. She shrugged a bit, as if his question was not a surprise or of particular concern to her, as if she herself had been thinking about it for a while, too.

"Now let's think about this… I can certainly see advantages and disadvantages either way. We are well set here, but on the other hand, this house is too big for us now, don't you think? I don't want you to rush into a decision just for my sake…" he trailed off.

Again she shrugged, and emphasized, "Oh Cedric, of course I would be doing it for you."

She went on to explained that she did not really mind where they lived, and her own job was not nearly as important to her as his was to him, and that she knew all this was in the cards thirty years ago when they first married. She patted him on the shoulder and added, "Look, the last thing I want is to have to put up with you pouting, the way you did the last time things did not go your way."

He felt guilty. He knew that their relationship had been biased toward his preferences, and he was feeling like a move now would be skewing it even further in his favor. "Let us talk about it," he suggested.

"Cedric, It is clear that you want to go," she responded. "You've been brooding about something for weeks, and I gather this must be it. So…let's just go. Besides, I think it may turn out to be a good excuse for me to do what I've wanted to do for a while now. I want to write, and a move would be good motivation to get going."

"Write what?" Cedric was puzzled.

"Fiction... Maybe a novel... I've been playing at it for years and now that we are financially set and we don't have the kids to worry about, I think I want to try it. Maybe take a class in creative writing. Maybe join a study group..."

Of course he knew about Lakshmi's interest in writing, but he'd never quite understood it. He took it to be something like his own interest in classic cars—a hobby. A fancy. Something one did in his spare time when restless or bored. But surely not the kind of a thing that one rearranges his life around. He would have loved to rebuild a classic car—maybe a 1972 Triumph TR6, or even a 1964 Jaguar E-Type—but of course he would never quit his job and move across the country to do it.

Yet the exchange reminded Cedric why he'd fallen in love with Lakshmi years ago, and why he still loved her. She was totally different from him; unfathomable, enigmatic, mysterious, confounding, mystifying, perplexing, puzzling, and wonderfully incomprehensible. He knew he would never understand her.

On the other hand, she seemed to know what was on his mind even before he was fully aware of it himself. It seemed like she had already thought the move through and made up her mind.

They talked about it for the rest of the evening, but the decision had actually been made. They would move to Phoenix because he wanted to continue in his vocation, and because she saw it as an opportunity to change hers. Besides, they still had friends living there, people she'd kept in touch with since their previous time in Arizona ten years ago.

They put their big Austin house on the market and bought a small ranch house in Scottsdale not that far from Taliesin West. It was a twenty-eight mile commute to Chandler, which was where the new EIInt fab was to be built, but the location was breathtaking, and the smaller house was perfect for them. After all, the kids were not coming home for more than a day or two at a time.

He went to work virtually the first day after they moved into their new house. He was eager to start, and besides, he knew that it would be easier for Lakshmi to do all the things she needed to do to arrange their new life if he was not in her hair.

He was to be a part of the core group of experts – hand-picked people – who comprised a kind of steering committee that was intended to oversee first the planning, then the equipping and eventually the staffing of a brand new mega-fab. His special mission on the committee was to champion the best yield learning curve on the planet—from fab layout to the equipment selection, and of course his Physical and Failure Analysis lab.

The fact that the fab was a part of the national drive to bring advanced semiconductor manufacturing back to the United States, and that the federal government, as well as the state governments and a consortium of tech companies were investing heavily in it was interesting, but ultimately meant little to him. The fact that even the president talked about the American Semiconductor Initiative in his State of the Union speech, and that the enterprise was driven by national security considerations was interesting, but not particularly important to him. The fact that it was apparently a personal pet project of the National Security Adviser—Matt, his patron, had told him all about a meeting where she had insisted on having an on-site Failure Analysis Lab—was gratifying, but also inconsequential. He had no interest in politics and all the talk about why they had to have a US based fab did not affect him in the least.

No, the thing that attracted him to the project was the opportunity to start from a scratch. The notion that even the powers-that-be recognized that an analysis lab was a vital part of any modern fab was refreshing, and that they were willing to fund it was downright invigorating. Designing and equipping an entirely new state-of-the-art lab—cost being no object—would be a once-in-a-lifetime opportunity.

And participating in, and even contributing to planning an entirely new fab, would be a privilege. Staying connected from groundbreaking to fully commissioning a manufacturing line would be special. "Quite a worthy achievement," he muttered to himself. "Maybe we can even manage to make the place friendly to left handers," he added wryly, having internalized long ago all the frustrations that he, and all the other left-handed people, had had to manage on a daily basis while living in a right-handed world.

Round 2:
The Implementation

t-0 + 15 months, Tainan, Taiwan

First, Cliff created a phantom business just for the purpose of managing these transactions—an entity that was destined to disappear within a few months, no traces left behind—a sure way to handicap any effort at following the trail of money.

Meanwhile, Argon confirmed that the Fine-Flow Industry model TLF SS316 Mass Flow Controller units were the type commonly used by the makers of semiconductor manufacturing equipment for very precise management of the flows of gasses and chemicals used in semiconductor manufacturing processes. Semiconductor grade MFC is a box, typically a few inches on a side, with fittings on both ends, for attachment to the gas plumbing, and an electric-connector socket on top for integration with a computer control system. This Fine-Flow model was common in the industry and fully certified by FSMC itself.

Then they acquired fifty of these using the fake business entity and had them drop-shipped directly to the machine shop that they had already vetted for the job. They obtained the micro solenoid valves through an over-the-counter transaction with a local industrial supply retailer and had them shipped to the same address. The Teflon ampules were acquired through a similar transaction but from a different retailer and shipped to a private address in Hsinchu.

Cliff chose a specialty semiconductor-grade machine shop mostly based on the reputation that it had with the department; supposedly they were both good and discrete. Besides, the test prototypes that they'd built—the second stage of the vetting process—were also first class.

In fact, Taiwan had hundreds of such machine shops. This sector of the industry was an unsung hero of the Taiwanese technological miracle. Everybody knew about the giant foundries and package and test service providers, but no one ever mentioned the specialized machine shops, glass blowers, plastic mold manufacturers, and other types of 'low-tech' craftsmen businesses that were essential for keeping the celebrated foundries supplied with the gizmos, gadgets, jigs, fixtures, and all sorts of unique items necessary for efficient operation of a fab or an assembly line. Over time many of these had become providers of different types of industrial products in their own right. For example, the founder of the Fine-Flow manufacturer of the Mass Flow Controllers had started as a contractor that happened to be good at installing the ultra-pure plumbing in semiconductor facilities. But others had chosen to remain as small family businesses, ubiquitous in the back streets of Hsinchu, Kaohsiung, Tainan and other high-tech hubs. The good ones, known mostly through word of mouth, could ensure a very good standard of living for the craftsmen who preferred the independence that working for themselves enabled. These shops were reputed to be able to make anything that could possibly be imagined given specifications and, of course, enough money. Lately some were reputed to have branched out into far more complex jobs and to have made the investment for the very high-end tools such as the latest German and Japanese computer-controlled machines, or even the American and Dutch 3D printing tools.

Once the MFC devices were received and properly logged in, the chosen machine shop performed the modifications per agreed-upon specifications. The metal covers were slid off the Mass Flow Controllers exposing the stainless-steel manifold, along with the associated valves and the PCB which held the control circuitry. A special jig that was designed and built during the demo phase was then used to hold the MFC device firmly in place. The detailed schematics provided by the client were used to program the computer-controlled drill presses to do the required modifications. Two pairs of precisely defined 1 mm. holes set 5.5 mm. apart were drilled into the opposing sides of the main manifold. Miniature 4.0 mm. long stainless-steel elbow pipe sections were cooled in liquid nitrogen and then wedged into these holes, such that on reaching room temperature they were cold-welded into the body of the manifold. The ends of these pipes were then machined off, leaving 2.4 mm. stubs. Four miniature cartridges, each a 5.0 mm. by 5.0 mm. by 7.8 mm. stainless steel block pre-machined to house a micro solenoid valve and a Teflon ampule, were then attached to these stubs using the threaded nut and the pre-machined stainless steel compression fitting. The entire assembly was then cleaned and leak tested to 100 psi pressure. The solder coated tips of the solenoid wires protruding from the cartridges were then plugged into the miniature socket on the main PCB and the operation of the valve was verified using a 5.0 volt power supply and a voltmeter. Then the little Teflon ampules with their chemical cargo were inserted into the cartridges—carefully—as per the warning that the contents could be toxic if spilled.

Each cartridge was then taped down, and all the electrical joints were cemented with silica – based conducting gel. To a casual observer there was nothing out of place. In fact, one would have to either be an expert intimately familiar with MFC construction, or put two MFC units side by side, to determine that one had been modified.

The covers were then slid back on, the labels with the revised serial numbers were affixed, the units packed into their Styrofoam molds, taped together for maximum protection, and inserted back into their shipping boxes.

After the first few trial runs, the modifications on each unit could be completed in about thirty minutes, including the manual assembly. The cleaning took an hour, the pressure and electrical testing was about twenty minutes, and the reassembly was a one-minute job—all for 25,000 NT plus 5,000 NT for machining the cartridges.

A man could live quite comfortably for an entire year off the 1.5 million NT that the entire job fetched. Easy money!

t-0 + 16 months, Taipei, Taiwan

Cliff did not think that they needed precautions like dead drop handoff or anything so clandestine.

"C'mon, we're on our own turf. This is Taiwan!" he declared and arranged another meeting in Snake Alley. They met in a street bar over a beer, and YouWen placed a USB stick on the table. He assured them in quiet and confident tones that the code would work as per specifications, and that on completion of payment he would permanently delete all traces of it on his machines. Cliff handed over an envelope, said that the testing would take a few weeks, and that if everything was verified, he would touch base to arrange the payment of the final thirty thousand.

There were no questions from either party. There was nothing to talk about. They finished their drinks and left in different directions.

Cliff had pre-arranged for the testing of the software by a cyber security lab at the National Tsing Hua University. Argon did not know the details, but, apparently whomever Cliff had recruited confirmed that everything was as expected.

They then met again at the Hsinchu Park and finally agreed to 'pull the trigger'. At the time, they were so engrossed with the mechanics of their plan that they did not ponder the bigger picture, or appreciate the enormous implications of what they were about to do. That would come later. At this point it was just another step in the process, and they saw no reason not to take it. Everything looked good. So, they authorized Cliff's man at the Laboratory of Cryptography and System Security at the highly respected National Tsing Hua University to enter the final ID numbers required by the code and then to proceed to inject the worm into their two pre-defined targets.

This was the point of no return.

Both prongs of their attack plan were intended to operate more like a 'fire and forget' missile than a 'command guidance' weapon, and once the virus was launched, there was no going back. They concluded that this approach was most secure, since it left fewer tracks that could be traced back to them. Besides, their targets were well defined and there was no need to broadcast the virus and infect many machines while searching for a specific victim, as was the case with Stuxnet. So, there was no need for post-launch communication with the virus.

They identified two, and only two, well-defined carriers. After all, the semiconductor industry was quite provincial, and narrowing the field to a specific target was not hard—especially with the plan like theirs, designed by a technologist who understood how the industry worked and who knew how to achieve their broad goals by focusing on just two narrow but very carefully chosen applications.

For the prong that they referred to as the 'cause' side of the equation, the carrier that they selected was the software driver for the Mass Flow Controllers manufactured by Fine-Flow Technologies. This was a low-level piece of code that any user of the MFC, including the manufacturers of the equipment bought by semiconductor fabs, would download and incorporate into their higher-level command and control software. Oxidation furnaces, plasma etchers, whatever... Like the printer driver software that is pre-loaded on every PC, or is downloaded whenever a PC needs to interface to a new printer. However, their driver had a virus that was 'trained' to activate if, and only if, the serial number of the MFC, manually entered by the user, matched the codes that were pre-programmed into the worm.

Otherwise it was to remain dormant and entirely harmless—and invisible. Like the millions of lines of legacy code that lurk everywhere, such as Stuxnet did in most PCs.

On the 'effect' side of the equation, the carrier they selected was Gwenevere Technology's *Merlin* software. Argon did the research and found that whereas there were a dozen or so makers of the various failure analysis hardware tools, they all happened to rely on a single software package for navigating their way around a chip—Gwenevere Technology's *Merlin*. Gwenevere Technology was a small software company started in Silicon Valley back in the late 1980s. It was acquired in 1998 by a bigger company, Electroglass, which specialized in making test equipment, and which was in turn acquired in 2003 by an even bigger company, FEI, which made Focused Ion Beam and Scanning Electron Microscope machines, which, in turn, was acquired in 2017 by an even bigger-bigger company, Thermo Fisher Scientific, which made analytic instruments of all kinds… Gwenevere *Merlin* navigational software had remained more or less unchanged throughout all the mergers and acquisitions.

This was sort of like every operating system in every laptop has some 'grandfathered' legacy code to control a mouse, and the fact that this code was originally created by XEROX PARC research center way back in the early 1980s was entirely forgotten. In the high-tech industry, it is always easier to buy a piece of software than to write your own, especially as the interface protocols become standardized, and users grow accustomed to specific features and attributes.

So, the Gwenevere *Merlin* tool became and industry-wide default way of steering any smart microscope, or spectrometer, or even an electrical probe, to a specific location on a chip. Fundamentally, this software navigated around a chip to a specific block of circuitry based on that chip's design and layout information. If you were in the business of looking for one particular device on an IC, amongst one to ten billion other similar devices, then this was an absolutely vital capability. Just like a software tool that you would absolutely have to have if you were in the business of locating one specific house in a giant city that had no street names or house numbers and only kept track of the neighbors' names. Which was the kind of challenge that Failure Analysts had to deal with on daily basis.

Consequently, *Merlin* was a software package that was embedded in every common piece of equipment used for failure analysis of semiconductor devices, which made it a perfect carrier of a virus. However, in this case it was to be activated if and only if the virus found itself hosted on a computer whose self-identification code was associated with an asset tag number that matched the format unique to ElInt.

For legal as well as practical reasons required by any accounting system, every company ascribed an 'asset tag' number to all items that were acquired, and written off, as capital—to differentiate money spent on durable goods from the expenditures for consumable items or labor. Except that ElInt used a unique alpha-numeric format for this—probably a legacy from the early days when it had to build a lot of equipment internally. It was presumably easier for ElInt to apply this tag number format for naming and tracking every computer used by the company, than to invest in new accounting software or to invent an alternate naming system. All suppliers were simply asked to implement this particular naming convention in gear that they sold to the company, which was a standard practice used by large customers like IBM or GE. This was common knowledge among Field Engineers for fab equipment. So the virus keyed off this format. Otherwise it was to remain dormant, invisible and entirely harmless.

"Fortunately," Argon had thought while doing the background research, since this made the targeting quite easy.

t-0 + 16 months, Beijing, China

The system worked as expected. When Houxi Wusheng logged on, he was alerted that the two individuals of interest, YouWen Zhao and Cliff Lingdao, had intersected again. He had to pull up the files, along with previous entries, to reacquaint himself with the case. Oh, yes: a Hong Kong hacker and a Taiwanese spy master.

The system did not tell him what exactly had precipitated the alert, but he suspected that it might have been the location data transmitted by their mobile phones intersecting in same place and time. That would be typical of the 'machine track and monitor' instruction that he had authorized the last time he'd paid attention to this case. Not that difficult to arrange—just hack into the meta data database captured by the Mobile Switching Center that controls the base stations in the area of interest, and look for the activity of the mobile numbers associated with the targeted individuals.

He scrolled down the menu of options and clicked on the 'human track and monitor-level 1' option and updated the comment section.

He knew that the meeting reported was probably nothing—maybe just a coincidence—the kind of coincidence not improbable at popular and crowded places like movie theaters, art galleries, train stations or even food courts. Nevertheless, he decided that an increased level of monitoring was in order. According to his training, that was the recommended option.

With this option activated, he knew that he would be receiving updates on the movements of the targeted individuals maybe two or three times a week. Maybe some photographs as well—especially if the two were to meet again. And the case status would then be reviewed with his superior officer on a weekly basis. Standard protocol...

t-0 + 19 months, Kaohsiung, Taiwan

It was easy. Well, easy if you had the kind of access that Argon had...

Figuring out what equipment was used in which fab was typically not public knowledge. Some companies would even treat that kind of information as a trade secret, especially before the installation was completed. The 'meta data'—information about which semiconductor companies were doing business with which equipment vendors was more accessible, but it was retroactive and understandable only if you were an insider who knew how to read press announcements, annual reports and other public releases. Getting information about deals that were still to be made, and specifically about what equipment was to be installed in the new American fabs, was much harder.

Argon knew that. He also knew that, ironically, the best source for that kind of information was the rumor mill—gossip that various technicians and field engineers happened to share. Fortunately, FSMC was probably the best customer for all reputable vendors of semiconductor manufacturing equipment; hence the best field engineers and equipment specialists spent a lot of time in Taiwan—servicing their equipment, performing routine maintenance and installing various upgrades. Fortunately, they tended to be chatty—lonely men who spent a lot of time on the road living out of their suitcases. Men like that knew exactly who was buying what equipment and when, because they themselves either serviced it at client XYZ or were about to travel to ABC to install it. Or their colleagues did. Within a specialized discipline, such as fab equipment maintenance, in an industry with a fluid workforce, field engineers were a tight group of people who typically did not keep client visits and jobs done secret. Often, they were colleagues who at some point in their careers worked together for a same company. Men like that knew that they should maintain clients' privacy, but it was so hard not to gossip. Especially after a beer or two... Such men welcomed an opportunity to go out for dinner and drinks with their customers.

Argon knew this, and he put out informal 'feelers' among the various FSMC process and equipment engineers, who turned out to be only too eager to be noticed by a Senior Executive office like his. And so he found out that the Arizona fab was buying oxidation furnaces from Yama and from ASM, plasma etchers from PicoWati and Hitachi, and so on...

Then it was just a matter of superimposing this information over the information that Cliff obtained from his man at Fine-Flow to figure out which Mass Flow Controllers were destined to go to the Arizona fab. And there was no need to narrow it down to a specific MFC and a specific piece of equipment, because they could rely on the smarts built into the virus to do that final targeting.

After that it was just a matter of substituting the modified MFC's for the ones that had been ordered by the specific equipment vendors.

And that is where Cliffs 'crew' came in...

They were flown in the night before, rented a car that was reserved for them and had a good sleep at the hotel they were told to go to. They spent the day hanging around the hotel pool. As per instructions, they then took the 6:00 pm ferry to Cijin Island, enjoyed a dinner (no drinks, though) and came back on the 9:00 o'clock boat. By the time they got back to their hotel the equipment that they needed had been delivered.

At 1:00 am, the four of them went in. One stayed in the car and kept an eye on the street, just in case they needed a quick escape. Another stayed outside the warehouse to keep an eye on things around the loading dock, just in case. One went in through a window that had been left ajar.

Thanks to the information provided by their 'client', that man was fully aware of the location of the two security cameras, and in order to stay in their blind spot he took care to hug the walls when he crept inside. He scaled a shelf unit next to one of the cameras, unplugged the co-ax cable, attached the little box that the 'client' had given them, and plugged the co-ax back into the port. This was supposed to put the camera in 'freeze' mode, and other than the couple of seconds that the co-ax was disconnected, the main security computer would carry on recording the same unchanging scene. And that glitch—a fleeting image of fuzzy snow—was something that would be noticed only by someone who knew exactly what to look for and a corresponding precise time stamp. He repeated the procedure for the second camera, and then opened the side door to let his colleague inside. They quickly found the cartons that they needed, and after double checking the clearly marked addressee and contents information versus their instructions, they replaced the dozen boxes neatly stacked inside each of the cartons with the ones that they had in their backpacks. They collected the replaced boxes, counted them to make sure that they were not missing anything, and closed the cartons. Then they repeated the procedure in reverse, collected the 'freeze' gizmos and, like shadows, left the place undisturbed.

They were done in less than twenty minutes.

This was the third time that they had carried out this job—each time trouble free. No need to reason why as long as they got paid. And they did get paid well for such a simple job. Easy money...

As per the instructions, the next day they checked out of the hotel, took the car back to the rental office, left the backpacks in the trunk, and caught their flight home.

The entire job had been arranged and managed through trusted intermediaries, and none of them ever met face to face with anyone connected to 'the client'. This may have been overly conservative, but it was always good to plant breaks in a possible chain of evidence.

Tradecraft 101...

"There is a Tide in the Affairs of Men"
—William Shakespeare

t-0 + 20 months, Chandler, AZ

Jane knew that this time around she would need to be nothing more than a wallflower. But she did not mind. In fact, she knew that her participation on this junket was something of a reward. In the political language of the capital, the proximity to the president that this trip offered was recognition for the part she'd played in the project. Besides, flying with POTUS on Air Force 1 was always fun. Even *Iron Brew* was impressed. And since all the attention would be focused on him, she would get to do what she preferred—observe rather than be observed.

Yes, this trip was to be a ribbon cutting ceremony to mark the opening of the first of her advanced semiconductor factories. POTUS would meet the CEO of ElInt, they would shake hands, pose for pictures, probably with one of those silly giant scissors, and then pretend to tour the facility.

Jane was however surprised by the many thousands of man-hours that went into orchestrating the event. The team that represented the hosting company—Matt Nowak, the site manager, and his tech geeks—were highly concerned about the prospect of a tour of the facility. Apparently, this would contaminate the line and once corrupted it would take them weeks to bring it back up to the needed standard. They kept going on about *Class-1*, whatever that meant, and insisted that the only possible way of supporting a tour was if the party was limited to no more than five people, and if everyone wore the full 'bunny suits' and followed standard procedures. Some amongst the nerd squad thought that even that would be unacceptable.

On the other hand, the Secret Service people went into conniptions at the idea of POTUS wearing a bunny suit. Apparently having POTUS in a disguise that would make him indistinguishable from the rest of the party was unthinkable. It seemed that having him out of sight of the full support team—aides, snipers, eyes and ears, the guy carrying 'the football', medics, and all the rest of the normal retinue—was totally against procedures. Not to mention that the level of protection provided by only a couple of agents who would not be allowed to bring in their weapons was entirely unacceptable.

And the White House political spin doctors were concerned about someone snapping inappropriate pictures of the president struggling to get in and out of one of those bunny suits—an awkward procedure that would apparently call for levels of agility that may be beyond the septuagenarian POTUS.

In the end, and many meetings later, they reached a compromise and agreed that the entire ceremony (ribbon cutting and the tour) would take place a month before the facility was fully commissioned. As such, the facility would not yet be up to full cleanroom standards and a so-called 'window tour' would not contaminate the line. This would involve the party entering only the service chases, as opposed to the actual cleanrooms, and would require everyone to wear only smocks and booties, rather than the full-blown bunny suits. It was a compromise that was acceptable to both the Secret Service and the White House people, and the technology geeks were happy that no one would be actually going into their precious fab.

Clearly a solution worthy of Solomon himself, Jane concluded. It fully justified all the time spent on it and ended up achieving a historic pact no less significant than the Peace of Westphalia or great Congress of Vienna, or something of equal importance to humanity, she mused.

Nevertheless, she had no doubt that the ribbon-cutting and the tour would be a great photo-op for POTUS: an opportunity to thump his chest, promote his national security initiatives, and advertise his technology renewal effort as well as job creation programs, which was probably worth at least a five point bump in the polls. And ElInt CEO would get to bathe in the glow of the president, and to advertise the new line of business that his blue-chip company was pursuing.

Of course, Jane thought, no one will talk about the billions of dollars of taxpayer money that was used to subsidize this brand new bleading edge high tech fab. Or all the pork that had to be distributed in order to get the congress—especially those prima-donna Senators—to support it. But Jane knew that that was simply how politics worked. The only thing that actually mattered was getting the high-end semiconductor factories back on American soil.

In fact, the thing that caught her attention the most was the list of the hundreds of suppliers for this facility. They all had to be vetted and approved, ranging from billion-dollar companies that made the amazing high-tech gear used to manufacture chips, down to mom-and-pop shops that provided some of the fittings for the utilities, and everybody else in between. Manufacturing equipment, computer control systems, software tools, contractors, employees, and probably even the damned toilet seats had to be certified!

It was not just a matter of ensuring that the appropriate industry and company standards of quality were met. ElInt had an army of highly trained inspectors whose job was to do exactly that; flashing all kinds of checklists and armed with tomes that spelled out the detailed specifications. None of that was comprehensible to Jane and she let that be.

No, her concern was more to do with security. She needed to ensure that nothing at all introduced anything like a 'back door' that could be used to spy on, or even worse, to sabotage, her new facility. After all, this factory was to be the crown jewel of American technological prowess. It would be surprising if rival nations, namely China and Russia, or maybe even North Korea or Iran, did not at least attempt to snoop on the project. It might not have been too far out of character for some of them to try and hinder its construction, or, later down the line, even its operation.

So Jane made sure that every piece of equipment, every computer, every box, every nut and bolt that was brought into the facility was properly reviewed and screened to the highest military security standards. She did not care by whom, as long as they had some suitable expertise. FBI, CIA, NSA, private security

conglomerates, software security companies, ElInt, whomever...
Even the National Bureau of Standards was recruited to the effort.

In the end the exercise turned out to be quite heartening
because virtually all of the suppliers met her national security
requirements. Because most of the supply chain for the semiconductor factories, including the makers of the manufacturing
equipment, and the owners of the associated ElInt intellectual
property, were entities from the United States, or from nations
friendly to the United States. The majority of the suppliers were
in fact domestic. Some were from the EU. Others were from Japan, Korea and Taiwan—all countries that were good allies of the
United States. They all already had laws in place that required
their companies to establish a fence of patent laws and export
compliance rules, and to verify the safe provenance of the components that went into their products, and in turn that of the
products from their suppliers.

Only around five percent of the suppliers had to be screened
out. A few were from China—manufacturers of the cleanroom
gear and air handlers. But replacements from Europe were quickly
identified, with only a relatively small hit to the budget. Surprisingly, most of the rejected suppliers were from Israel—not because
it was considered to be an unfriendly nation, but because they did
not yet have sufficient protocols in place to warrantee the security
provenance of their products.

That exercise was quite encouraging. Clearly, The West was
still very much the dominant power in the technology field. If,
or when, China was to conduct a similar screening of suppliers
for the semiconductor facilities that they, too, were scrambling to
build, they would be in trouble. They would be forced to cheat or
steal to acquire much of the critical gear, because it was available
only from nations that they would consider unfriendly.

That realization made Jane feel good. We are still number-one,
she thought smugly.

And the ceremony went as planned. Unusually, there were not
many protesters trying to draw attention to their causes. It was
exactly what POTUS had wanted it to be—a veritable Ameri-
ca-the-Great fest, with media lapping up all the talk about American technological prowess and the re-shoring of high-tech jobs.

The window tour of the facility was a bit surreal, too – like staring through a portal into an alien world populated by humanoid beings wearing space suits.

Jane enjoyed it all.

"Something is Rotten in the State of Denmark"
—William Shakespeare

t-0 + 25 months, Chandler, AZ

It was late and everyone was gone, including the keenest of the engineers on his team—those who were always so comically reluctant to leave before the boss. Even the night cleaning crew was long gone.

Cedric liked the feeling of a deserted lab. His realm was now totally unmarred by the noise and interruptions of others. Only the soothing hum of vacuum pumps, occasionally interrupted by the soft thumping sound made by various solenoids, filled the lab. These were the normal background noises made by the equipment that maintained the proscribed ambient, pressure and temperature inside the most delicate of his instruments—like the sounds of a heart pumping blood to the vital organs in a body. Dimly lit only by soft office night lights, neat and tidy, with the loose paperwork, various samples for analyses, miscellaneous bits of equipment normally scattered around the lab now stowed away for the night in their proper holding places. This was the kind of tidiness and discipline that he insisted on.

Everything was copasetic in his brand new 'Failure & Physical Analysis Lab', which was attached to 'his' brand new mega-fab. This orderliness infused Cedric with a general sense of peace and calm that was a prerequisite for deep thought. Yes, he was now armed with some of the best physical and failure analyses tools out there: SEM, EDX, TEM, SIMS, FIB, AFM, FTIR, SAM, CT, PEM—a veritable alphabet soup of acronyms naming the various analytic tools and techniques used in the semiconductor industry.

In addition to those flagship instruments, there were a number of the run of the mill optical microscopes, a couple of fully shielded and exhausted chemical benches fitted with various acid baths and de-ionized water rinses, several plasma etchers, and a myriad of other 'ordinary' pieces of equipment.

For Cedric this was heaven. He had all the instruments required to literally take a picture of an atom, or to fingerprint even the minutest trace amount of any element on the planet, or to capture and characterize a photon or two. These were tools and techniques whose discovery and development were collectively recognized by about half a dozen of different Nobel prizes and that he now had at his fingertips. The cost was well in excess of twenty million dollars, but this was still just a drop in the bucket relative to the twenty billion that the overall fab had cost. And worth every penny! Yes, he was confident that if, or when, a yield or a reliability issue arose—bound to happen sooner or later—each and every of his 'babies' would prove its value.

The fab had been commissioned a few months ago and the lead material processed through the line looked pretty good. Just the usual kind of teething problems that would be expected from a brand new line. The various process recipes had to be fine-tuned and the parametric yield was coming up the learning curve nicely. Some of the equipment, and specifically the wafer handling robots, also needed tweaking. Now, the particulate counts and the consequent defect yields were closer to the expectations.

And then it happened… Along came a rogue lot which seemed to have zero yield.

Chips are produced on 12-inch discs of pure silicon material—referred to as 'wafers'—that go through a series of as many as a thousand manufacturing steps. Some of these manufacturing steps are batch operations, where a group of wafers—typically twenty—are kept and processed together, and are tracked through the manufacturing line as a single unit that is normally referred to as a 'lot' in the lingo.

He'd known that it would happen sooner or later, but this lot was very odd.

The normal process control metrics performed on all the wafers—the usual data that even a newbie process engineer would know to check at first sign of poor yield—were within their statistical limits. Furthermore, all the equipment monitoring measurements—the second thing that would be reviewed—were normal, and none of the thousands of in-line sensors, controllers or other kinds of instruments that monitored temperatures, pressures, purities, flow rates, and whatever else could possibly be measured in a modern fab showed anything that was out of bounds or notable in any way.

And yet, this one lot had zero yield, with one hundred percent of testable die exhibiting out-of-spec performance metrics. This was odd for several reasons.

Firstly, most chips from all wafers in that particular lot showed the same failure signature. This could normally be indicative of a bad batch of bare wafers—the incoming 'raw material' for a fab—except that the other hundred or so wafer lots that came from the same source crystal ingot were fine. Or it could be indicative of something going wrong with a particular machine performing a given process step that happened just to this lot. Except that none of the in-line run-cards that tracked everything that happened to a given lot of wafers indicated any such coincidences.

Secondly, the failure mode was strange. The failing material showed a significant increase in leakage currents; but the currents were consistent and pretty much the same magnitude across the entire lot, with no catastrophic outliers. This indicated that the problem was a systematic issue rather than some kind of a discrete defect causing electrical shorts somewhere on the chip.

This was like a balloon that had no puncture but was still leaking air.

And all failing chips showed aberrant behavior in the timing sensitive tests; but again, no catastrophic failures; just material that was consistently off target.

It was as if every clock and watch in a jewelry store had started to run too slow at the same time.

And yet all the usual parametric process control data was normal and well within the statistical bounds...

Naturally, Cedric's first instinct was to suspect that something was off with the test program or the test equipment and that the failing lot was actually OK. 'Test' is a procedure that is performed at the end of manufacturing line to verify that every one of those billion or so devices on every chip was operational. It is performed using the so called 'Automated Test Equipment' (ATE): complex and large machines that look like old mainframe computers and that ran on software programs with millions of lines of code. An error somewhere in that procedure would not be unusual. Not at all. The traditional old-timers' wisdom was that when a new failure mode appeared, one should wait a month or so, to allow for all the tests to be properly de-bugged, and react only then. But that rule of thumb normally applied to new designs and the IC that was failing had already been fully tested and debugged. Furthermore, his counterpart in the test center assured him that there was nothing wrong with the Test process because, (a) the same test program run on the same design behaved normally with chips drawn from other manufacturing lots, and (b) they had confirmed and replicated the failure mode through detailed electrical tests with a bench-top set-up on packaged samples of the failing die. This eliminated not only a bug in the test program, or in the ATE machine, or even in any of the auxiliary hardware such as the wafer probers and handlers, as possible culprits.

'His' fab was doing something funny; not ha-ha funny, but funny as in strange and different, and Cedric needed to figure out why.

Even though he knew that another old timers' adage was that if you look hard enough at any one chip you would find something wrong with it, he had to look. He also knew that just looking at a chip, with its billions of transistors on a die no bigger than a thumb nail, was truly like looking for the proverbial needle in a haystack. In fact, worse. Every now and then he was known to preach to his junior engineers that if he were doing nothing other than counting seconds, 24/7 and 365 days a year, it would take him around thirty years to get to a billion! This was his way of making sure that they maintained a suitably humble attitude toward the enormous numbers that were taken for granted in their business—because they were so ubiquitous. Day in and day out. Billions of chips per year… Billions of transistors per chip… The size of each measured in billionths of a meter… Operating in a billionth of a second…

Nevertheless, he had to look. Blindly, so to speak, for something among a few billion features that just might catch his eye. So he did, not so much because he really expected to see something, but because that was how his mind worked. He had to visit the crime scene before trying to solve who did it.

He first inspected a few of the failing samples using an optical microscope—instruments that use light and special lenses to magnify features by a factor of about a thousand. But there was nothing that caught his attention there.

Then he inspected several samples in a Scanning Electron Microscope (SEM). This is a microscope that uses electrons rather than visible light to scan the surface and to image its features, and that offers magnification of the order of a million times. No, nothing to see there, either.

Then he took a shot in the dark, and inspected the samples at various oblique angles, at various electron beam energies and with all kinds of other settings—usual tricks that sometimes highlighted different aspects of the surface under inspection. No, nothing there.

He even looked at it with a Focused Ion Beam (FIB) machine – an instrument that scans a surface with a beam of fairly heavy ions—typically Gallium—which often brought out different attributes of the surface under inspection. Still nothing... He then considered inspecting the samples in an Infrared Microscope that would allow him to look through the back of the chip—like through a piece of glass—to see the bottom side of the circuitry. But it was 1:00 a.m. already, and that technique required fairly extensive sample preparation and offered magnifications of only ten to hundred times...

In the end he rationalized what he'd suspected to begin with; that this was a case where he would need to work backwards and do a complete Failure Modes and Effects Analysis: FMEA. This is a standard engineering practice where all the known types of failures are tabulated, the improbable candidates are eliminated based on laws of physics, and the list is pared down only to the modes that could conceivably exhibit the observed behavior. Then, failure mechanisms that might cause these remaining failure modes are postulated, and then, and only then, physical analyses is done to identify the culprit and prove out the theory. That way he would have a better idea about what he was looking for—or at least what type of a thing he was looking for. Otherwise, it was truly a blind search—something like groping around in total darkness through hundreds of rooms of Buckingham Palace looking for a dropped contact lens...

Except that (a) FMEA was a painstaking and lengthy procedure that burned many man-hours, and (b) it required input and information from the chip architects and designers and lay out engineers, all of whom worked for a third-party company that owned the chip. That was one of the things that made pure-play foundry business particularly difficult. In this case that company was Qualcomm, and, being based in San Diego, at least it was the same time zone as the fab.

Round 3:
The Discovery

"The Game is Afoot"
—Arthur Conan Doyle

t-0 + 28 months, Scottsdale, AZ – Part 1

Cedric awoke with a start. It must be something in the FEOL!

To a seasoned engineer like Cedric the term FEOL—short for 'Front End of Line'—carried subliminal meaning. It referred to roughly the first half of the thousand or so individual steps that it took to build silicon chips, and specifically it referred to the portion of the manufacturing flow that formed the transistors and was hence shorthand for the actual active devices.

There was nothing dream-like about his state, no wondering where he was, or confusion between what was real and what he might have imagined in a dream. No, he was completely alert. Clearly, even though he'd been asleep, his mind was still working on his little puzzle.

He got up quietly and looked at Lakshmi, snoring gently into her pillow. He covered her and smiled to himself, remembering how mad she became when he told her that she snored and even drooled a bit while she slept. Funny that... She was normally so patient and balanced that she rarely allowed things to upset her. She took good natured teasing from him, from the kids or from friends, with class and poise. And yet, for some reason, she really was miffed when told about her snoring. Of course, he'd mentioned it once, and only once. He told himself that it did not matter why it upset her, and that it really did not have to make any sense to him. Even though it went against the grain, he knew that Lakshmi deserved the respect and he worked hard to leave that topic alone...for whatever irrational, spurious, or otherwise illogical reason that she might have.

He quietly padded off to the den. There was no point trying to go back to sleep right then. That was not going to happen for a while.

Yes, the nature of the failure mode—leakage currents and reduced performance—was indicative of something going on within the silicon devices themselves—FEOL in the lingo, as opposed to something going on within the metal wires used to connect those devices.

He knew that it was not necessarily one hundred percent sure that this was so. It was possible that some charged particles—ions or electrons trapped within some interface—were forming a parasitic device which then leaked electricity. It was possible that the insulators wrapped around the metal traces were contaminated or de-natured allowing some kind of a leakage path.

Possible, but his instinct told him that it was something within the silicon.

Yes, they'd had similar failures a few months ago, and he determined that a full FMEA—Failure Modes and Effects Analysis—was necessary. He'd contacted the chip designers at Qualcomm, and they were willing to investigate. A tiger team was formed, and the process was initiated in good faith.

Then the problem mysteriously went away. Subsequent lots all yielded fine—no trace of anything misbehaving. Other things came up that required his attention, and the Qualcomm guys got busy. As usual, the FMEA analyses slid down the list of priorities, and eventually everyone was reassigned to deal with other more urgent issues.

But now it was happening again—this time not on Qualcomm's chip, rather a design from nVidia. Still, the failure mode was similar: shifted distributions of leakage currents and some performance metrics, and an absence of catastrophic outliers.

"It has to be the same thing," he mumbled to himself. "So now what?" He was just as stumped as he'd been the last time, and he still concluded that a full FMEA assessment was the right thing to do...

And then, the realization that woke him up.

"Oh, Cedric, trust your instinct. What is it telling you? Short-cut the FMEA."

This brought to mind the scene from the *Star Wars* movies. *Trust the force, Luke…* He smirked at the subliminal comparison, shook his head and concluded, "Yes, it has to be something in the FEOL."

This was significant because it narrowed the scope of his search. He knew that the Front End Of Line manufacturing involved process steps which formed the devices in silicon, creating the tiny little pockets of precisely altered material properties which enabled the transistors to do what they did. But it was all in silicon, as opposed to things happening in the dozen or so layers of polycrystalline metal traces or in the glassy insulators between them. And silicon was a crystalline material that came as close to perfection as was possible, with atoms precisely ordered in exact orientation and with fixed distance to the nearest neighbors in a pattern that was perfectly repeated throughout the wafer. A pattern that allowed only one out of a billion atoms, or so, to be out of place!

Cedric knew that crystal environment like that was typically susceptible to only two types of failure mechanisms.

One was some kind of a disruption in the ordering pattern—either the so-called 'point defect', where an atom was missing or was sitting in a wrong place; or a 'dislocation' consisting of a line or a plane of atoms misaligned to the rest of the crystal. Like, say, a street, or even a whole block that is offset or misaligned relative to a neighborhood in a city that is laid out on a perfect grid. Such phenomena typically caused issues that were relatively localized—a single bad device, or a discrete leakage path due to a cluster of devices that were sitting on the dislocation, or something of the kind. But this did not match the observed failure mode.

The other type of failure mechanism that was possible with crystal structures had to do with impurities—where other types of atoms were incorporated in the crystal lattice, either in place of a host atom or wedged inside the crystal lattice framework. Of course, some impurities—the so called 'dopants'—were added intentionally, to alter the properties of silicon in desired ways. That was the intent of most of the process steps associated with FEOL. But sometimes other impurities might also sneak into the silicon

crystal. These could then cause different and often undesirable be-
haviors, such as higher leakage currents.

Cedric knew all this. "If we are looking for impurities in silicon," he muttered to himself, "it's likely that they would be widely
distributed, rather than clustering." He knew what every technologist knew: that the FEOL process steps involved repeated exposure to high temperatures—on the order of a thousand degrees
or so—and that such treatment would cause impurities to diffuse
throughout the host crystal.

If so, the issue then would be that of resolution. Were there
enough of these undesirable impurities to be detectable by his
failure analysis tools? For once the challenge was not that of spatial resolution of his various microscopes, i.e. the magnification
required to see something awfully small. Rather the challenge
would be the detection resolution of his various spectrometry instruments required to identify trace amounts of some impurity.

He reviewed the inventory of techniques available in his lab
and immediately zeroed in on SIMS.

SIMS (Secondary Ion Mass Spectroscopy) was a tool that relied
on something like an atomic version of a sand blaster to abrade
the material under analysis, and then fingerprinted the nature of
the debris that was kicked up. Like an extremely sophisticated
sub-atomic version of 'Scratch and Sniff', except that it used a
stream of high energy ions to bombard the surface for the 'scratch'
part and a mass spectrometer for the 'sniff' part.

"Yes, for silicon contaminants, SIMS would have the best resolution. Inorganics. Possibly heavy metals…" he again said to himself, trying to guess what kind of impurity would match the observed failure mode. "*If* that is our problem…" He was excited but
careful not to leap to conclusions.

In the earlier days of the industry, contamination of silicon
crystals by unintended dopants—copper, gold, carbon or the so-
called heavy metals—was fairly common. "Or at least it was not
*un*common," he corrected himself.

The wisdom from those early days was that such contaminants
tended to increase leakage currents and to degrade carrier lifetime,
which tended to affect some of the device timing characteristics.

"That fits," he mused.

But since then the industry had learned how to cope with the issue. All sorts of techniques were developed in the initial crystal pulling process to ensure the highest levels of purity in bare wafers—parts per billion kind of purity. And many so-called 'barrier films' were invented to keep the 'bad' dopants out of the silicon crystal structure during subsequent processing, to the point that such contamination was not an issue any more. Cedric was sure that younger engineers would be entirely flummoxed by the phenomena that accompanied such impurities. In fact, if anyone was going to recognize the mechanism, it would have to be him, or someone just like him: an old geezer who had spent decades looking at how things went wrong in silicon chips. It had been twenty years since he'd last faced this kind of problem.

"Besides," he again cautioned himself, "so many things have changed since then. The device dimensions have all shrunk and the operating speeds have increased. Under these circumstances other sources of leakages might dominate," he carried on trying to play devil's advocate in his own head, arguing why his out-of-date experience might be irrelevant, and why his instinct might be wrong this time.

He knew what he had to do next. The only question was whether he would be able to go to sleep that night, and if this could wait until morning, or if he should get dressed and test his theory before everybody else arrived to the lab.

He went back to bed and snuggled up to Lakshmi's warm body. Then he tossed and turned and eventually gave up trying to sleep. He got up, showered in the guest bathroom so as not to wake her, got dressed, made himself breakfast, and was on the road by 3:30 am. It was night and the sky in the east was only beginning to show traces of lighter hues. There were still a couple of hours until sunrise, and the spectacular display of the starry sky typical of deserts was clearly visible—until he got into the built-up areas with streetlamps, neon signs, and brightly lit shop windows.

"Morning, Dr Dyson." The night guard buzzed him into the building—probably hoping for a conversation, or at least a short chat. Clearly this was not the first time that Cedric had decided to go to his lab in the middle of the night, and the security guard knew him by name. But Cedric was on a mission, and just nodded a quick hello.

He rummaged through the closets in the lab used for storage of the samples for analyses, and retrieved a section of a wafer of the Qualcomm material that had had a problem a few months ago, along with a handful of die of the same product drawn from lots that showed none of the failing symptoms. Whenever he could, he insisted on getting specimens from both the failing lots and the good lots. It was always helpful to have a reference. He also found an equivalent set of the recent 'good' and 'bad' samples for the suspect nVidia product.

In this case he actually had plenty of 'bad' material, and therefore he did not have to tread as carefully as he normally would if he were dealing with one of the more typical one-of-a-kind failures. He scribed the back of the failing wafers and fractured off suitably sized slivers. He decided that he would go straight to the end point to test his theory, and simply etch off all the dielectrics and metals to expose the bare surface of silicon. This was the failure analysts' equivalent of a slash-and-burn approach, but he was in a hurry, partially because he was anxious and excited to see the results, and partially because he wanted to be done before the first shift arrived.

Using heavy rubber gloves he mixed his chemicals in the special PTFE beakers inside a well ventilated, hooded wet bench. He was careful to treat all the specimens equally, and to keep everything clean, and after a few minutes he flushed the beakers with deionized water and retrieved his samples. This was 'quick and dirty', and different from standard FA procedures that required meticulous care to stop the etching at a precisely desired level, usually involving iterative etch-and-inspect cycles to ensure that appropriate features of a sample chip were unharmed. But he knew that the liquid acids that he'd chosen—a suitable mixture of pure water and hydrofluoric and phosphoric acids—had excellent selectivity for silicon and would dissolve the copper metallization and the glassy insulators without touching the crystalline silicon. They would have also dissolved the glassware, if he had not taken care to use PTFE beakers. Ergo, it was okay to over-etch these samples. Slash-and-burn.

By the time he had everything prepared and ready for SIMS analysis it was already 7:30. In the back of his mind he was aware that people would soon start rolling in and he felt like he needed to hurry. He wanted to be done before the day shift started and his experiments interfered with the regular workload in the lab. Of course, he could commandeer the SIMS machine, but even though he knew that the problem he was working on was of the highest importance, he always hated to pull rank and instead preferred to honor the sign-up list, which showed that the SIMS system was booked for the next few days.

He loaded the samples into the chamber, closed it, and initiated the pump-down cycle. Like most of his instruments, SIMS worked in a vacuum environment. When the pressure reached the pre-scribed level, he aligned the first specimen, selected a high setting for ion beam energy, and picked a large spot-size, meaning that he would be ion-milling a relatively large area. Well, it would be an area less than a square micron, but relative to the scales that he was accustomed to, this was big. This was like looking at the debris kicked up by blasting through a city block with heavy-duty ordinance as opposed to analyzing the dust after shooting up a single building with a small caliber Uzi. Slash and burn. He set the end point, which dictated the depth that his test run would probe, and initiated the sputtering procedure.

Nothing...

He looked at the screens that presented the data in the usual graphical format: a plot that displayed the number of a given kind of atoms on the y-axis, versus their mass on the x-axis—that is, a plot of the amount of a given element that was sputtered off the surface of the specimen.

And he saw nothing. No trace of anything unusual. Just the normal peaks for silicon, and for phosphorus and boron dopants. Nothing out of norm.

He repeated the procedure for the other three samples...

Nothing unusual.

The normal signals for silicon and the intended dopant ele-ments that one would expect to see in a semiconductor grade wafer exposed to the standard CMOS manufacturing process flow were all there, indicating that his machine was working.

Probably...

"Well Cedric, you might be all wet this time," he muttered to himself.

His instrument told him that there was nothing there, but his instincts insisted that there must be some impurity present. It was not just stubbornness or a determination to prove himself right—he really did feel that this was the most likely failure mechanism. It was the only thing that fit the observations, except for the data staring him in the face, produced by his own SIMS analysis.

He was not ready to give up—not yet. He knew that even if there were some alien impurities in his silicon sample, there were several perfectly good reasons that could explain why SIMS might not see them.

Maybe the level of the impurities was below his detection limits? He knew perfectly well that the resolution of his instrument was a complex function of the nature of the impurity, the sample, his ion gun, the sputtering rate, and all sorts of other factors. "And probably the phase of the moon!" he mumbled. "On the other hand, the shift in leakage currents was quite large, and if it were caused by some impurity, then its concentration should be higher than parts-per-billion and ergo detectible by SIMS!" He would have to repeat the analysis but go slower to maximize the resolution.

Maybe his 'quick and dirty' method was just too dirty, and his sample preparation had somehow contaminated the evidence. He would have to prepare a new set of samples, much more carefully… Maybe the impurities were not uniformly distributed, and he happened to be looking in the wrong region. He would have to test more sites on his specimens and sooner or later, just by the laws of random statistics, he was bound to hit the right area… Or maybe his instrument was out of calibration. He would have to ask one of his engineers to double check it against standard calibration samples…

All in all, he knew he would have to dig deeper. Much, much deeper…

t-0 + 28 months,
Scottsdale, AZ, – part 2

Nothing checked out. Or everything checked out, depending how you looked at it.

During the subsequent week Cedric followed up his initial quick-and-dirty analysis, this time double and triple checking everything, ranging from his instruments to his sample preparation and all the other details in between. He did everything carefully and properly, and still, nothing. The SIMS results were always the same and showed only the usual presence of the intended dopants. And, of course, silicon and oxygen.

But the more he thought about it the more certain he felt that the cause of the problem had to be some unintended impurity in the crystal lattice. Something like heavy metals...

At a loss about what to do next, he closed the door to the SIMS room to make sure that he would not be disturbed and went into a kind of a trance. Staring at the screen and seeing nothing, while absent mindedly flipping through the data files and scrolling through rows and rows of eight-digit numbers separated by sixteen spaces, and followed by four-digit numbers. This was just raw meaningless data displayed in the format produced by the mass spectrometer, the 'sniff' part of his microscopic 'scratch and sniff' technique. He was in a daze, on auto pilot, using his muscle memory rather than conscious thought to control the mouse, looking through the raw unprocessed data before it was sorted and massaged to be presented in the form so elegant that a human operator could readily digest it at a glance; a simple chart of number of atoms versus their mass/charge ratio...

Going through the raw data files was a habit that Cedric had developed in the early days when he first started doing Failure Analyses. Thirty odd years ago… Because back then we had to…

…Back then, when our FA instruments were much cruder, and we were happy with resolutions of the order of a tenth of a micron. Even the wavelength of visible light was not too large to see individual features on a chip, as opposed to the current state-of-the-art where electron beams or X-rays were necessary to image things that were only a nanometer in size…

…Back then, when the computer hardware that ran the FA instruments was so clunky, running on the original Pentium processor, built on a 0.8 micron technology with all of its three million-odd transistors per chip, and operating at just 60MHz. If memory serves. As opposed to the modern processors built on a 5nm or even a 3nm node, featuring more than thirty billion transistors and running at a few GHz. Despite living with the silicon technology day in and day out, Cedric was always awed by its evolution, and as a matter of habit he automatically reminded himself of the mind-blowing statistics…

…Back then, when the software that automated the analyses was almost non-existent and we used to have to look at the raw data and plot the results by hand…

"Hello, hello, hello!" Cedric sat up with a start. Something was not right. Something… "What do we have here?" He scrolled back and forth through the data file. "Bloody hell!" he exclaimed as he noticed—or really his subconscious 'reptilian brain' first noticed—that there was something wrong with the pattern of the digits. And now that his cerebral cortex had taken over, his conscious mind confirmed that the pattern of the digits corresponded to three peaks in the data, in addition to the baseline signals for silicon and the primary oxygen ions used by the ion gun. Not only the two that he saw displayed on the chart! "What the hell?"

The raw data showed a trace of another atomic species—a small count but one that was definitely there. He looked back and confirmed that there was no trace of a corresponding peak on the chart that the analytic software produced. "What the fuck? Something heavy by the looks of it," he mumbled to himself. His observation was based on the values of the numbers in the second column which he knew to be related to the atomic mass of the species responsible for the signal.

He retrieved the box that contained the samples of materials with known composition that were meant to be used as references for calibration of the SIMS instrument. But all that he found were the usual n-type and p-type silicon wafers of various resistances doped with boron, phosphorus or arsenic. All light elements... No good... He suspected that this would be the case, since these addressed most of their normal requirements, but he had to look.

So he did a sanity check on the instrument itself (another old timer's trick) and focused the sputter gun on the pedestal that was used to hold up the samples of material under analyses—a kind of a platter about two inches in diameter. "Probably 316 stainless-steel," he muttered, and initiated the SIMS run.

When the run was completed, the computer displayed the usual graph of the results with peaks for iron, chromium, nickel, molybdenum, and so on... He then went into the raw data file. Everything matched. The raw data and the summary graph both showed eight peaks corresponding to the eight elements that should be present in that type of stainless steel.

Good, he thought, feeling somewhat relieved. This made sense. There was sanity, after all.

He looked again through the raw data for the failing silicon samples, just to verify that he was not imagining it. "Yes," he confirmed. "There is definitely a signal in the raw data that is not there in the graph."

"Hmm... Looks like something heavier than iron or nickel," he muttered, looking at the relative mass corresponding to the missing peak and comparing it in his mind to the peaks from the stainless-steel sample. "Almost twice as heavy as iron..."

In his head he went through the Periodic Table of Elements that he had memorized when he was a kid and that he still remembered, and quickly sorted through the atomic weights for the common elements. "Twice as heavy as iron? Palladium, silver, cadmium, indium, tin..." He recited a list of metallic elements with atomic mass that was roughly twice that of iron.

He knew that the proper course of action now should be to get the reference samples for these elements and to re-run the full and proper calibration runs. But that would take days...maybe weeks. He was too impatient for that and rummaged in his head for something that he could use. Something that included heavy transition metals...

"Nickel-Cadmium batteries!" he announced to the empty room. "Of course."

He knew that the materials used for batteries were not nearly as pure as semiconductor grade silicon, and that the cadmium electrode in the NiCad battery would likely include significant amounts of elements that were its neighbors in the Periodic Table. Therefore, he thought that this could be a handy reference for the heavy metals that were about twice the atomic mass of iron. To him this was 'common knowledge'.

He went on the hunt and eventually found a precision Dremel tool—a miniature rotary saw that they occasionally used to cut open some types of packaged ICs, and which used rechargeable NiCad batteries. He pulled out the battery, potted it in quick-set resin, and cut out a cross sectional slice. Impatiently, he polished and cleaned this dime-sized disc, gave it a quick rinse in acid, loaded it into the SIMS instrument, and repeated the analysis runs.

The graphical output clearly showed major peaks for nickel, cadmium, potassium, hydroxyl groups and oxygen, along with tiny peaks corresponding to the various impurities—trace amounts of sodium, calcium, zinc, tin, sulphur... He double-checked the raw data output by the mass spectrometer itself. And yes, the raw data showed the same number of peaks as presented by the graph. Nothing missing. Everything was copasetic.

"Good," he muttered again, quite excited now. He compared the raw data numbers of the major peaks from his homemade NiCad battery reference to the raw numbers from the silicon samples and determined that the missing peak corresponded to the mass-charge ratio of cadmium.

"Cadmium!" he exclaimed. "Ha! I got you!"

Just to make sure, he decided that using an alternative tool to perform the same material analysis would also be a good sanity check. So, he repeated the analysis on both, his NiCad reference and on the samples of failing silicon, using a Scanning Electron Microscope and its EDX attachment. This tool used a beam of electrons to bombard a sample and relied on X-Rays emitted by the surface atoms to fingerprint the material in the area under analysis, as opposed to the ion gun and a mass spectrometer used in SIMS. But, in principle, both techniques were similar and were normally used to identify the elements present.

He detected cadmium in his homemade reference and its corresponding graphic output, but not in the slivers of Silicon wafers. And again, when he looked through the raw data for his failing samples, he could see a peak that was missing from the output chart.

Both tools worked properly but his instruments were blinded. They could see cadmium by itself but not when it was embedded in Silicon! Like some color-blind people do not see certain colors, or like some deaf people do not hear specific frequencies of sound...

"No wander that I did not see anything wrong with the failing Qualcomm and nVidia chips. The failure mechanism *is* heavy metal contamination; cadmium to be precise. But my tools have been blinded!"

The sense of elation—that of feeling 'dead chuffed'—because his gut was correct was fleeting because the strongest emotion that he experienced at that point in time was that of anger. Even outrage. "Some shite is fucking with my tools...and with my fab!"

This was no accident: two entirely different analytical tools, both operating properly, but both blind only to specific type of heavy metal contamination in silicon. And just when his fab line was showing symptoms of heavy metal contamination, precisely of the kind to which his tools were blind. No, this was *not* a coincidence.

Cedric was overwhelmed by a sense of deep concern. Without a doubt, this was intentional. This was sabotage.

t-0 + 29 months, Chandler, AZ

On April st at 4:07 am the random number generator module in the computer that controlled a furnace built by Yama Thermal Systems of Nara, Japan produced the 'right' number.

The output of that module was sampled once every ten seconds and that particular time the number fell between the pre-programmed minimum and maximum set points which were defined to cover just 0.00005% of the statistically pure random distribution. This triggered a subroutine buried deep in the code of the master control program of this particular furnace, which was one in a bank of the three identical pieces of chip manufacturing equipment neatly lined in a row in the 'Oxidation Bay' module of the new Arizona fab.

The subroutine, awakened by the 'right' number, first verified that the specific piece of manufacturing equipment was in the 'purge' phase of its process cycle (when the main chamber of the furnace was flushed with inert Argon gas). A furnace used in full production mode is typically in this phase about 25% of the time. Next, the subroutine verified that the heaters of the furnace were in power-up mode (when the temperature of the chamber was either ramping up or holding the prescribed set point of 980 degrees centigrade, $+/-0.5$ degrees). This was expected to be the case about 20% of the time.

Since all these conditions were met at that particular instance, the subroutine issued a command to the control circuitry in the Mass Flow Controller made by Fine-Flow Industries of Kaohsiung, Taiwan, to turn on a specific power transistor. This pulse of current set a miniature solenoid valve into its 'open' state, which in turn allowed dimethylcadmium to fume out of a two cubic centimeter

PTFE ampule into the manifold of the Mass Flow Controller. The toxic organometallic compound was then picked up by the argon gas and carried into the main chamber of the oxidation furnace, where the high temperature caused it to decompose into metallic cadmium and gaseous methane.

The methane, together with the rest of the byproduct gasses, was harmlessly exhausted from the furnace through the chemical scrubbers intended to ensure that no toxic fumes would be released into the atmosphere.

The metallic cadmium was deposited as a thin film that coated the silicon wafers, the twelve-inch discs neatly stacked in the quartz 'boat' used to hold the wafers in the furnace. Like cassettes in the old-school CD changers. At the high temperature of the chamber, cadmium atoms quickly diffused into the host material, replacing approximately every ten-millionth silicon atom in the crystal lattice of every wafer.

The minimum and maximum set points that the random number generator had to meet in order to trigger that sequence were selected so that these conditions would be met approximately once every couple of months or so, if and only if the specific fab equipment met all the other pre-screening conditions, including the make and model of the equipment, the serial number of the MFC, and so on. The conditions were not deterministic and the variability in the frequency of occurrence was expected to be of the order of $+/-30\%$, coming from natural statistical variation in random number distribution, from the exact nature of the processing recipes, and from the frequency of time when the furnaces were taken offline for regular maintenance. This particular event was the third time that all the conditions had been met since the 5th of September of the previous year, when the fab was fully commissioned and qualified for mass production.

Seven weeks later, on June 3rd, these same wafers would complete the last step in the manufacturing process flow and would be tested and found to fail for excessive leakage current and abnormal delay metrics. The entire wafer lot would then be rejected, and, per the standard procedures, put through a detailed electrical characterization test, and forwarded to Dr. Cedric Dyson's Physical Analysis lab for root cause failure analysis.

If standard procedures were to be followed, then a sample of the failing material would be subjected to any of the usual physical analysis evaluations, and a signal corresponding to cadmium incorporated in the bulk of silicon wafers would be detected.

However, cadmium metal—an element that is rarely used in semiconductor industry—was also a trigger for a virus that infected the analytic tools used in Dr. Dyson's Physical Analysis lab. The virus—imported by *Merlin* navigation module—inserted a specific subroutine deep in the control software that ran this type of instruments. On detection of both, the trace amount of cadmium and the dominant amounts of silicon, the subroutine ran a check that verified the identity of the analytic equipment. If, and only if, the equipment identity code matched the pre-programmed format, and both signals were present, then the virus would issue a command to generate additional data that was an exact inverse of the signal produced by cadmium. Subsequent natural data manipulations would then combine and sort all the signals and present the results in a form of a graph that displayed the net signal amplitudes. That graph was all that the 'normal' human users looked at. Everything would look perfectly normal except that the net magnitude of the signal corresponding to cadmium would be zero.

All that would have happened *if* the standard procedures were followed…

"There is nothing more deceptive than an obvious fact"
—Arthur Conan Doyle

t-0 + 29 months, Chandler AZ and Washington DC

Cedric's first reaction to the ugly realization that dawned on him was almost intuitive. He reflexively recoiled from the situation and said nothing to anyone. Instead, he put away the samples that he was working on, and even deleted all the files associated with his analysis. Something within him told him that maintaining total secrecy was of paramount importance if they were ever to identify the culprit behind the very clever acts of sabotage against *his* fab.

Later—much later—he rationalized that the reason for his behavior was probably shaped by the programming of World War II legends that every boy and girl growing up in the United Kingdom in the 1960's and 70's received. The heroic exploits of the allied forces, 'Britain's finest hour ', the RAF victory of the Battle for Britain, Monty outfoxing the Desert Fox, and on and on… For a shy boy with a bit of a stutter and with a natural bias for technical things, it was the Bletchley Park legend of cracking of the Enigma code that rang the loudest. He was very familiar with the full history of the brilliant effort to decipher German secret messages and he remembered all sorts of minutia about it. Not only the way that Alan Turing and his team had broken the code and how a byproduct of their approach had shaped computer science in the second half of the twentieth century, thereby incidentally triggering his own interest in semiconductor technology, but also irrelevant things like the name and date of birth of Alan Turing's favorite punch-tape typist (Jennifer Maxwell, 1919). And he was also fully aware of the extent to which the allies had gone in order to keep their knowledge of the German Enigma code secret—even to the point of knowingly suffering losses that could have been prevented but that might have revealed to the Germans that their secret code had been compromised.

So, almost intuitively he understood the importance of keeping secret the realization that his fab was *compromised*—he shied away from using the loaded word 'sabotage'. Even if that meant that his fab had to suffer incremental yield losses.

So, for a few days he did absolutely nothing. At least no one is going to die over this, he comforted himself.

Then, after things settled down in his mind and he'd had a chance to digest the enormity of his discovery, he was ready. He knew that he must tell someone. So, he called his patron, Matt Nowak, the fab manager. He'd known Matt for many years and believed him to be someone who could not, and would not, be corrupted—someone who could be trusted.

Busy as a man in his position must have been, Matt humored Cedric, managed to clear a slot on his calendar and even agreed to meet outside and go for a walk in the park area of the ElInt campus. He thought that Cedric's request to meet out of the office was a bit odd and suspected that Cedric wanted to gripe about some people and hence needed privacy, or something of that kind. But as he listened carefully and understood immediately both the serious nature of Cedric's finding and the need for secrecy, he asked, "Are you sure?"

"Yes," Cedric confirmed. "It must be sabotage. If it were just an odd instance of cadmium contamination in the fab, I would believe it to be a technical problem. Even with contamination that seems to be random, like what we have seen so far. If it were just one of my FA tools missing a cadmium signal, I would believe it to be a technical problem. But two tools showing the same symptoms, at the same time when the fab is experiencing waves of cadmium contamination, no way! That is a human problem. It must be sabotage. Very subtle, obviously orchestrated by some clever bastard who understands the technology and the fabs, but sabotage nonetheless!"

Matt's first reaction was that of denial. "Can't be! In my fab? Here? In America? No way!"

Then, despite his trust in Cedric, he tried to pick holes in the argument. "How do you know that there was a master plan? Co-incidences sometimes do happen." Or, "How can you be sure that it is cadmium in both cases? Maybe the yield issue in the fab is due to something else, and your tools just happen to have a cadmium problem that you would normally never see. You are just trying to put two and two together." And so on…

But in the end, Matt had to accept it. "Yeah, you are probably right," he concluded. "I do not want to believe it, and don't like it, but… The broader implications are particularly alarming to me, but I guess that does not change the conclusions. So, I agree."

He also agreed that they must keep this knowledge between themselves and that no one should be trusted, at least for the time being. But he felt that the need for the extreme secrecy was dictated by possible national security considerations, not just so that they could keep the culprit in the dark until they figured out how to nab him, or her. Or them…

"This is not just any silicon fab," Matt insisted. "It is also the symbol of a very high-profile national initiative. For Christ's sake, we had the president attend the opening ceremony. Sabotage here is much bigger than just you or me or our fab."

And he went on to explain the extreme interest that the National Security Adviser personally showed for ensuring security, even as the fab was under construction. He described some of the bureaucratic hoops that she'd made the vendors jump through before they were allowed to bring anything on-site. "She not only made sure that the vendors met all sorts of national security criteria, but even insisted on fully documented provenance of the vendors' suppliers. Two or sometimes even three layers deep into the supply chain. She even nixed a few suppliers who could not provide such proofs."

"Who knows, maybe she knew something even back then," Matt suggested.

After a short discussion they agreed that they should probably try to call her directly rather than using other channels.

"Internal security, or the local police? No, not within their scope. The local FBI people? Probably not, they likely won't get it anyway. This is complicated esoterica. Besides, who knows who may or may not be involved in this?" Matt emphasized.

Fortunately, Matt was a meticulous record keeper, and he readily retrieved the contact information that Jane Stewart, the National Security Adviser, had shared during one of her visits. They placed the call from Matt's office and worked their way through various tiers of White House operators and assistants and aides and deputies until they reached the person who agreed to pass the message that Matt Nowak, the site manager of the ElInt Fab-8 in Arizona, had some critical information that was sure to be of interest to the National Security Adviser. Two days later, Matt received a call from the same assistant, and a time slot for the following week for a direct conversation with Jane Stewart was arranged.

On the day of the call, Matt opened with, "Madam, thank you for taking this call. I am not sure if you remember me, but I—"

"Yes, yes, Matt, you are the site manager of the Arizona fab. Please call me Jane. Your message said that you had some critical information that I need to hear," she interrupted brusquely.

Matt then introduced Cedric who proceeded to explain his observation and conclusion in as succinct terms as he could manage but bearing in mind that he was talking to an outsider who was probably unfamiliar with the technical lingo.

When he'd finished, Jane asked only two questions: How sure of the findings were they; and who else knew?

She seemed satisfied when Matt responded, "One hundred percent sure," and "no one other than the three of us and whoever else might be listening in on this call."

She took a few seconds to collect herself and then responded, "Thank you. You did the right thing to call me and no one else. Please keep it that way for now." Then, after another pause, she speculated, "This might turn out to be a very big deal. Both on a national and an international scale. I need to think through who should be involved, and how... Not only to prevent a possible leak to whoever is responsible, but also because in this town a story like that could lead to all sorts of reactions and overreactions."

And she signed off with an admonition, "Gentlemen, let me again insist that this is a matter of national security and that this must remain secret. Please do not talk about it to anyone. Not your most trusted colleagues, not your wife or family, not even your pet dog—no one! And please do not *do* anything until you hear from me personally." She sounded very serious. "It is critical," she repeated.

Few days later Matt received a text message that said that JMS would be in Phoenix next month, and that they must meet face-to-face. The message stressed that this was to be a below-the-radar 'personal trip', that she preferred to remain incognito, and that no one should be made aware of it, and indicated that the details of the place and the time of the meeting will be forthcoming. It closed with a request for confirmation of the proposed dates.

Matt checked back with Cedric, and then replied: "Yes."

"You have a grand gift for silence, Watson.
It makes you quite invaluable."
—Arthur Conan Doyle

t-0 + 29 months, Hsinchu, Taiwan

Fifteen time zones and seven thousand, one hundred and eight miles away, Argon Zhi was entirely unaware of the events in Arizona. At the instant dimethylcadmium was released into the oxidation furnace of ElInt's new fab—an occurrence that he had instigated and that was possibly fated to bring two world powers to the brink of a major war—he was just sitting down to have dinner with Akemi in their home in Hsinchu, Taiwan.

In fact, it had been months since he'd even thought about their 'project'. As far as he was concerned, that chapter of his life was over. He was confident—perhaps even smug—that the plan he'd hatched would work and that there was no reason to believe that things would unfold in any way other than as intended. After all, his plan was a 'belt-and-suspenders' solution that worked on both sides of the equation, making it quite robust. Almost foolproof. On the cause side of the equation, the mechanism that introduced contamination into the Americans' new fab was subtle and random, resulting in irreproducible and inconsistent behavior whose root cause would always be hard to trace down. And on the effect side, they had made sure that the source of the problem would appear to be invisible, or at least extremely difficult to pin down. This was bound to make finding a solution to the yield problem that much more difficult. It was a good plan.

Yes, his plan was something that only an insider—a good engineer—could dream up. And quite devious, too. Blinding the

117

doctor while at the same time poisoning his patient was downright clever, and he was quite proud of it. And even if the plan was not as foolproof as he thought it to be, and the Americans did unravel the plot, it would be impossible for them to trace any of it back to him or Cliff.

Hence, he was confident, and felt secure enough, to push the entire affair to the back of his mind.

Argon also knew that it would be very unlikely for him to find out anything concrete about the actual events that his ploy might have triggered. Even if an issue was discovered, people just did not advertise their yield problems and certainly no one talked openly about contamination in their fab. If ElInt, or some of its suppliers and contractors, or even some of the organs of the US federal government, perchance understood and appreciated what was going on, it would nevertheless be kept very quiet.

Still, he was curious. Especially with all the fanfare and publicity that accompanied the launch of the new fab, what with the President of the United States attending the opening ceremony and with mighty ElInt gushing about going into the pure-play foundry business and bragging about new clients like Qualcomm and nVidia—rightfully FSMC's clients.

He pinged his rumor mill a few times, trying several industry talking heads, trying people he knew at ElInt and people he trusted at the various equipment vendors, and even trying some of the FSMC process engineers who might have talked with the field service engineers who, in turn, knew everything. Roundabout questioning of all sorts of people who might know something about the performance of the ElInt new foundry. A man in his position had legitimate reasons to ask about it…

But there was nothing. Certainly nothing that indicated that there were yield issues in the new fab.

And he knew better than to ask Cliff to use his channels to keep an eye on the events in Arizona.

In his mind the only residue of the entire affair was his increased awareness of the importance of failure analysis to the overall business. He came to appreciate that failure analyses activities were undervalued, and typically viewed more as a necessary overhead rather than a way of differentiating the entire business. And this in turn caused him to ask one of his analysts to do a market study to see if there were suitable manufacturers of FA equipment that FSMC could acquire. He thought that if FSMC could lock up some FA tool or technique and make it proprietary, it may give the company an edge in achieving—and cementing—best yield learning curves. But there was no suitable pinch point in that portion of the supply chain. FA hardware seemed to be produced by at least three different and credible sources, and software was too esoteric to form a good lock-out mechanism. That exercise also touched on the makers of various types of inspection equipment, which sometimes relied on similar techniques as those used in FA, such as, for example, scanning electron microscopes. He toyed with the idea of pursuing an acquisition of Lasertec—a manufacturer of tools for inspecting the latest generation of mask plates used in chip manufacturing—the so-called 'actinic' Extreme Ultraviolet mask inspection. But he decided that this was unlikely to be good value for money. The field was too new and volatile, and disruptive new solutions might crop up at any time, potentially making his investment useless.

Round 4:
The Response

*"The fact that you can only do a little is
no excuse for doing nothing"*
—John le Carré

t-0 + 30 months, Scottsdale, AZ

They met in a modern, smoked glass and desert-sandstone villa tucked away in the back of the *Sanctuary at Camelback Mountain*, a posh resort just north of Scottsdale. Of course, Matt and Cedric first had to clear hotel security, who made sure that they were indeed on the list of pre-approved visitors, and who then double checked their ID's. They were then escorted to the villa, where they were screened by her Secret Service agent—not a stereotypical six foot, five-inch goon, but a regular guy whose jacket with leather elbow patches gave him something of a scholarly look. He did not ask for their IDs but instead photographed them and verified on his computer that they were indeed who they claimed to be, and who then scanned them with an electronic wand to confirm that they had no weapons and that they were not wired. Clearly, the 'muscle' portion of her security detail must have been out of sight. They were told to leave their laptops and phones in the foyer by the door and ushered into the main area of the villa.

"So much for an incognito personal trip…" Cedric mumbled to Matt.

"Come in, come in…" Jane closed the file she was reading and waved them into the open plan room which was tastefully decorated in desert hues and Maricopa tribal art that contrasted nicely with the modern angular furniture. They shook hands and were invited to sample coffee, drinks or snacks in the kitchenette. Then she invited them to take seats at the large conference table positioned on a kind of a dais in front of floor-to-ceiling windows that offered a spectacular view of the valley.

Perhaps it was because she overheard Cedric's comment, or because she noticed their awed reaction to the sumptuous surroundings, or because she just wanted to break the ice, Jane explained that people in her position did not get to travel without an approval from Secret Services, and that they insisted that a separate villa would be easier to secure than a regular hotel suite. She added that she shuddered to think how much all that cost, but that she was assured that this was cheaper than bringing her entire security detail, and that this is as low a profile as she was allowed to be.

Cedric was impressed by her personable tone that seemed to show 'everyman' values and decided that he quite liked this National Security Adviser lady.

"First," she started, "we must take care of formalities." She then explained that whereas they had been vetted when they first took their position with the new facility, she'd had them thoroughly checked out, and that from this point on they should consider themselves under all the restrictions that went with full US government Level-1 'Top-Secret' clearance, as defined by the Title 50 U.S. Subsection 3341 executive order. Reacting to their blank stares, she clarified, "It just means that you now have Top Secret clearance and that if you misappropriate or mishandle any classified information, you could be charged and tried for espionage or even treason under appropriate US laws. Standard stuff." She gave each of them a packet of papers to sign and said, "As of right now, I am defining everything and anything to do with the supposed act of sabotage in your factory as a classified US Government Level-1 Secret. Is that clear?" And then after a short pause, she added, "I am sorry, but it is a matter of National Security. You are now obliged to keep quiet about it. The papers are just an acknowledgment that you have been informed of this. Furthermore, you should assume that you are under twenty-four-hour surveillance to ensure your safety and your compliance with the gag order."

She laughed a bit at their apparent alarm and added in a lighter tone, "Don't worry. It's nothing like what I have to put up with. For you it just means that you should carry on doing what you have done so far and talk to absolutely no one about this case unless I personally authorize it."

Cedric of course protested that he would not sign anything without reading it first; and judging by the heft of the packet that she gave them, that would take him a while. Jane looked at him and simply said that he should just sign it since it was not as if he could change the verbiage, or as if he had a choice. "Standard stuff," she repeated. They had a bit of a staring match, but finally he shrugged to acknowledge his capitulation, and signed. Matt did the same.

They then settled around the table and Jane dived in. "After our phone conversation, I alerted the president about the possibility of sabotage in your facility. Let me tell you, he went ballistic. He said that sabotage is a long way from espionage, and that whereas espionage was routine and practiced by all sides, sabotage was more like an act of war, and therefore we must mount a suitable reprisal, and that he suspected—no, that he knew—that it was China, and..."

Cedric felt sick with tension. Matt turned pale, too. The surroundings and legal warnings were intimidating enough, but a term like 'act of war' that Jane had dropped so casually, was positively frightening.

"I had quite a time," she continued in a business-like tone, "bringing him down to earth. I told him that in the first place we were not yet one hundred percent sure that there was sabotage, and that I was just giving him a heads-up; and secondly, that even if confirmed, we certainly did not know who was behind it, and therefore talk of reprisal, especially against China, was premature." She tapped the table in cadence with the points she made. She paused and clarified in slightly softer tones, "I am telling you this so that you understand the background. We must plan the next steps and, gentlemen, we do not have a lot of latitude." She looked at them, appraised their reaction, nodded, and proceeded.

"The president has calmed down since then, but he still insists that he does not want to appear weak on something like state sponsored sabotage, particularly against a high-profile asset that is so directly associated with his administration. Therefore, even a hint of anything of the kind must be kept secret until we are really sure; and that once we are sure, he will want to react quickly and resolutely.

"Bottom line," she concluded, "he is directing us to come to a definitive position that (a) this was an act of sabotage, (b) it was conducted by a state or an organization rather than some individual, (c) that we know exactly who did it, and (d) that we know how it was done." She counted off on her fingers for emphasis. "Meanwhile, he is constraining all activities to the minimum footprint."

"What exactly does that mean? Cedric asked.

"It means that POTUS wants to keep the US government machinery uninvolved and entirely in the dark, because he knows that it would leak. He does not want to be caught in a situation where there is talk of sabotage without a ready plan of action. He wants to keep a lid on it until he either hears that nothing actually happened and that talk of sabotage was a mistake, or we have a demonstrable proof. And, incidentally, he let it be known that he wants to make sure that this all plays out a year or so ahead of the elections. If it works out well, he will use it to position his administration as a strong defender of US interests; if it goes badly, he will still have time to re-focus the electorate on something else. He also thinks that planning a suitable response would take the Pentagon and the Intelligence Community a couple of months, so we only have until around September-time. Until then, we are on our own."

Matt and Cedric exchanged surprised looks. Orchestrating anything like an act of war to coincide with the election cycle was just the kind of a corrupt and cynical activity that people despised politicians for. And she was talking about the President of the United States doing exactly that!

Jane studied them calmly with her piercing green eyes.

"Okay," she picked up when their body language communicated that they had understood and were ready to move on. "Until then, the president has put me in sole charge of leading the investigation. And I am now recruiting you gentlemen. So, welcome aboard and what do you recommend we do?"

Cedric took that as his cue, cleared his throat, and volunteered, "I have been thinking about that. Of course, we could go through the entire fab with a fine-tooth comb to find the source of cadmium contamination. But that would take months, it would be very disruptive to the fab, and it would be very visible to anyone who was paying even the slightest bit of attention."

"Yes," Jane cut in, "not only do we have to do whatever we are going to do without alerting the parties involved—even though we have no idea who they might be—but we also must do it all with our hands tied behind our backs, so to speak. By insisting on total secrecy, the president has not only asked us to work alone, but he has also ordered us to remain invisible. So, since we do not know who might be involved, whatever we do must not be noticed either by the people at this site, or for that matter by anyone in your entire company. And absolutely nothing should be even suspected by the media, or any of the various government organizations. This is awkward since we most likely will need their help. I might be able to recruit an individual here or there—off the books so to speak—but the security apparatus of the government—the professionals like the FBI, CIA, NSA—must remain on the outside." She leaned forward and slapped the table in frustration, revealing that she felt like she was set up to fail.

Cedric mumbled, "I suspected that we would have to stay below the radar as far as the rest of the Company is concerned—at least for a while—but I did not expect to have to hide from our government."

Jane gave him a helpless shrug, as if to say that there was nothing that she could do about that, and repeated. "These are the orders of the President of the United States, whether we agree with them or not. Experience has thought him that there is no such thing as a secret in Washington DC."

After a pause Cedric continued, "So we will just have to be clever. But we do have one big advantage. We do know the exact thermal history of the contaminated material, and given the concentration profile of cadmium, we should be able to work backward through T-CAD simulations and pinpoint the step in the process where the contamination was introduced."

Matt nodded slowly in understanding, but Jane looked entirely puzzled, so Cedric elaborated. "We must assume that cadmium was deposited on the surface of silicon wafers at some point during manufacturing. Subsequently, every time the wafers were exposed to elevated temperatures the contaminants would diffuse deeper into the silicon. The higher the temperature or the longer the exposure, the further they would go. There are mathematical expressions that define the interdependence. So, if we measure the distribution of cadmium—basically determine how deep the cadmium atoms went—and since we know the exact nature of all the thermal cycles the material has seen, then we can work backward to figure out the origin of that contamination. We have computer tools that can help with that. That way we can narrow the search down to one or, at worst a few, pieces of equipment. We can then take those apart to find the source of the contamination. And presumably that would give us the hard evidence of sabotage that you need. And maybe even a hint as to who is responsible…"

"Oh, I see," Jane muttered, but she did not sound convincing.

"I must measure the profile of cadmium distribution in the contaminated material," Cedric carried on. "But, since our lab is compromised, I need to go off-site for that. Maybe I can call in a favor or two and use Charles Evans' lab in the Bay Area. Jim Doi, the director of surface analysis there, is a friend, and I think that I can get him to let me use one of his older machines which is not connected and on-line, and therefore, by definition, is presumably virus-free. Insurance, just in case that their machines have been infected, too."

Matt hesitated. "Are you sure? I would think that the famous Dr Cedric Dyson showing up at some commercial lab to use their equipment might raise some eyebrows."

"Possible," Cedric reacted, "but I would think that using other labs within the company would be even more suspicious and would surely start busy tongues wagging. So, if I go to a commercial lab and rely on a friend's discretion? Maybe go over the weekend and invent some suitable cover story… Like a side job for some start up?" He then turned to Jane and asked directly, "What do you think? Do I have your permission?"

She nodded and said, "Yes, of course. Do what you need to do. I do not care about which lab you use and what cover story you make up as long as no one suspects the real thing."

"Furthermore," Cedric continued, now mostly addressing Matt, "if we tweak the manufacturing flow and use 'mini-lots' to maintain a direct one-to-one correlation between specific process equipment and unique wafer lots, the next time we have an issue we should be able to identify immediately the suspect machine."

"Makes sense," Matt confirmed. "That is obviously a less efficient way to run a fab than merging multiple lots into larger batches." And then, after a few seconds, he added, "Maybe an argument about trading off efficiency until we have eliminated all the fab teething problems would stick. I will put out a policy statement that calls for use of these mini-lots until we iron out our biggest yield issues. That way the change will not confuse people." And he jotted something down in his notebook.

"The other big problem," Matt observed, "is that our computer systems have clearly been infected with some bug, and we have no idea of the extent of the penetration. It could be just the machines in your lab, or it could be every computer on the site, or it may go even beyond the corporate firewalls? Identifying and cleaning that up might be harder. Certainly so, if we must keep corporate IT guys in the dark."

"Good point," Cedric reacted. "Clearly the computers in my lab have been infected. I suppose it is possible—even likely—that other machines in the fab have also been compromised. And I suppose that it is possible that any tampering with the bug might alert the culprit. Who knows? But other than that, this is a topic that I know nothing about."

"Nor do I," Matt responded. "This is something where we must involve additional people. The three of us are just not technically capable. Jane, we do need help in this area."

"Okay," Jane nodded. "Let me look into that. Maybe some techie from NSA? But obviously, he or she will have to operate with blinders and be restricted to a very narrow scope. We need a cover of some kind for him to operate unnoticed even by your IT. Matt, can you, as the site manager, come up with a suitable excuse?"

Matt nodded and wrote something else in his notebook.

They stayed in that villa the entire day, planning and brainstorming. Lunch, and later, a light dinner, were brought in. At that point in time, none of them had the detachment required to note the contrast of the sinister topic that they were discussing versus the idyllic setting in which they were discussing it in. The view of the valley was truly spectacular, especially in the evening when the sunset tinged everything with the amber and orange glow that went so well with the desert hues, and later, at nightfall, with the streetlights and desert sky stars fading in at about the same time. But they did not notice.

However, by the end of the day, they did have a definite plan. In closing, they went over their specific action items, each confirming or adding tasks to their respective to-do lists.

Before they left, Jane gave them two phones which were supposed to be very secure and bug-proof and were to be used exclusively for communications between the three of them. They agreed to touch base frequently.

And then Matt and Cedric left the villa, each wearing the shell-shocked look of one who had gone through a traumatic experience. All this was far beyond anything that either man had ever experienced in his thirty-year professional life.

But it would not remain so for long. And this was only the beginning...

t-0 + 31 months,
Singapore and Taiwan

It was important to ascertain whether other fabs and other companies were also infected, or if the problem they saw was limited only to the new ElInt fab. Jane felt that this would go a long way toward proving whether it was indeed sabotage, and further, whether it was a state sponsored act or an act of some individual with a gripe. She thought that the kind of thing that an unfriendly state might sponsor would likely be a broadside attack on U.S. technology prowess, and that therefore other U.S. fabs, as well as the fabs of US allies, including Taiwan, Japan and Korea, should be expected to be hit as well. Versus something like a disgruntled employee, or some deranged activist, who might have a bone to pick with ElInt.

However, given the order for utter secrecy, they could not use official channels, such as any of the U.S. government agencies, to reach out to other domestic semiconductor companies, or companies of various allied nations. It was not like they could do the obvious and just call and ask an outright question; "Hey, have you experienced any issues with heavy metal contamination in your fabs?" Such a question would ring all sorts of alarm bells. Similarly, reaching out through non-governmental channels like industry associations, trade groups, or standard-setting bodies would be equally counterproductive, not just due to their need for secrecy, but also because semiconductor companies were known to be uncommunicative about yield problems. Understandably so, since yield numbers rolled directly into corporate cost structure and hence impacted pricing and margins. "Thou shalt not talk about yield numbers" was the eleventh commandment in the industry.

So, they agreed that the best way to obtain the needed information was for Cedric to ping his personal network. After all, if anyone was going to know anything about fab contamination, it would be Cedric's fellow Failure Analysts. They also felt that professional courtesy, colleague-to-colleague kind of informal discussion would not raise any eyebrows. Just a part of an off-the-books exchange of war stories that FA engineers apparently loved.

Therefore, one of the tasks on Cedric's to-do list from their meeting at the *Sanctuary at Camelback Mountain* was to chat with as many of his colleagues as he could, without raising undue suspicions. The chip industry is fairly provincial, and given the fluidity of its engineering workforce, people within a specialty field, such as Failure Analysis, knew each other, or at least knew *of* each other—from various conferences and industry events, or from working together at this company or that, or from various publications and scientific papers, or maybe just through gossip. This was especially so when it came to an old and a well-known figure such as Dr. Cedric Dyson—a name on hundreds of technical papers and a personality who had been in the field for decades.

Cedric did get busy and made multiple calls to various friends, colleagues and failure analysts he knew. However, socializing did not come readily to a person like he was, and after a few awkward phone conversations he concluded that he might be more successful at ferreting out subtle information that he was after, if he were to meet select analysts face to face.

So, he dropped some hints to the right people, and soon he was invited to give a keynote speech at the IPFA (International Symposium on the Physical and Failure Analysis of Integrated Circuits)—a suitable conference that he selected primarily because it was to be held at a convenient time and place.

With ElInt's recent entrance into the foundry business, a speaker like Dr. Cedric Dyson giving a presentation at a premier Asian Failure Analysis conference made a bit of a splash, and he was duly invited to stop by and tour the Physical and Failure Analysis labs at FSMC in Taiwan, and to visit Samsung facilities in Korea, and Sony labs in Japan.

Since the three of them felt that if some enemy was attacking

U.S. technology interests, then they would also be sure to go after FSMC, he accepted that invitation and declined the rest. Also, co-incidentally, the FSMC FA lab was managed by one of the people who had worked for him ten years ago in Austin, and Cedric felt that he was most likely to get the real story from someone he already knew.

Cedric was supposed to maintain his cover and therefore he had to come up with a keynote presentation for the conference in Singapore. He did not have the time, or the inclination, to prepare one of those typical highly polished PowerPoint presentations that included fancy graphics, animations and sound effects. Instead, he prepared his talk mostly during his flight to Singapore. ElInt's travel policy allowed flying Business Class, and the relatively spacious seats, and lack of interruptions for much of the seventeen-hour flight, made for excellent conditions for just that kind of a task. The set of black and white slides that he prepared, using simple text and a few hand-drawn graphs, was quite atypical for a keynote presentation, but the prosaic style suited his image. And the points that he intended to make were very appropriate and popular. He used the data that he had gathered in his own labs over the last few decades and claimed that the standard metrics usually applied to the Failure Analysis activities—such as the Turn-Around-Time (TAT) or No-Defect-Found (NDF) rate—had mostly remained constant over the last few decades. That was well received by the audience of FA analysts. His second point was also appreciated; that when that data was presented in context of the complexity of the devices under analysis, then those same metrics showed the usual exponential growth in productivity that was typical of Moore's Law. The audience lapped that up, since they knew all too well that technology evolution resulted in an enormous increase in not just the number of devices per chip, but also in the types of materials and the number of layers that it took to build them. And hence, the effort required to take them apart—to 'de-process' them, in the lingo—has also ballooned. He was quite amused when he overheard some fawning junior engineers referring to this as 'Dyson's Law'. But he was satisfied that the message that failure analysis labs had managed to keep pace with the head-spinning technology evolution seemed to have come across.

That finished, he enjoyed a free half-day in Singapore, still one of his favorite places on earth. He did not have the time to visit with Lakshmi's relatives who lived there but could not possibly miss a chance to gorge himself at one of the famous local Hawker Centers. He ravenously ate a plate of Black Pepper Crab at Maxwell Road Center, his favorite since the days when he'd lived there, so many years ago. It was still as good as he remembered it. Then he took the evening flight to Taipei, where he was met by a limo that drove him to his hotel in Hsinchu.

Next morning he met John—John Lin—the Director of all Physical Analysis facilities at FSMC. Over breakfast they mostly talked about the 'old times' that they'd shared in Austin, and gossiped about the people in the field that they both knew. Afterward, John took him to the famous FSMC Fab-12 complex and proudly showed off his central Physical and Failure Analysis lab; a state-of-the-art facility that was very good—but not as good as his own lab at EllInt.

Then, contrary to Cedric's expectations, instead of ending up in John's office where they could have a private chat, he was ushered into a conference room filled with a dozen people, who all seemed to want to meet him. John then asked him to give a synopsis of his plenary talk at IPFA and to 'endure' a Q&A session with the people present.

After his presentation, one of the members of the audience who identified himself as Argon Zhi, asked if he could talk about the kind of issues that he had to address in EllInt's new fab, and whether there were any surprises… The question was notable in two senses. One was that it came from a man who, judging from the way he handled things, was a leftie—an attribute that Cedric, being one himself, was very practiced at picking up, almost at a subliminal level. The other was that according to his business card, that question came from an EVP from the Office of Strategic Planning—not a type that Cedric would have expected to understand, or care about, the intricacies of failure mechanisms in modern ICs.

So, of course, he gave the usual fluffy response. It was not like Cedric would share his 'dirty laundry' in an open setting, and he was certainly not going to break the gag order from *Madame*

Secretary—the title that he had ascribed to Jane, after the TV series.

He then tried to turn the question around and asked the people present about any new issues that might have been noticed in the FSMC fabs, and he received an equally fluffy answer. He could not detect even a whiff of the furtive exchange of glances typical of people who shared a secret.

Then a fancy lunch that supposedly highlighted the best of Taiwanese cuisine was brought in and they all had the typical business-casual meal accompanied with the usual superficial conversation. Altogether, given the list of invitees, it became clear to Cedric that John was milking the occasion of his visit to score some internal political points, and that the topic that was most of interest to that audience was not Failure Analysis but ElInt's business in the pure-play foundry market. So, Cedric steered the conversation toward less sensitive topics and said something about how he loved visiting the east because chop sticks were one of the few inventions that did not favor right-handed people. Argon reacted to that with a comment about how this was ironic as in their culture leftism was not only not condoned, but was positively and actively deterred, and confessed that he was a leftie himself. Which then led to quite an exchange of stories of woe between Argon and Cedric, each lamenting the prejudices and the everyday difficulties that left-handers faced even in the modern world. This dominated the conversation through the lunch and there was no further talk of chip failures or ElInt business.

Finally, just before he was due to leave, he and John had a private moment, and Cedric probed with all sorts of leading questions and comments. But there was nothing in John's response that led Cedric to believe that FSMC was in the middle of a yield bust battle, or that there were any novel failure mechanisms. No mention of contamination of any kind. He even asked leading questions about the types of reference samples that John might have acquired for calibration of his SIMS machines, hoping that John might slip and mention cadmium. Still nothing... Finally, in exasperation Cedric threw caution to the wind and asked directly if John might have seen something like heavy metal contamination in any of his fabs. John's seemingly frank and unguarded surprise at the question convinced Cedric that the FSMC fabs were not experiencing anything like what he had seen. Or if they had, they were not aware of it.

Cedric flew back the next morning believing that the problem was localized to ElInt's fab in Arizona.

"Survival...is an infinite capacity for suspicion"
—John le Carré

t-0 + 32 months, Hsinchu, Taiwan

Argon was alarmed. It was not due to something that Cedric said during the meeting because Cedric's commentary was sparse and addressed only generic issues. What was it that he said? Something like: "The dominant source of failures in advanced ICs is not caused by some new mechanism; it is due to the same old parametric issues that have been exacerbated by erosion of design margin." Everybody knew that.

No, it was the fact that Cedric was there at all that alarmed Argon. Based on everything that he could dig up on Cedric—both from informal chats with John and other people who knew Cedric, and from the formal background report that he'd requested—it was out of character for Cedric to travel for business. Apparently, it had been a long time since he last attended any of the open industry events. And giving a presentation—especially a non-technical overview—was also out of character for him. Particularly at what was, realistically speaking, a second-rate conference. From what Argon could gather, Dr. Dyson could score a keynote speaker slot at any one of the premier industry gatherings: IRPS in Monterey, DAC in San Francisco, or VLSI in Hawaii, or even IEDM in Washington. Instead, supposedly he had chosen IPFA in Singapore for his first public presentation in fifteen years. Argon found this to be unlikely. And probably not just a coincidence.

Then again, Argon was fully aware that the sole reason that Cedric's visit had caught his attention at all was because of his connection to the new ElInt fab. Which was significant only to

Argon because of the secret that he and Cliff kept. Perhaps he was being overly sensitive, or myopic, or paranoid. So, he called Cliff for a sanity check, and they arranged a meeting a few days later, again at Hsinchu Park.

By that time Argon had calmed down, but he explained the situation to Cliff and elaborated how he *felt* that something was not right, and that it might possibly be connected to their ploy. Cliff listened carefully and then took a long time to articulate a response.

"The worst-case scenario would be that your intuition is right, and that this Dr. Dyson has uncovered our little time bomb," he started. "Was there anything in his behavior that gave you a feeling that he was in the middle of dealing with a yield problem or that he knew its source or that he suspected you?"

"No, definitely not," Argon answered readily. He sounded more certain of this than he really felt, partially because he thought that more time would be needed to solve the problem, and that it was unlikely that anyone would have found its source so soon. According to his model, ElInt's fab should have experienced only three to five occurrences of cadmium poisoning by that date. He knew that under normal circumstances more data points would be required to unravel the puzzle. But partially, it was because he felt safe since he was confident that it would be impossible to trace the problem back to them.

"Exactly," Cliff confirmed. "I think we are covered. Therefore, the worst that can happen is that our plan is neutralized. That they stop it prematurely…"

"Which would mean that we spent all that effort for nothing," Argon reacted to Cliff's point. "It is too soon for that fab to have earned any kind of a reputation. This was supposed to be all about establishing a pattern which would be sufficiently believable to affect normal business flows. As we discussed, somewhere between five and ten occurrences of yield busts—probably closer to 10— would be required for a reputation to take hold in the industry. And so far, I certainly have not heard anything in the news or even through the rumor mills to indicate that anything of the kind was happening. So, if they do 'neutralize' our plan now, we will have failed," Argon concluded.

"Is it possible," Cliff continued, seemingly following his own train of thought rather than listening to Argon, "that they have a suspicion but have not quite solved it? Perhaps this Dyson knows something is wrong, but does not yet know specifically what it is…"

"Yes, definitely," Argon confirmed." In fact, that may even be probable. From what I've heard about Cedric Dyson, he is exactly that rare kind of 'mutant' who might have had a chance to find the root cause very quickly. He's supposed to be one in a million." Argon used the term "mutant" in reference to an earlier conversation that they'd had, when he tried to explain to Cliff that good Failure Analysis engineers were rare because of the unique mix of 'mutations' of traditional engineering specialties that were required.

"So, perhaps not all is lost," Cliff concluded. "If we eliminate Dr. Dyson before he neutralizes us, then our plan would remain active. Maybe we can still make sure that we succeed."

"Eliminate Cedric Dyson? What do you mean?" Argon blurted.

Cliff waved the question away impatiently. "Think about it. If Dyson is everything you think he is, and if you are right and they have not yet discovered the problem or its source, then removing him from the picture would probably prolong the game. Eliminating *him* would maximize our chances of success." He spoke slowly, as if feeling his way through a logical puzzle.

"Cliff, what are you saying? Are you thinking of having him killed?" Argon was dumbfounded.

"Don't be dramatic, Argon. You've seen too many movies," Cliff responded laughing it off. "There are various ways that an individual can be eliminated," he added cryptically.

"No!" Argon insisted. "Whatever you do…get him fired, or…I don't know…somehow discredit him, or… God forbid, have him killed, or whatever else you may be thinking of as a way of 'eliminating' him, it is all equally wrong!"

"Well, logically, according to what you've told me, the most constructive thing that we could do now would be to remove *him* from the equation," Cliff persisted. "If sabotaging a twenty billion dollar fab of our ally was the right thing to do for our island republic, then eliminating one person to ensure the success of that enterprise would surely also be the right thing to do."

"No, no and no!" Argon repeated. "When it comes to people, ends do not justify the means. Any person who uses force will find that he accomplishes nothing," he quoted *Tao Te Ching*.

Cliff just grunted and muttered something under his breath about countryfolk's 'bullshit'.

Argon knew that Cliff was the type of a person who was hard to divert once he set out on a particular path, so he fervently pressed on trying to reel him back. "Cliff, we are talking about a human being! A good man. A professional man. He is just like you and me. I met him only a couple of days ago and had lunch with him and we chatted about the troubles that left-handers face, and... And now you are talking about 'eliminating' him as if he were an inanimate object. No!"

Cliff shrugged and looked into the distance—a look that signaled to Argon that he was no longer listening.

Argon knew that look. It was like a cold shower for him. A shock... A disappointment... Of course, what Cliff said made logical sense, but Cliff was now talking about peoples' lives!

For the first time, Argon saw things in a different light, almost as if he'd just awakened. In the past he'd thought about this project as an abstract exercise. An engineering challenge. A puzzle. The brutal terms that they were now considering had not previously come to his mind: sabotage; neutralization; elimination... In addition, for the first time their enterprise somehow felt personal rather than purely intellectual. Now he could attach a name and a face to his 'opponent'. Such new perceptions triggered a range of emotions, and for the first time Argon began to question what he had done. Had it been the right thing to do? Was it moral? Would it hurt people? Was it consistent with Tao?

But the worst of it was the disappointment he felt toward Cliff. Suddenly, he saw Cliff in an entirely new light, and he shrank in horror. A flood of realizations came pouring at him. He realized that when it came to Cliff, he had failed to practice his own dictum: 'over, under or through, but never around'. Over the years he had skirted *around* Cliff's actions because they had been friends since childhood. He had danced *around* direct questions to avoid embarrassing his friend. He had looked *around* the realities of Cliffs role with the government. Doubts surfaced in his mind about whatever Cliff might, or might not, have been involved with during his years with the Military and National Security.

And perhaps his disappointment with Cliff was equaled only by the disappointment he felt toward himself. Yes, he realized that not only had he failed to question Cliff, but also, he had failed to question his own ethics, and his own involvement in the 'project'.

And now Cliff was talking about murder?

"Cliff, I am not sure that I know who you are," he spluttered. "Don't tell me anything more. I do not want any part of it, and I do not want to know."

But it was no use. Cliff was beyond reach.

t-0 + 33 months, Beijing, China

Houxi Wusheng was surprised. He had entirely forgotten about the case of the Hong Kong hacker and the Taiwanese spymaster. It had been a long time since he'd had any involvement with that incident, and the surveillance operation had been suspended a year ago. The 'human track and monitor-level 1' option that he'd authorized had yielded no results, and after a consultation with his superior officer, it had been terminated.

But now, he was staring at a set of photographs, taken from various angles and with various levels of resolution, of some man, entirely unknown to him, meeting with the Taiwanese spymaster, Cliff Lingdao, who he could barely remember. He clicked on the image of the unknown man and the usual summary came up: name, age, affiliation, address, etc. The notable thing was that there were two red stars next to the name of the man: Enchong Dee, aka F Gordon Liddy, with a note that read 'a private operative, known to the MSS'.

Strange alias, Haoxi thought to himself, ascribing it to the known Filipino propensity for use of odd nicknames drawn from multiple cultures, so instead he just focused on the red stars.

Houxi knew that the red star system was a way of rating various known intelligence assets. Four stars next to a name meant that a person was probably an active agent of the MSS—certainly someone who must not be interfered with, and whose dossier was not open to regular analysts. Sometimes the system even censored the image of four-star people and automatically blurred out their faces. According to the rumors shared among the analysts (people do talk despite what the rules say), dealing with four-star people was above their pay grade, and apparently, the wisest course of action was to steer well away from whatever that person might, or might not, be involved with. Three stars next to a name meant that a person was associated with the Ministry, but just as a trusted, friendly asset, rather than as an active field agent. Although he did not know it for sure, he believed that he, himself, was probably tagged with three stars. Two stars meant that a person was an external, and possibly a foreign operative, but who was a known asset. Usually, this designation was ascribed to people who might have collaborated with the MSS in the past, which, in practice, meant that the Ministry already had established and proven methods of interfacing with those individuals. One star meant that a person was a known operative, but not necessarily a friendly one. Typically, it was applied to 'non-aligned' people: professional operators who worked for money. And no stars meant that the subject was a 'civilian' (not an agent or a person in any kind of security or intelligence business). This of course covered 99% of the people.

He suspected that there was probably an analogous mechanism for tagging enemy agents, but that would be something for which he had not been cleared.

Furthermore, Houxi understood that there were usually two layers around every government institution involved in covert operations, such as the America's CIA, or Russia's KGB, or the British MI6, or, for that matter, China's MSS. One layer was above the organization and intended to contain powerful people, such as political or business leaders, who needed to maintain some distance from the reality of covert operations but who were aware of, and sometimes even initiated, those same dark ops.

The other layer was a tier below such government organizations, that was intended to contain people who might be useful but who needed to be kept separate, and at a distance, from the institution, for security, political or just practical reasons. These were mostly people who were either too shady or too greedy to recruit on permanent bases, but who could be used to perform specific, and perhaps onerous, tasks. Or they may be people useful for foreign operations, who had connections to, and could blend with, the local population. Or they might be people who played on multiple sides. Or they may be miscellaneous kind of people with useful skills or services, such as arms dealers, or local guerillas, or so-called terrorist, or even lone-wolf operatives.

He knew all this from the training that he had received. Now that China, under the leadership of President Xi, was assuming its rightful place in the world order, the Ministry was exploring taking a more active international role and had therefore put together a course about the workings of other, similar organizations. He was very proud to have been one of the few analysts chosen for this training. In fact, just the week before, he was privileged to sit through a presentation about the recent history of CIA, who was apparently very good at using that 'lower' layer of external resources even for massive international operations such as removal of unfriendly governments.

Houxi guessed that the man in the picture was some kind of an operative from that lower layer. In his limited experience, most of the two-star people were. His name and appearance was Chinese, but perhaps he was just a *Chinoy*—a Filipino term that he knew the locals used for Chinese people born there.

The AI System notes at the bottom of the report read:

- What: a field operative meeting a high-ranking member of the ROC secret service.

- Where: Akrotiri Greek Restobar, 146-B Jupiter, Makati, 1209 Metro Manila, Philippines.

- When: 23:12 Philippine Standard Time (23:12 China Standard Time), 1st of August.

Houxi's curiosity was naturally peaked, and he clicked on the image to bring up the information on this two-star person. The dossier indicated that Enchong Dee was a descendent of a Chinese family that emigrated to Philippines in 1965, that he had twenty years of service with the Philippine Army, twelve of which were with the elite Ranger unit, and that he still kept in touch with cousins in Fujian province. It said that he was currently operating as a security specialist and a private agent for hire, that he'd adopted a business alias, F Gordon Liddy (which meant nothing to Houxi), and that MSS had had some dealings with him. The rest of the dossier was full of redacted paragraphs, indicating that Houxi did not have a clearance to access the details of whatever operations this Enchong Dee may have been involved with. There was the usual note on the bottom of the screen that said that he would have to work through his superior officer to access any further information.

He conjectured that Enchong Dee was probably a freelance agent who worked for money. Or, that he may have been persuaded to cooperate with the MSS in the past because he had family in Mainland China. Or perhaps he might have been recruited by some other means. Or maybe he just was simply not trustworthy enough to be a permanent four-star name...

Houxi thought that all this was probably some kind of error in the system. He suspected that he was notified of this specific meeting because it took place in his territory—the Philippines—and because he'd had a prior interest in one of the people involved. However, he also suspected that the pictures were a part of some ongoing field operation; because the photographs were clearly 'harvested' from multiple sources, possibly ranging from satellite images to pictures hacked from neighborhood security cameras to high-resolution photographs taken by a field agent. This would have been typical of an active, ongoing operation. Furthermore, the man in the photographs—Enchong Dee aka F Gordon Liddy—was evidently an experienced agent.

Houxi knew that as a simple analyst he was not meant to be involved with covert ops unless he, himself, had ordered them; and currently he had nothing of the kind going on in the Philippines. So, informing him about it must have been a glitch. Even *the Oracle* could make mistakes sometimes.

Regardless of the specifics of the men in the photographs, and whereas sharing the pictures with an uninvolved analyst might have been a glitch, it was an interesting one. Why would the ROC spymaster be meeting with a freelance operative who was friendly to the Peoples Republic of China? Who was turning whom? Was Cliff Lingdao converting a friendly asset, or was it the other way around?

He would certainly report this to his superior officer, and ask for guidance on what, if any, follow-up steps were merited. After all, if the picture showed people engaged in a current dark op, then the glitch should be reported to the Internal Security Department. And if the picture showed people not engaged in a current operation, then their two-star free agent was potentially cooperating with Taipei security services, and the External Security Department should be alerted. Either way, (a) it must be reported to the higher-ups, and (b) someone in MSS would have to determine the exact nature of that contact.

t-0 + 33 months, Scottsdale, AZ

They got it!

The absolute and indisputable proof that it was indeed sabotage. It was sitting right in front of them on the fancy conference table at the villa in the *Sanctuary at Camelback Mountain*, which has become their usual rendezvous spot.

So far, in addition to direct phone calls to report on specific tasks, Jane had managed to come to Phoenix for three-way, in-person, sync-up meetings on monthly basis. This time they had a lot of significant new material to cover.

"Do you see it?" Cedric asked, pointing out the differences between the culprit and reference Mass Flow Controller units, both with their outer covers taken off, exposing their internal structure.

Jane and Matt, wary of getting too close, nodded hesitantly. As if it were a bomb, or something equally dangerous…

Cedric retrieved the culprit unit from a Yama VF-5900 Vertical Furnace. His SIMS analysis and T-CAD modeling had narrowed the source of contamination down to the oxidation step in the manufacturing process, and once they implemented a mini-lot manufacturing flow and the third instance of cadmium poisoning had been found, it was not hard to triangulate on a specific piece of manufacturing equipment in the oxidation module of the fab. The suspect furnace was taken off-line, disqualified for fab use, disconnected from the factory pure gas, water supply, computer control systems and exhaust lines, and wheeled into a separate bay in the back of the fab. Cedric then dismantled it, working by himself and mostly at night. Matt injected a story into the rumor mill that Cedric had come up with a brilliant idea for advanced oxidation and was tweaking the equipment for the new process step, and that everybody should give him space. This fit well with Cedric's reputation as an eccentric, and after a while everyone pretty much shrugged their shoulders, ignored him and got on with their regular work.

Cedric went into his hyperactive mode, and despite Lakshmi's protestations that he was not a young man anymore and that he should take care of himself, so he did not drop dead like his father had, he was operating on only four hours of sleep per night. He had to admit to himself that a part of him really enjoyed it—not only the detective work, which was spiced up by the conspiratorial secrecy around the effort, but also the sheer mechanics of 'bunnying up' and working in the fab, just as he had when he was a young engineer.

He was meticulous, and while disassembling the machine he carefully labeled and bagged each and every part, down to individual sections of the Swagelok stainless steel pipes and fittings. He knew that cadmium was a toxic substance and used appropriate precautions, wearing gloves when handling anything and examining the individual parts of interest only in the well exhausted chemical bench in his lab. It took him four nights to zero in on the Mass Flow Controllers, mostly because he focused on the bits and pieces that were directly in contact with the gasses and ignored the thousands of other components associated with wafer handling, robotics, temperature controls and other aspects of this sophisticated piece of manufacturing equipment. Once he got down to examining the individual Mass Flow Controllers, and he took the outer covers off, he immediately spotted that some were different than others. He then examined a 'doctored' Fine-Flow Industry model TLF SS316 Mass Flow Controller unit in detail, and carefully took it apart, until he ended up with the four cartridges that contained the Teflon ampules. He analyzed the content of the ampules and identified dimethylcadmium. After that, reverse engineering the details of how exactly cadmium contamination was introduced into the line was trivial.

"These little ampules contained an organometallic compound of cadmium, which was vented into the process gasses, and which then contaminated our silicon wafers," he explained to Matt and Jane, pointing out the specific features with his pen. "Don't worry,"

147

he added when he noticed their reluctance to look closely, "I have flushed the toxic compound; it is safe now. And," he added, "I have been very careful to handle everything with gloves—not just for health and safety reasons but also so that any fingerprints that might have been carelessly left by the perpetrators could be lifted." He was pleased to have thought of that—courtesy of the CSI TV franchise.

"But it would be surprising if these people made such a careless mistake," Matt conjectured. "By the feel of the entire operation, they knew exactly what they were doing."

"So, we now know how it was done, but not by whom," Jane concluded.

"Well, the Mass Flow Controller was made by Fine-Flow Industries from Taiwan. The furnace was designed and built in Japan by Yama Thermal Systems and installed here by our regular American contractors. But these facts in themselves are not particularly revealing. I checked, and we have many other pieces of Yama equipment throughout the fab and many machines were installed by the same contractors in this, and other fabs. And Fine-Flow MFCs are fairly common and are used by equipment makers other than just Yama. There are probably hundreds of them just in our fab," Cedric elaborated. "Ergo, so far, we know that it was a purposeful, elaborate scheme, and we know the mechanics of how it was done. What we do not know is (a) how was it triggered; and, (b) as you said, by whom."

"We may have the answer to your point 'a'," Matt interrupted. "Per your instruction, Jane, I have been in contact with your NSA whizz-kid and told her about the specific furnace that is now known to be the source of the contamination."

Jane and Cedric turned to him in anticipation. This was news to both.

"Apparently," Matt carried on, "having two independent computers—the one in Cedric's lab and the one that controlled the oxidation furnace—potentially infected by the same, or at least somehow related, malignant code, was of great help. It is amazing, and a bit frightening, how easily she has managed to hack past our standard firewalls into both of these computers—remotely, too— all the way from Fort Meade, Maryland. It seems that both machines were infected by the same virus, and that she has managed to isolate the common denominator code. She said many things that, frankly, I did not understand, but it seems that the virus is dormant in multiple computers, not only in our fab but possibly in many machines throughout the semiconductor industry. Furthermore, it seems that the virus was armed by a set of specific MFC serial numbers, and then triggered by a random number generator. This was why the problems we experienced were so inconsistent and irregular."

"How does that explain what happened to my SIMS machine?" Cedric asked.

"Don't know yet. She is working on that part still," Matt responded. "But in a way that does not matter. What *does* matter is that NSA apparently has some fancy Artificial Intelligence tools which are intended to fingerprint the malignant code, which would help identify the source. However, so far, they have not been able to typecast our virus. Meaning that this is either some new hacker, or an established party that is using an entirely new virus."

"That is not good," Jane stated the obvious. "So, we are no closer to finding out who did it. We know that it was a deliberate act of sabotage, and we know exactly how it was done, but we still need to find out by whom," she summed up.

"True. But now we do know enough to eliminate the problem," Matt said. "We could easily go through Fab-8 and remove all the doctored MFC's, and we could comb through the computer systems and delete the virus," he added hoping to get his facility back into full and normal operation.

"No," Jane reacted instantly, "let's not do that yet. The risks of alerting the perpetrator are too high. If we do, then we might never find out who they are. Based on the sophistication of the attack, I would guess that it was some organization—possibly sponsored by an enemy state—rather than an individual. As such, they very well might have eyes and ears here…" she trailed off. Then she added, "but, on the other hand, your facility seems to be their only target, which just does not fit a typical profile of a state sponsored act," she voiced the conflicting argument. "So, we just do not know. Not to mention the risk of a leak to the media, and the political ramifications of the public firestorm that would ensue. We are not ready for that," she carried on, mostly to herself. "Not yet."

"Once again, true," Matt concurred. "But, on the other hand I believe that we have gone as far as we can go with the current constraints. I don't know what more Cedric or I can do while working alone and in secret."

Jane nodded. "I will have to take that up with the president."

"The cat sat on the mat is not a story. The cat
sat on the other cat's mat is a story"
—John le Carré

t-0 + 33 months, Washington DC

Jane had a problem. A serious problem.

A couple of weeks ago, she had apprised the president of their status and confirmed that there was a proof positive of sabotage against the ElInt facility in Arizona. His reaction was the same as the last time she'd updated him, and he again declared that this was an act of war. She then obtained his permission to bring the core of the National Security Council up to speed, and convened an emergency meeting of the statutory members.

She opened the meeting with a summary of the events to date and brought everybody up to speed regarding all the known facts and the obvious conjectures.

Some of the people around the table read the president's mood correctly and speculated that given the current frosty relationship with People's Republic and Chairman Xi, the responsible party must have been China, and that this could not be allowed to continue without a response.

But cooler heads prevailed and suggested that China's role must be proven beyond a shadow of doubt and that therefore a broader effort, involving all the appropriate organs of the US Intelligence Community, must be launched before National Security Council formulated any conclusions, or directed any concrete retaliatory actions.

Jane agreed that this was the right thing to do. She felt that the data they had so far was conflicting, and not at all as unambiguous as some wanted to believe. She also thought that the people behind the attack were quite sophisticated, so that only a thorough and committed effort by the professional Intelligence Community could uncover the real perpetrators. She needed the CIA, FBI, NSA...

The president commented about how this might make it impossible to keep the lid on the story, but he authorized an in-depth probe anyway. He then made it clear that he was very concerned about the optics and the politics of the affair, and that once hundreds of agents and analysts of the broader Intelligence Community, got involved, a story like this was bound to leak out. Hence, he believed that they were in a race against time and directed Jane to assume that it was indeed an act of an unfriendly state and to come up with a list of options of possible responses coordinating only with State, Defense and DNI.

Jane, along with a few others, cautioned that since they did not yet have positive proof of the identity of the perpetrator, it was too early to plan a response. But POTUS emphasized that he did not want to be 'caught with his pants down' and that for the time being he was just looking for a list of options so that they could start shaping the narrative in the media, as opposed to asking for a detailed execution plans and the associated risk assessments.

So, he gave her only a couple of days and again directed her to maintain as low a profile as she could, and to confine the activity to just the top echelon.

This worried Jane because she knew that the said 'top echelon' was biased toward the political rather than the technical end of the spectrum of skills, and that as such it had a tendency to oversimplify. And she knew that oversimplifying weighty and complex matters, such as crafting a response to a very subtle and surprisingly pointed act of sabotage, was dangerous.

But she had her orders, and scrambled to set up and coordinate a series of meetings to produce the list that POTUS had requested. Once all the usual disclaimers, excuses and cautionary notes were pared away, the list that they came up with, had four broadbrush possibilities.

First, the president could order a military operation against the responsible party and limit it to some target of technological significance. To maintain the sense of a pointed response, he could, for example, order a missile or a drone strike and destroy something like an enemy semiconductor facility. It was clear that this option would involve collateral damage and would possibly, maybe even probably, lead to an escalation, especially if the target turned out to be China, who had recently been quite belligerent anyway.

Secondly, the president could order a commando operation against a selected target, sending a highly skilled team to destroy or damage a suitable high-tech facility of the culprit nation. This would probably decrease collateral damage but could lead to loss of personnel. In order to contain the risk of a broader war and maintain 'plausible deniability', the operation could be conducted by professional mercenaries rather than the US armed forces or US intelligence operatives. Or, perhaps, if the target ended up being Iran, someone like Israel's Mossad might be counted upon to perform a strike. Or Korea's NIS if the culprit was North Korea. Then a suitable back channel could be used to inform the culprit that this was a US sponsored limited and focused response.

Thirdly, the president could order limited covert op, and focus the operation on disabling or damaging an enemy's high-tech asset. It was possible that such an undertaking could be conducted entirely out of public eye, and would likely avoid a broader war, limit collateral damage and minimize risks to US human assets. An operation like that could be scaled to maintain the feel of a balanced response, one to match the attack that had targeted a single US factory. Again, some suitable back channel could be used to subsequently inform the culprit government that this was a punitive response.

And finally, the president could order a cyber-attack against an enemy asset by hacking into the control systems of a high-tech manufacturing or research facility to scramble their data bases or delete critical information. This would also have the effect of a balanced response, but in addition it would eliminate all risks to US personnel, or any collateral damage. They could leave sufficient traces behind to make it clear to anyone doing the forensic analysis that this was a one-off action in response to the act of sabotage.

This list of options in itself was not Jane's problem. Sobering as it was, Jane put it together with the help of assigned Defense and Intelligence personnel because she had an explicit order to do so. Her problem was that she was not sure *how* to present it, especially because the isolated nature of the sabotage bothered her, and she was not one hundred percent convinced that it was a state sponsored act.

On one hand, she could simply follow her orders and present the list to the president. But she knew that Defense and DNI tended to be hawkish—especially toward China. That would leave only herself and possibly State arguing for caution. At best, two against two. And with POTUS convinced that China was the culprit and feeling like he was under pressure to act well ahead of the election, he might make a rash decision.

So, she could play the Washington game and involve a few other select Secretaries in discussion and tilt the balance toward caution. Maybe the Chief of Staff and the UN Ambassador? Maybe AG? But that would be playing politics with her own boss, which, in her book, could not possibly be the right thing to do…

Or she could simply wait and see, and if a decision was made that she felt was wrong or premature she could tend her resignation in protest. But that would be like going down in glorious flames of self-righteousness, which would leave her hands clean, but accomplish nothing other than inconveniencing the president at a critical time—not a nice way to repay for the trust he had shown her.

Or she could leak it to the media and create an uproar that would limit the president's options. But that would be sabotaging her own side and hurting her boss, which would be worse than simply failing at her job.

She was not sure. She needed balanced and ethical advice but could not trust anyone in the Cabinet or the NSC since they all had their own agendas.

So, she called the professor.

Professor Bartholomew Harriman—Bart—protested that he was packing to leave for his vacation the very next day. But, despite fretting about being too pushy, Jane pressed him, and he agreed to meet her for Happy Hour drinks somewhere in his neighborhood. He lived in Lyon Village, an area of Arlington that had comparable look and feel as Georgetown, but that still had a somewhat lower profile and was less exclusive—and only slightly less expensive. The professor suggested the Ambar Restaurant, an ethnic Balkan food establishment close to his home. When they met, he was atypically keyed up, and went on how the Balkan food served in this restaurant was quite an appropriate warm-up for his vacation, because he and his wife were going just to that region. He said that he was taking a month off and that they had chartered a forty-two-footer and were planning to sail it themselves down the Adriatic coast, from Trieste, probably all the way to Corfu, and...

But Jane was hardly listening.

"That's nice, Professor, but I have a problem and need your help," she started.

"Well, you caught me just in time. One more day and you would have had to fly an extra 4,500 miles to get me. And one day after that, and you would have to swim to find me," he joked. "What's up?"

Since the professor did not have the appropriate security clearances, she had been worrying how to answer that question for a few days. It was not that she was concerned that he would be indiscreet, or that he would pass the sensitive information on to someone else. Still, she also did not want to break the law, so she framed her question at an abstract level.

"It's like this: there has been... an *incident* in a high-profile facility in Arizona. It is perceived as an act of aggression against the United States sponsored by some foreign government. I was told to compile a list of options for an appropriate response. Which I did, of course. But I now have reservations about delivering the list, because I am not fully convinced that the incident was the act of an unfriendly state, and because I am concerned that it may precipitate rash decisions. And an overreaction in this case could have *extremely serious consequences*. So, I am wondering if I should *influence* the decision and try to bias the audience, or if I should present it just as an unvarnished finding. Or something else? What do you think?"

"Hmm, thank you for keeping the details to yourself. I appreciate that—masterfully done," the professor joked, and then, getting serious, he said, "I gather from your level of concern that this '*incident*' is something far more serious than just some embarrassing event, like say, a sex scandal with a foreign honey that might have compromised some secrets... Scandals like those do tend to kick up a lot of dust in this town, and I presume that you are worried about a lot more than just hurting someone's political career."

"Yes, definitely."

"Well, Jane, I know that in the court of history, with all the brilliance of 20:20 hindsight, Superior Order Defense—along the lines of the usual I-was-just-following-orders—have typically not been deemed to be an adequate cover for doing something wrong. On the other hand, in *your* position, if you are given an order, you must follow it. Unlike the AG or the Cabinet Secretaries, who could hide behind an oath to defend the constitution, your position does not carry obligations toward anyone other than your boss. Your sole duty is to the president. Not even to the Republic or One Nation Under God…"

"Exactly," Jane affirmed, glad that the professor had immediately grasped her problem.

"I am afraid that in that case there is no right answer. Or, really, that the only answer is to make sure that whatever you do leads to a correct decision—the one that will at some future date be deemed to be on the right side of history." Bart smiled cryptically.

"What do you mean."

"Jane, the reality is that no matter what you do, if the president makes a decision that turns out to be a bad one, then history will deem that you made a mistake. And vice versa, no matter what you do, if the president makes a good decision, then history will either say that you were irrelevant, or maybe allow that you did not do anything wrong. So, my dear, you have no choice. Just make sure that he makes a decision which will be perceived at some future date as a good one."

"But…" Jane started. His logic was circular; it made no sense in reality. And it certainly was no help to her…

"As trite as that may sound," the professor interjected, "in the end it does boil down to having to follow *your own* ethic. One could argue that you are paid precisely for that: your opinions and your judgment, not just for your time and labor."

As always, Jane had enjoyed her meeting with the professor, but ultimately, it was no help to her. She scurried back to her office at the White House after only an hour with her old friend and mentor.

t-0 + 34 months, Kotor, Montenegro

"Ah, life is so very good," Bart sighed, reclining on the deck of *DeMiRaLi*, inhaling the aroma of fresh coffee and admiring the sunrise over the beautiful Bay of Kotor in Montenegro. "Doesn't get much better than this."

The bay—more like a fjord—was surrounded by naked rocky mountains that went almost straight up some five thousand feet, leaving just a narrow strip of relatively flat coastline, in places just wide enough to accommodate the road that circumvented the bay. The sun had just rounded the top of the mountains making the one or two rows of stone houses hugging the coastline on the west side glow white and terracotta. Amidst the shadows on the east side, still to be warmed by the morning sun, a thin layer of mist hugged the mirrorlike surface, giving the inlet where they anchored a mystical aura with a sense of tranquility that was almost palpable. And the only sounds that could be heard were a few birds screeching, and the somber chiming of the hours rung in by the churches that seemed to crown every prominent position around the bay.

"Spectacular! Easily deserving of the UNESCO World Heritage designation," he mumbled, thinking that this was his favorite of all the places that they had visited so far.

They had chartered *DeMiRaLi*, a spacious monohull sailing boat, in Trieste and had been enjoying a leisurely sail down the Dalmatian coast for the past couple of weeks. To begin with they were a little concerned about crewing her by themselves at their age and in unfamiliar waters. But in the end, they'd decided to err on the side of comfort and privacy and opted for the bareboat charter arrangement. In fact, the forty-two-foot boat was too big for the two of them, but Pamela was as accomplished a sailor as he was, and features such as the self-tacking jib and other modern gizmos made operating her very easy. The Adriatic was also quite calm and friendly at that time of the year—far less challenging than Chesapeake Bay, and certainly an easy sail relative to the waters around Cape Cod, where both had earned their sea-legs. Their Bavaria C-42 sailing yacht handled nicely indeed, and the rental rate of three thousand, five hundred euros per week was well worth it.

In hindsight they were glad to have avoided the summertime crowds and heat waves, and now enjoyed the moderate autumn seas and the post-tourist-season calm in the ports. Places like Hvar, Trogir, Split, Dubrovnik and Cavtat in Croatia were amazing—not just due to their natural beauty, but also because of the many monuments, buildings, artifacts and colorful stories left behind by a few thousand years of fascinating history, and, of course, the excellent Dalmatian cuisine.

And now, this Bay of Kotor in Montenegro; actually a set of four interconnected bays that form a complex that looked more like mountain lakes than salt-water inlets.

It was all very lovely and they were truly having the time of their lives.

They had arrived just the day before, sailed to the local big town to clear the usual customs and immigration procedures, duly took down their yellow Flag-Q, and anchored on the north end of the innermost bay just before sunset. According to all the gossip they had picked up on the Internet, it was apparently not wise to sail there at night, mostly to avoid getting snared in the illegal fishing nets that the locals tended to leave overnight. So, they anchored early last evening, but planned to spend the next day exploring the old town, to enjoy a meal or two, and whatever other small luxuries they might find.

An aroma of fried eggs and toast wafted from below, signaling that Pam was making breakfast, and he got up to join her. "Good morning, cookie," he said. "Smells good." He gave her a hug and a loving pat, and sat down, ready to eat.

"I was thinking," he said, this time more seriously, "what would you think of changing the plan, and instead of going all the way down to Corfu, we hang around here, and just sail to the Port of Shëngjin and check out the north portion of the Albanian coast. Then come back in a year or two and do the southern portion, along with Corfu and the Greek islands?"

"Really? What prompted that?" Pam asked looking over her shoulder.

"No particular reason. I like it here. And I don't want to hurry. And Albania will be mostly blue water sailing…"

But before she could answer there was a knocking noise on the outside of the boat…

"Ahoy, DeMiRaLi! Permission to come aboard…"

They looked at each other, puzzled, and Bart went above.

He could not believe his eyes! It was… Bart frantically searched through his memory banks to retrieve the name. Ah, yes! Zheng Jing! But there was no doubt about the face: This was a man he'd met many times over the years of his service; first as a minor party functionary serving in some northern region of the Peoples Republic, then as a negotiator for some of the US-China trade deals in which Bart was involved. Then, of course, as the mayor of Beijing. And finally, as an ambassador, first to Britain and then to Australia. Not a man that Bart would call a friend, but one that he'd come to trust as a serious counterpart, with a style that was unusually direct for a Chinese official. Comrade Zheng Jing had clearly done very well and had risen through the party ranks at a stellar pace. Recent rumors had it that he was even slated to be the next head of their diplomatic corps—the Alpha of the 'Wolf Pack', referring to the so-called Wolf Warrior diplomatic style lately espoused by the Peoples Republic of China.

"Mr. Zheng… Jing! To what do I owe this pleasure?" Bart spluttered as he reverted to the forced familiarity of using first names that, if memory served, they had adopted the last time they'd had met. But that was five or six years ago… He offered a hand to steady the visitor coming from the rowboat that he was standing in, straw hat in hand, and smiling broadly. "This is certainly not the place I expected to have the honor of meeting you again." Bart automatically adopted the polite and somewhat stiff way of expressing himself, knowing that form was important to Chinese.

"Well, Dr Harriman—Bart—a little bird told me that you were

in the area, and I thought that perhaps you would not mind a surprise visit. We are moored just there," Jing intoned in his perfect,
but somewhat formal, English, pointing to a motor yacht anchored
less than half a mile away. "May I?" he repeated, as the crewman
skillfully brought the rowboat alongside *DeMiRaLi*.

"Of course, please come aboard. And do join us for breakfast,"
Bart helped him up. "You remember Pamela, my wife," he asked as
Pam came up to see what was going on.

"Of course," Jing bowed slightly and shook her hand. "I hope
you will forgive my intrusion."

Pam, herself a veteran of many years in foreign service, picked
up the cue from Bart, insisted that the honor was all theirs, and
also invited him to come aboard and to join them for a simple
breakfast. After all, a wife of an ambassador had to be just as tactful,
if not more so, than the ambassador himself. So, after the usual polite protestations, Jing Zheng, a slight sixty-something year
old man with striking mane of snow-white hair and a somewhat
scholarly look about him, accepted the offer with a deep bow of
his head, and joined them for breakfast. His humble attitude, even
pitching in and helping to bring the cutlery and dishes up to the
dining area on the main deck, helped to set a relaxed atmosphere.

They settled around the table, politely passed the eggs, toast, butter and jam, poured coffee for each other and offered the creamer
and sugar bowl, and talked about the place, about the weather,
about how each happened to be there, about their respective boats,
about the last time they had met… About everything other than
the topic that clearly brought someone as important as the head
diplomat of the People's Republic of China to this most unlikely
location. Regardless of the appearance of spontaneity, both Bart
and Pam were too experienced and knew very well that this was
far from a chance encounter.

After breakfast was cleared, Jing gave a slight signal to the crewman who rowed the skiff some hundred feet away. Pam took the
hint and made her excuses and went below, leaving the two men
alone on the deck.

"Actually Bart, I must confess," Jing began, "I did seek you out
because I needed to talk with you," he said, acknowledging the
obvious. "So, I have you to thank for giving me an excuse to visit

this beautiful place," he added a bit wistfully.

"Oh, yes?" Bart said, waiting.

"We need you to convey a message to Washington," Jing said directly.

"Of course you know that I have left the service and am now just an academic, so..." Bart's explanation veiled a mild protest.

"Yes, we know. But you are a man who is well respected in certain government circles. And you have always been straight with us. We know you to be an honest man who understands our country."

Bart inclined his head to indicate his appreciation of the compliments but said nothing.

"The message is, shall we say, delicate," Jing began. "We have learned from certain sources that a new semiconductor manufacturing facility in Arizona has experienced some difficulties, and that the problems are believed to be caused by...sabotage." He lowered his voice and almost whispered the last word.

"Sources?" Bart asked, wondering if this was the same 'incident' that Jane had talked about the last time they'd met.

"Obviously, I cannot go into details. But we believe our source to be credible. Very credible. We believe that this source is very well connected with certain organs of your government, and that therefore he or she would reasonably have access to such information." Jing seemed to blush a bit. "And, we have recently picked up some collateral information from an entirely different source that could be best interpreted as independent corroboration. If they are both wrong, then that would be the best-case scenario. Then nothing has happened, and we can just celebrate meeting in this wonderful place," he added as an afterthought.

"I know nothing about this," Bart protested again. "I really am just a professor at Georgetown."

"Yes, we know. Bear with me, please," Jing persisted politely. "Some people in Washington believe that the events in Arizona were our doing... Perhaps this is not surprising, since the Peoples Republic of China is always a prime suspect. Accordingly, we are led to believe that it is assumed in some circles that we are behind this act of sabotage." He paused for a second and concluded, "The message that we need you to convey is that it was not us."

The professor sat in silence for a half minute, contemplating what he'd heard, and then asked, "Why do you need me? Why don't you send this message through the usual channels?"

"Well," Jing protested, "we cannot really deny something that we have not been accused of ... yet. Officially, in fact, no one knows what I just told you. Even if—or when—it does leak out, we will not comment. It would not be appropriate for the Peoples Republic of China to react to random rumors that come up in your media. If an accusation is made through more credible channels— say, a formal diplomatic communique, or even an interview of a suitably placed government functionary—then we would react, and of course deny it with all the usual vigor and vehemence. But until then, if it came up only through informal channels, then we would have to ignore it, like we ignore all the unfounded claims that lately seem to be surfacing in your press."

Bart thought about this, then asked, "Why the hurry? Why don't you just wait until there is an accusation? *If* there is an accusation..."

Jing nodded to signify that he understood. "Because, if we wait for a month or two for this story to break, then some minds might be made up, or some regrettable decisions might be taken. It would be much more difficult to un-make those certain minds, or to prevent events from spinning out of control. By then our denials might be interpreted as rote responses and might be useless."

"I can see that," Bart acknowledged. "But again, why do you need me? Why don't you send the message of denial through more conventional back channels? Your ambassador could whisper in the right ears, or there could be an opinion piece in some suitable outlet, or...I am sure that your spies talk to our spies..."

"Yes, that is true," Jing responded. "But in *some* circles, that kind of message would be greeted with skepticism, and seen as contrived misinformation, and interpreted to be pre-emptive canned damage control—even something that was planned ahead of the time. Likely, it would not be believed."

"Possibly," Bart again acknowledged, "but in *some* circles your denial will not be believed anyway, regardless when, how and by whom it is communicated. Presumably, there is evidence that leads some people to believe that it was a purposeful act. You will need proof to show that it was not."

"Yes, we know. And the problem is that it is hard to prove a negative, an absence of action. So, at this time we do not have incontrovertible proof of our innocence. If we were to collaborate, then we, the US and China together, could presumably, and jointly, discover the true culprit at some time in the future. Until then, I am afraid that all we can rely upon is a *preponderance of circumstantial evidence.*" He made air quotes around the typical phrase used in American legal dramas.

"Which is…" Bart challenged.

"At this point of time, the best that we can offer is logic. The motive, or really, the lack of it. Anyone who knows China would understand that it would make no sense for us to sabotage a semiconductor facility in the US. That is where you. Professor, come in. You do know us very well. You could confirm that as long as we are playing catch-up with the US technology, it is in our interest to keep the barriers between our countries as low as possible. Low barriers make learning easier —even if some people on your side call it spying. It is against our best interest to provoke America into putting up protectionist walls around its semiconductor technology. And that would be the best-case scenario… Only an idiot would expect America *not* to react to a perceived attack. The very least that would satisfy the US in case of an act of sabotage would be to put up protectionist walls and probably to impose retaliatory sanctions of some kind. And we are not idiots," Jing said emphatically. "So, just a little bit of thought would lead any unbiased person to a conclusion that it really does not make any sense for us to provoke America, just to inflict minor damage to one little manufacturing facility. Why would we do that?"

The professor said nothing.

"In addition," Jing continued, "we believe that time is on our side. We are not blind, and we fully appreciate that in the current unfortunate atmosphere between our two countries, and the consequent unravelling of the world trade system, the United States is driving to reduce its dependence on global supply chains and is ramping up its investments in *domestic* technology sources. We are too, of course. The facility in Arizona is an example of that drive. So, whereas today you could not afford to be cut off from Asian sources of, say semiconductors from places like Taipei, tomorrow you might be. And your readiness to go to war over a distant island far away from your shores may decrease. So, we believe that time is on *our* side. Therefore, again, why would we want to hurry a potential confrontation with America? Delay is favorable for us."

"Conjecture and subjective speculation," Bart responded, now sounding professorial. "One could also argue that time is on the side of Taiwanese people, whose connection to the Mainland is weaker, and whose love of independence is stronger with every successive generation. Unification is progressively less popular with the people of Taiwan ..."

"True," Jing shrugged with a ready answer. "But let *us* worry about the twenty million people and their so-called popular sentiment. Don't forget, for us that number is roughly comparable to the population of just one of our cities. We know how to manage such local misguided expectations... Honestly Bart, who do you think we are more concerned about: a noisy crowd of misinformed and misguided civilians, or the mighty military-industrial complex of the United States of America?"

There was a long silence. "And," Bart prompted to break the apparent impasse.

"And," Jing concluded, "*you*, Bart, can make those arguments in Washington DC like no one else. Because *you* know us. You would be believed. So, yes, *we* do need *you* to transmit this message. You would be doing a service to both of our countries," he said, repeatedly stressing the '*you*'.

Bart eyed him thoughtfully. Yes, what Jing said made a lot of sense to him. No, it was not because he trusted Jing, who was, after all, an agent for Peoples Republic of China. It was because he trusted the logic of self-interest. He believed that Jing's arguments about China's best interests made sense. Yet he just shrugged and said nothing.

"Bart, you and I have worked with each other for more than twenty years. In all that time, have you ever known me to lie?" Jing challenged. "Believe me, the incidents in Arizona are definitely *not* us," he repeated, pointedly looking Bart straight in the eyes, in a gesture that he hoped communicated the right message to the westerner he was trying to convince. "And, if mishandled by either side, this kind of situation could very well have dire results. An act of sabotage on the territory of one power, believed to be conducted by another power, would demand a response. A reprisal. And an undeserved reprisal would, in turn, demand a response from that second power. Wars have been started over far smaller issues," he concluded ominously. "Avoiding such a spiral is the only responsible thing that any rational and moral man can do!"

They set in silence for a good minute or two while Professor Bartholomew Harriman was making up his mind. Analyzing the tradeoffs and risks. Then he nodded and said simply, "Okay. I will try. I will convey your message to some people in Washington. If asked, I will even add my personal editorial comments. But note, please, I will do nothing else. The rest—the proof—is entirely in your hands."

Jing nodded and reached out to shake Bart's hand. Relief shone in his eyes. "Blessed are the peacemakers: for they shall be called the children of God," he quoted the Bible in another attempt to communicate in terms that would resonate with a westerner, and then waived to the crewman, asked Bart to give his regards to Pamela, and left as soon as the skiff came about.

Round 5:
At the Brink

"If you want to kick a tiger in the
ass you'd better have a plan for his teeth"
—Tom Clancy

t-0 + 34 months, Taipei, Taiwan

Cliff Lingdao, Senior Permanent Consultant to the Minister of
Defense of Republic of China, felt accomplished. Maybe even a
bit self-satisfied. He was back from his little side trip to Manila
and he had taken care of business as he always did. Even when it
was 'distasteful'.

Of course, it bothered him that Argon, his friend since childhood, had turned cold and would not return his calls, or even
respond to his messages.

He'll come around; Cliff encouraged himself. He always does.

In fact, Cliff knew that he was sheltering Argon from certain
ugly realities in the world, just as, years ago, he'd protected his
younger, smaller comrade from the bullies at school. "Maybe it's
better this way," he consoled himself.

But whether Argon liked it or not, or understood it or not, or
even approved of it or not, Cliff had done what needed to be done.
He had analyzed the situation and determined that in order to
maximize the chance for success for his operation—an operation
that was very critical for ROC National Security—a loose end
had to be addressed. Surely it was good—even commendable—to
take precautionary steps. As always, he was careful. He was, after
all, a professional.

He searched for, found, vetted and finally engaged a free agent
operative who was to do what had to be done, and most im-
portantly, who was discreet and could be relied upon to keep a

secret. His own hands, and by extension, those of ROC, would remain clean. Based on everything that he had managed to learn, Enchong Dee, aka F Gordon Liddy—where, according to his sources, the 'F' apparently stood for 'Filipino'—was the right man for the task. It seemed that the strange moniker under which he had chosen to operate was appropriate—or at least it demonstrated what the man was aspiring to become. A gun for hire. A 'fixer'. A capable man who got the job done—no matter what. According to the people that Cliff trusted, all the terms that had been applied to the original G. Gordon Liddy seemed to apply to this Filipino incarnation too. Unscrupulous, dedicated, discreet, gutsy, professional…

Cliff, of course, knew of the original G. Gordon Liddy. This was a part of popular lore for people of Cliff's generation—especially those who were drawn to the dark side of the tradecraft. G. Gordon Liddy, ex FBI agent and the leader of the so-called 'White House plumbers' of the Watergate scandal in the 1970's… G. Gordon Liddy who became notorious by unrepentantly choosing to serve time in prison rather than leak information about his employers… G. Gordon Liddy who joined the speakers' circuit, hosted a wacky radio program, and became something of a real-life James Bond persona…

Expensive, though, Cliff mused. But it would be stupid if he now chose the wrong man for such a delicate task just to save a few NT. You get what you pay for…

Best of all, Enchong Dee was an ethnic Chinese who was known to have done a few odd jobs for the Chinese Ministry of State Security. If things went astray, and the project failed, any reasonable post-mortem analysis would likely point at the PRC, not Taiwan. Even the money that he'd used to pay the man—if anyone ever managed or bothered to trace it—would lead to Singapore and then to Mainland China.

Furthermore, Cliff was very careful to cover his tracks, and even selected a time to meet this operative when Manilla was 'dark' and not in the field of vision of American spy satellites. Paranoid? Maybe. But one could not be too careful, and it was always good to plan for the worst. Tradecraft 101. Well, maybe 201 in this case," he thought to himself smugly.

The agreement was simple and clear. Half down, half on completion of the job. A target, a certain resident of Scottsdale, Arizona in United States, was to be eliminated. The necessary details of the target—name, address, and pictures—were provided. F Gordon Liddy should travel to Las Vegas, incognito among the thousands of Asians who enjoyed the gambling mecca. Once in the US, he should secure a weapon and ammo through his ex-Filipino army buddies who lived in the States. To maximize the probability that the job did not raise undue attention, and that the local police wrote it off as just another example of gang violence, the weapon should preferably come with a genealogy that would lead to one of the Latino gangs in the area—maybe the Sinaloa cartel. Once so equipped, he should take a road trip to admire some of the spectacular sights of the American Southwest, go to Scottsdale, and complete his mission there. He was supposed to make it look like a random act of road-rage. Such a uniquely American phenomenon. Better that than a robbery gone bad because it minimized the chances of collateral damage. He should then return to Vegas and fly back to the Philippines. There was to be no questions asked and no contact between them until the task was done, and even then, just a coded message through burner phones. It was agreed that the entire operation would be completed within the next six weeks at most, allowing plenty of time for proper planning and flawless execution. And that then everything would be forgotten. No questions and no traces.

That was the purpose of Cliff's last month's side trip to the Philippines. Even with all the prep work, these kinds of deals had to be sealed in a face-to-face meeting. You had to look into the man's eyes before handing over that much money. But it took less than twelve hours, including the decoy visit to the Taipei Economic and Cultural Office, which was his official pretext for the trip.

Now he just had to wait. His part was done.

t-0 + 35 months, Beijing, China

Unbeknownst to Cliff, who was focused on remaining below the American radar, his activities were detected in Beijing. What Houxi Wusheng had first thought to be a glitch had turned out to be a feature. The range of options that the latest release of the MSS's AI system could exercise automatically had been expanded. For example, the ability to simultaneously harvest multiple sources of information, such as a number of different cameras, that Houxi interpreted as a telltale sign of a human directed operation, was now a capability that the AI system could access autonomously. So, the very appropriately named, *All-Seeing-Eyes* system, aka *The Oracle*, picked up on Cliff's trip to the Philippines—probably by monitoring the airlines data bases. Based on a fundamental directive to observe the activities of known agents of the ROC's NSB while they travelled abroad, it automatically-activated the mechanisms that were made available to it. Accordingly, the system directed the cameras on a satellite that was at the time positioned over the South China Sea to track Cliff's movements in Manila and tapped other readily accessible sources of information in the area. This resulted in the report that Houxi Wusheng saw in his office in Beijing, China, less than twenty-four hours after the event took place.

Peoples Republic of China, keen to catch up with its rivals, had been deploying a network of satellites of its own since 2003, both in Low Earth and Geosynchronous orbits, all, of course, in full compliance with the rules issued by the *United Nations Office of Outer Space Affairs* (UNOOSA) and associated legal framework. Some of these satellites were, naturally, for military and intelligence purposes. If the Americans knew which of the three

hundred eighty-three Chinese vehicles that have so far been officially registered with the *United Nations Register of Objects Launched
into Outer Space* (UNROLOS) were spy satellites, then they did
not share that information with their allies in East Asia—perhaps
in order to protect their sources—and Cliff was entirely unaware
of their existence.

So, careful as he was to schedule his meeting with F Gor-
don Liddy during the window in time when Manila was dark to
American satellites, it took place in full view of the Chinese *All-
Seeing-Eyes* system.

Up to that point in time, that combination of Artificial Intelligence and spy satellite capabilities was unknown to Houxi. But,
while reporting what he thought was a glitch, the Tech Department informed him that this capability was new and, apparently,
still under evaluation, and that if no major bugs were found during
the beta phase assessment, it was to become a standard feature in
all future revisions of the system.

Having been brought up to speed, Houxi and his superior officer enthusiastically agreed that these new capabilities were extremely valuable. A perfect proof was in front of them. In this
particular case the system autonomously identified a suspicious
event and automatically generated excellent data points, including high-res photographs, map of movements, log of contacts, the
usual metadata, and so on. Outstanding! After a short discussion
they also agreed that the situation they faced merited a follow-up.
They knew that according to standard procedures, they should
find, and then coax the cooperation from the MSS functionary
in Fujian province who was listed as the appropriate contact that
had worked this Mr. Enchong Dee in the past. However, obtain-
ing the contact information for this handler required two levels
of signatures, and his superior officer's supervisor was out of town
and unreachable. So, they rationalized to themselves that this pro-
cedural requirement made perfect sense for active field operations
conducted abroad by the MSS, but felt that in their specific case
that rule need not apply, because they were just keeping an eye
on the activities of a foreign asset. So, they decided to place this
two-star operative from Manila under observation using the usual 'machine track and monitor' directive. They felt that especially

with the new system capabilities, such an approach would produce results far more quickly and at a significantly lower cost, than if they followed the rules.

Accordingly, over the following few days the *All-Seeing-Eyes* system generated regular reports that kept Houxi informed about the target's movements and activities. In addition to the minutiae of daily life that Houxi thought to be irrelevant—things like going out for lunch, doing some grocery shopping, picking up the laundry, going for a run, and so on—the system reported that the target had:

(a) Conducted a number of Google searches that added up to a total of seven hours and twelve minutes of online time. The most frequent search parameters included key words 'Cedric Dyson', 'ElInt', 'Lakshmi Dyson', 'Motorola'...

(b) Spent an additional eight hours and fourteen minutes on Google Earth, Google Map and Waze apps, exploring routes, traffic patterns and trip durations at various times of day, and street views of multiple sites in the US, all in the Phoenix metro area,

(c) Made several international calls to mobile numbers in Los Angeles, Las Vegas, and Phoenix areas, with conversations lasting between three minutes and twelve seconds and twenty-seven minutes and forty-five seconds,

(d) Cancelled an appointment that was made five months ago, for 9:45 am on September twenty-fifth at Aventus, a dental clinic in Times Plaza Building on the corner of Taft and UN Avenue, in Manila,

(e) Booked a business class seat on Philippine Air flight 116 to Vancouver on Wednesday, September twentieth, with a connection to Air Canada flight #1898 to Las Vegas, and with the return scheduled for Thursday October fifth, and

(f) Booked a Deluxe Room with a view of the Strip at the Hilton Resorts World Las Vegas site for a stay from September twentieth to October fifth. He was granted a special rate of ninety-nine dollars per night, offered exclusively to 'The Ace' members of the Genting Rewards Alliance network.

Houxi was pleased with these reports because they demonstrated that the new system was working really very well. The activities reported felt like the kind of information that was likely obtained by hacking into various computers and data bases. This was something that MSS was good at, and Houxi knew that there was a set of specialized software tools that could penetrate most computer systems. But in the past, access to these tools was restricted, and extra signatures were required to authorize their use. The Ministry had been very protective and had repeatedly emphasized that it was a matter of policy that these tools be used sparingly and judiciously, and only to observe and to passively collect information—never to do anything malignant or disruptive or even intrusive. That way, supposedly no harm was done, and the targeted entities mostly had no idea that their computers were invaded. Even if they detected the intrusion, hacked businesses like the airlines, or doctors' offices, or hotel managers, or mobile operators, or even individual users, were only marginally disrupted and were therefore typically not motivated to invest in better firewalls, which would be harder to penetrate. So, making this kind of capability accessible to the AI system was new, and possibly still in beta. Clearly the Ministry was more confident that the strict hacking policy would be implemented correctly by the AI system than by the human operators. Nevertheless, this was all very promising and exciting.

Whereas they could not be sure, Houxi and his superior, both felt that the reported activities were most likely a direct consequence of the meeting with Cliff Lingdao. They felt that it was unlikely that a reasonable person would cancel a long-standing doctor appointment on a random spur-of-the-moment urge to try his luck in Las Vegas. Besides, they thought, it was more likely that a person in the Philippines would satisfy such an urge by hopping over to Macau; a mere two-hour flight that cost ten times less than the seventeen-hour journey to Vegas. So why the sudden trip to Las Vegas—especially by an individual who, given his *The Ace* status with Genting establishments, must have been a frequent visitor to the casinos. In addition, why would an individual in the Philippines suddenly take such interest in an individual in the United States—this Cedric Dyson. And why all the interest in the Phoenix metro area?

No, they felt that this F Gordon Liddy, aka Enchong Dee, was on an assignment for the ROC and that all evidence pointed to something suspicious that was due to take place in the United States. Possibly—maybe even probably—a hit? Why else would they outsource a task to a free agent from the Philippines? If so, this surely was explosive stuff. It was possible that they inadvertently—or with the help of the AI system—stumbled onto a potential gold mine that was somehow significant to Taipei. And anything to do with Taipei had always been of high interest to the Ministry. They were even glad that they chose to bypass the handler in Fujian province, as this way they would not have to share the credit with him—if credits were indeed due.

Since many of the capabilities that they normally had at their disposal, such as the machine tracking options or satellite observation capabilities, were not yet enabled for the continental United States, they asked for authorization to place Enchong Dee under 'human track and monitor level-2' observation. All MSS activities in North America were controlled by an entirely different department within the Ministry, so that deploying a team there required extra levels of approval.

They prepared a summary of the data and their suppositions that justified the request, emphasizing that what they were asking for was just monitoring, and that in the United States the only method available was using human agents. The report ended with a series of questions that they thought would be an effective way to amplify their suspicions:

- Why did a commander of the Taiwanese secret services make a separate trip just to meet a free agent based in the Philippines?

- Why did this free agent then appear to drop everything to go to America?

- Why did this free agent do a study on a particular American citizen working in the semiconductor industry?

- Why did this free agent do a detailed study of sites and traffic patterns in the Phoenix area, which was not on his itinerary?

175

Houxi was surprised that it took only thirty-six hours. Based on his past experiences he was expecting at least a weeklong delay. As per standard procedure, the office administrative system was meant to report the status of an open request as 'pending', 'granted' or 'denied'. In this case not only was 'granted' posted within thirty-six hours, but there was also a special note from no one less than the chief himself! It simply said: 'Good job. Resources approved'. Houxi was elated and his superior officer had included a print-out of that note in his file. It could mean a promotion and a raise!

He was even more surprised when, a few days later, another note from the chief was posted, only for the eyes of the individuals assigned to this specific case. The note directed the team to observe and monitor the target, to make sure that they documented all his activities in the field, and to disrupt him if, and only if, it was necessary to prevent him from 'anything more than gathering intelligence'. It also identified General Laosheng as the Case Manager and ordered everybody to contact him directly for further instructions and/or clarifications.

Houxi did not know this particular man but was very impressed that such a senior ranking officer had been assigned to lead the operation. He also did not fully understand the chief's message and rationalized the directive to prevent 'anything more than gathering intelligence' as the usual an-enemy-of-my-enemy-is-my-friend thinking. But he was certainly excited that his case had received such attention from the higher-ups. Clearly, they were paying attention—for whatever reason...

t-0 + 35 months, Washington DC

This was serious. Hard, unsmiling faces of the most powerful people on the planet sitting around the large conference table in the secure operations room in the West Wing.

POTUS had asked Jane to convene the NSC because he felt that time was running out and he wanted decisions to be made. The first item on the agenda was an update on the status of the investigations into the sabotage of the ElInt facility. The DNI deferred to the Directors of the CIA, FBI and NSA to do all the talking. The investigation of the incident was mostly in their respective arenas, so it made sense for them to report on the status.

Besides, DNI knew that there was nothing new, and she preferred not to be the one to take the heat for the lack of progress.

She was right. The president was frustrated, but no matter how much he pushed, all the Directors could do was to elaborate on the avenues that were explored and the dead ends that were encountered. Fundamentally, none of them had anything new to report.

...Yes, sir, it was without doubt an act of sabotage. A clever two-pronged approach that simultaneously contaminated the facility and blinded the inspection tools...

...No, it was not catastrophic. The facility was hobbled but not shut down...

...No, sir. Two more identical occurrences had been reported since full discovery, bringing the total to five incidents...

...Yes, the software virus has been isolated and fully characterized, and could now be eliminated. No sir, the virus has not yet been removed because it was found to be benign in every other case, and leaving it in place may (a) help lead to the culprit, and (b) keep the lid on the incident...

...No, no other facility has been affected, as far as it is known. Yes, they had polled US companies other than EIInt, and even friendly foreign entities... Yes, it was a very low-key assessment. No waves...

...No, there was still no evidence to who was, or was not, involved... Forensics were not revealing...

...Yes sir, the profiling studies were completed, but the incident does not fit any known models. The sophistication and complexity of the attack would indicate a state sponsored or a terrorist group, but the limited scope and footprint match a lone operative...

...Yes, they did follow up with the manufacturers of the compromised equipment in Taiwan and Japan. No, neither party had managed to isolate anything out of the ordinary, and yes, both parties were very cooperative...

...No, none of the ears on the ground, or eyes in the sky, had picked up any chatter that could possibly be related to the incident...

And on and on...

The president then asked Jane to go over the list of reprisal options that she'd pulled together a month before. She, of course, had shared the full assessment with him at the time—albeit in a private setting. She used her regular bi-weekly one-on-one slot, so that she'd ended up presenting her report just to him, with no hawks in the room who might bias the discussion. But now the president clearly wanted the report presented to the entire National Security Council because he wanted to move on to the next step. So, she had no choice but to present the material, concluding with a slide that summarized the four options that were identified:

Option 1: military strike
Option 2: commando strike
Option 3: covert op
Option 4: cyber-attack

"First of all," the President said, "I do not want to use Option 4. I do not want to be the one to open that can of worms. State has reached out to the cyber powers and now we have a kind of détente with Russia and China, with informal agreements about things that are off limits. I do not want to be the one to break that tacit understanding. So, cyber-attack is off the table..."

All in attendance seemed to hold their breath, waiting for a decision.

"I think I want a combination of Option 2 and 3. Could you," he pointed at the Director of CIA and Chairman of the Joint Chiefs of Staff, "prepare a set of possible action scenarios for us to review?"

Several people around the table, including Jane, squirmed and fidgeted in their chairs, ready to argue for caution. But before anyone could say anything, the president held his hands up and said, "Look, I just want to see the detailed plans for possible action scenarios. I think we should have something ready, locked and loaded, in a month or so. But I will not pull the trigger until we all agree that we have proof of the identity of the perpetrator. Positive and unambiguous proof."

That qualifier seemed to bring down the temperature in the room.

"Mr. President, do you want us to propose action scenarios for all five possible targets who meet both the technical capability and the possible motivation criteria," the Chairman asked, "for each of the prime suspects: China, Russia, Iran, North Korea, Belorussia?"

Of course, as soon as she heard from the professor, Jane communicated the message of denial of involvement that the Chinese had sent, along with the professor's rationalization of why he believed it. She'd shared it two weeks ago with POTUS and with a few of the prominent players seated around the table. But she found that the reactions were predictable. The hawks mistrusted it because of where it came from and wanted cold hard proof. The doves found it sufficiently credible because it confirmed their opinion and argued for rapprochement and diplomacy. And the president just requested a deep-dive session with the professor, where he first listened patiently and then pointed out that since the Chinese were already aware of the incident, either there was a leak in the government machinery, or they were the perpetrators. He emphasized that he found either scenario believable and that he was right to guard against both possibilities, noting that the Chinese seemed to have acted only *after* the Intelligence Community was engaged in the case.

Nevertheless, the consensus amongst the technical and supposedly unbiased analysts drawn from the many different branches of the Intelligence Community was that China was the most likely culprit—the prime suspect. POTUS knew this, of course.

"Let's start with China first and Russia second," the president responded. "The others do not worry me that much. And note, I do feel that doing nothing is *not* an option." He slapped the table for emphases. "An act of sabotage on our soil is an act of war, and therefore we *must* retaliate. "They started it and the longer we wait the weaker we look... Maybe they—whoever they are—are just testing us. Playing with us. Maybe that is why the first attack was so limited in scope. Probing to see how far they can push. Maybe this is just step-1 in a broader attack on the technology infrastructure of our country. We *must* act!"

"Yes Mr. President," rang around the table.

"And perhaps, at the same time, we should also prepare a plan for nuclear and conventional war with China first and Russia second," the Ambassador to the United Nations—the most vocal of the doves in the room—suggested. The pointed paraphrasing obviated the need to elaborate on why.

"I am aware of the danger," POTUS snapped. "I am simply asking for a plan now. Let us see what it would look like, what would the operational risks be, and so on. We can talk separately about when, and if, we would act... I also believe that when faced with the reality of war, they want it as little as we do, and they will back down. So let's make sure that we give their governments an out and not paint them into a corner where they feel that they have no choice. The operation should be structured so that they can present it to their people as an industrial accident. And we can use other means to make sure that they understand the reality. I want something that would be proportionate. And limited..."

"Yes Mr. President."

"However," the Chief of the White House Staff, and the principal political adviser to the president, hesitated, "we may want to make sure that it is presented to *our* people as a reprisal."

Everybody turned to look at him.

"Yes," he reaffirmed, "we all know that we are entering an election year. And let's face it, a sitting *war-time* President is *always* re-elected."

They all knew—or believed —that the president would not run

for re-election. He was not in good health. But he had said that while in office he would behave *as if* he were running for re-election so that whoever actually did end up as the nominee of the party would have the best chance of winning as a continuity candidate who would carry on the policies of the current administration. He'd said on a number of occasions that his approach to the elections was that the presidency—not the president—was running.

POTUS readily picked up on the topic. "I agree. And I think that we should start preparing the nation for a period of tension. We should inform the country about the… incident in Arizona. But carefully…be circumspect. Just a leak rather than a formal announcement. Float the story and maintain an aloof position by invoking the usual 'no-comment-on-ongoing-investigation' line. And then, when, or if, a reprisal is conducted, we must preserve some level of plausible deniability and yet let the country *believe* that it was in a response to an act of sabotage on US soil. We must shape that message very… carefully." The president was clearly choosing his words, almost as if trying them out to see how they might play in soundbites. "Jane, please circle back with C.J. and give me some proposals for messaging strategies," he directed, using the initials of his White House Communications Director.

"Yes, Sir."

"A resolute response might play well at the ballot box," POTUS mused aloud, "but it will play well," he carried on, looking pointedly at the two men he tasked with the planning, "if, and only if, the operation is successful. So, make sure that the plan is sufficiently simple and adequately modest so that it *will be successful*. Nothing too fancy. No cowboy diplomacy. No heroics. Nothing as spectacular as Entebbe," he emphasized, referring to a daring hostage rescue mission carried out by Israel in the 1970s. "I want a cool, calm, surgical operation… I do not want American boys and girls coming home in body bags. That *never* plays well at the ballot box. And I most certainly do not want an ostentatious failure on our hands. Nothing epic like our hostage rescue mission in Iran. Not on my watch…"

All somberly nodded their understanding.

"The difference between fiction and reality?
Fiction has to make sense"
—Tom Clancy

t-0 + 36 months, Washington DC

The packet in the large manila envelope was dropped off by stern looking middle-aged man wearing a bullet-proof vest and trailed by a uniformed armed guard who stood warily between the door and the van that advertised their concierge courier service. The man demanded to see Bart's ID and insisted on a signature to acknowledge receipt before handing over the package.

The envelope was addressed to Professor B. Harriman and had his correct home address on the front, but the back flap was secured with a string that was sealed with one of those old-fashioned dollops of red wax that bore the imprint of a star, and a label that declared the contents to be protected by Article 27.3 of the Vienna Convention on Diplomatic Relations (VCDR). The standard insignia that marked diplomatic pouches brought back a lot of memories to Bart, but it had been a while since he had personally handled anything of the kind, or even seen it used, and it had been forever since he'd last seen an honest-to-goodness wax seal used to secure it.

He was unsure if it were even legal for him to open it. It *was* addressed to him, and he knew that, strictly speaking, this voided the VCDR rules that were meant to cover only government-to-embassy communications. He obviously had no official diplomatic status, and especially no status as an agent of... He turned the manila envelope over and examined it. Other than a date stamp there was nothing to indicate where the package had come from, or to whom it belonged.

Just then his phone rang, and even though the display indicated that the caller ID had been blocked, he automatically swiped to answer the call. It was Jing Zheng!

"Hello, Bart! I am told that our little package has been delivered... Good, good. I just wanted to call and let you know that we consider this ... how shall I say it... an act of goodwill. We *are* sharing with you information that is potentially compromising *our* security services, and ... let us say this is Part 1 of the proof that we talked about. Please treat it with discretion and share only as a part of your mission. Feel free to contact me if you have any questions regarding its content."

Jing Zheng hung up before Bart had a chance to voice his resentment that despite his protest he was being pulled into something that he did not want to get involved with.

"*Shazbat!*" Bart swore aloud, borrowing a meaningless oath from a Robin Williams' TV show that ran back in the 80s. "My mission? Really?"

He took the package to his study, looked it over again, shrugged, and slit it open. His curiosity had obviously gotten the better of him.

Inside were photographs of people and places that meant nothing to him. The back of each photograph was marked in neat handwriting denoting names of places, dates and some letters. Las Vegas, Kingman, Phoenix... a set of dates, written in what he assumed was the non-American DD/MM/YY format... and what he presumed were the initials of the person or persons in the photographs.

And there was a letter. He glanced through it, skipping through all the disclaimers and headers that proclaimed the material to be secret and urged him to handle it carefully. If they wanted it kept secret, then they damn well should not have sent it to me, he thought. He skimmed through it and felt that he'd grasped the gist of its content, but there were some details that were confusing to him.

So he called Jane's private number and left a message...

They met the next day—this time at Café du Parc at the Willard hotel. Jane managed to clear an hour in her calendar by skipping lunch and juggling some meetings and this location was a quick walk from the West Wing.

As she flipped through the photographs she blanched when she came across one that showed a weedy looking man driving a car, remarkable only due to his messy head of red hair. "I know this man. That is Cedric Dyson," she exclaimed.

"Who?"

"He is the chief scientist, or chief something at EIInt. Chief nerd. The man who first discovered the sabotage and then figured out how it was done," she blurted, before she'd had a chance to check and censor what she was saying.

"Well, according to the letter, he is alive and well today thanks to the good graces of Chinese secret service agents operating on the soil of the United States of America," the professor reacted, perhaps somewhat sarcastically.

"Let me have these," Jane said, waiving the waiter down. "I will have my staff check the police reports and other details. If true, this is serious," she said to the professor. And to the waiter, "Please pack mine to go."

Bart enjoyed his Beef Bourguignon by himself.

The following day, Jane called the professor, and sounding quite agitated, said, "Well, so far it checks out. Of course, we have not had a chance to follow up on everything, but yes indeed there was an incident in Mesa, Arizona that was confirmed by the local police and that fits the events in your letter. We need to talk."

Before the professor had a chance to say anything, she carried on, "Can you come to my office? This evening, at 6:30? Just us… Oh, and Bart, I have decided to ignore your request and have asked for your security clearance to be updated and upgraded. Let's face it; whether you like it or not, you *are* involved. I will let the White House security staff know that you are coming."

The professor smiled to himself for several reasons. Firstly because he was pleased that he had removed himself from that rollercoaster that a high-level job in Foreign Services always turned out to be, and that had precipitated the manic flurry that he'd just heard from Jane. She was clearly amped up and all over the place—a feeling that he knew well. And partially because he was glad to be getting back on that same rollercoaster—if only for a little while. This was gearing up to be an interesting international intrigue and, in spite of himself, he thought that it would be a fun ride. But mostly because he noted that, for the first time ever, Jane

Stewart had called him by his first name. Finally!

Going to the White House was a nostalgic experience for him, even though he was now processed through the security hurdles as a visitor, as opposed to a person of rank that he used to be.

There was a time when they knew me by sight, Bart thought, almost wistfully.

He was escorted to Jane's office on the second floor of the West Wing and just as he sat down, Jane dove right in.

"Fact:" she started, "Sometime around 7:45 on the morning of Tuesday, October 3rd, the Arizona Highway Police received a report of a crashed vehicle on State Route 101 in Mesa—a city in the Phoenix metro area. The responding officers found a vehicle crashed into the barrier wall with its driver badly hurt and unresponsive... No witnesses... The vehicle was a Cadillac XT5 rented in Las Vegas on September 23rd. According to the papers retrieved at the scene, the deceased is believed to be a Mr. Enchong Dee, male, age forty-nine, citizen of Philippines... Arrived to the US on September 21st on a flight from Canada, staying at the Hilton in Vegas. The police notified the embassy... A weapon—a Herstal FN57 pistol—was also found at the scene. But it had not been fired recently and the cartridge was full."

She slid the folder across her desk toward him. Bart flipped through the contents, glanced at the gory photographs, but said nothing.

"Fact:" Jane pressed on, looking through another folder, "The postmortem report indicates that the deceased died of two bullet wounds; one to his head and one to the upper torso. Nothing to do with injuries sustained in the crash. The shots came head-on, full frontal, possibly fired from another vehicle. The bullets retrieved from the body were 5.8mm caliber rounds that are supposedly rarely seen in Arizona. Apparently, not used by weapons popular with the local *enthusiasts*..." she emphasized the word, clearly communicating her cynical attitude towards the standard language used by the gun lobby. "According to an expert that forensic pathologist consulted, this type of bullet is standard issue in China, and is used by Norinco QBU-88 rifle that is rare but not unheard of among the marksmen in the US. Still, the police are treating the incident as a gang shooting of some kind, possibly with foreign roots. Maybe Filipino gang moving in on someone's territory? Maybe road rage?" she said, tossing the folder toward him.

"Hmm, they can tell all that from a bullet pulled from somebody's head?" Bart marveled somewhat sarcastically.

"Fact:" she went on, "Enchong Dee, the deceased... I had our local station in Manila do a quick search. A Filipino of Chinese origin. Many years in the Philippine Army... Distinguished service record. Elite Rangers unit. Retired from the army in 2014 and now supposedly a free agent operative, a security consultant and a gun for hire... Get this, he is doing business under the name *F Gordon Liddy*."

Bart rolled his eyes and groaned, "Oh, God, that's all we need... A loose cannon and a bag of trouble, if he is, or was, anything like his chosen namesake." He reached for the folder.

"Turns out he had some history, and our people believe that he has done some contract work for the Chinese secret services, but that is mostly rumors. They could not dig out any specific details, but his bank account does show an unusual wire transfer of fifty thousand US dollars from the Development Bank of Singapore, dated August thirtieth."

Jane leaned back in her chair.

"All that proves is that *an* incident did indeed take place," Bart countered, "but not much about *why* it might have taken place. Even if this Enchong Dee was, as the Chinese claim, a hit man, *who* paid him?"

"True," Jane conceded. "I also called Cedric Dyson. He *is* alive and kicking. He confirmed that he normally does commute to work along that route and at that approximate time, and that to the best of his recollection, he did follow his usual routine on Tuesday, the third. But he did not notice anything out of the ordinary," Jane continued her update. "I also asked the local FBI to reinstate their watch over Dr. Dyson—just in case."

Bart raised an eyebrow, a bit surprised at this level of protection for a civilian.

"Everything checks out," Jane asserted. "The claim that China had reasons to believe that this was an attempt on Cedric Dyson's life, and that they foiled it, *could* fit actual events. If true, and if we discount mere coincidence, it is possible—even probable—that this was somehow connected to the sabotage incident… And if so, then it is a matter carrying serious national security implications." She then caught herself and added, "Remind me to fill you in about the sabotage. But for now, I think you have the gist?"

Bart nodded, and even though he was curious about the 'sabotage incident' that everyone kept mentioning, he reverted to the main topic, "Or, the whole affair was theater. Staged for our benefit, presumably by the Chinese secret service. Kicking up the dust to compound our confusion, and presumably delay, or suspend, or even abort any reprisal… After all, they do acknowledge that they will not share the details that have led them to their conclusions, supposedly because that would be too revealing of their methods. That sounds a bit lame to me, but, then again, who knows?"

"By the way," Jane broke in, "so far I have kept it all just between these walls," indicating her office. "I have not told anyone— my boss or my peers—about the letter from your Chinese friend, or the 'random' incident in Mesa. Yet… Because something like this could very well fibrillate NSC decisions that are far more significant than even the MSS operating on US soil and supposedly saving an American citizen. As is, the decision-making balance is delicate, and this could very well tip the scales. Not sure that I want to open that door based on an unverified story that comes to us from our prime suspect through an unusual channel."

"Understandable. Which way do you think it may tip that scale?"

Jane shrugged, obviously not sure, and said, "Could go either way." Then, after a pause, she folded her hands in her lap and asked, "So, what do you think we should do?"

After a brief silence, Bart opined, "Well, in my humble opinion, this does not constitute anything like a proof that China was *not* connected to that sabotage. At best, it may indicate that there was more to that incident in Mesa than a random gang shooting. So, I would suggest that we pass these folders, and everything else that you have, to the professionals. Let the FBI boys and girls do their thing and let's see what else they dig up."

"Agreed," Jane responded. "But what about their request? Do you think we should humor them and pass the virus on to China?"

Bart indicated that this was the part of the letter that he did not understand, and Jane quickly recapped the role that a computer virus had played in the act of sabotage.

"Clever," Bart reacted, and returned to the topic. "So, they want a copy of that virus because they think that it can help them connect the dots and lead them to the real culprit? Hmm, let's think about that…"

"Or it could help them add more confusion to an already complicated case," Jane added, seamlessly swapping roles. Bart and Jane automatically reverted to their old style of conversation that they'd honed over the years, each one alternately assuming the role of 'advocate for the opposition' and 'advocate for the case' to avoid polarization and independently identify which position felt truer.

"I would," Bart concluded. "There is nothing that we lose by giving them access to that virus. If they are the culprit, then they already have it. If they are not, then they can knock themselves out studying it, and either it will produce some helpful information, or not. Either way, we have nothing to lose…"

"Agreed," Jane nodded.

"In my opinion," the professor carried on, "I'm inclined to believe them. As a cultural rule, Chinese tend to be sensitive to loss of face, so if they had something to hide and were guilty, so to speak, then their normal tendency would be to evade a topic and to obfuscate. Instead they are asking for more information and looking for more involvement. And even though the communication has been through back channels, via Yours Truly, the entire conversation *feels* like a formal government position, rather than some loose individual talking. And once they have taken a formal position, the Chinese government rarely changes its mind. Normally… So, my sense is to believe them and assume that they are trying to build a case to prove that the sabotage was not them."

Jane looked at the professor for a long time, then rapped on the table and said, "Agreed!"

t-0 + 37 months,
Washington DC—Part 1

"Mr. President, sir, we do have a proposal for your review and authorization. This Hybrid Action Plan meets the constraints that have been specified and is rated 'Minimal Risk' by the standard operational risk assessment metrics." The Associate Deputy Director and head of the Directorate of Operations of CIA, stressed 'hybrid action' as if this was a special selling feature of the plan. An aide passed out neatly bound copies of a report that looked like it was tens of pages thick and that was prominently stamped 'Top Secret'. The Associate Deputy Director was standing erect and at attention, with hands clasped behind his back in an unmistakable military style, ready to present to the National Security Council.

POTUS nodded.

"First, the target. There are three elements to consider: the company, the facility, and the specific equipment," he began. "One: the company..." and a PowerPoint slide that described China Manufacturing International Corporation—CMIC—came up on the screen, while he continued without emotion. "By unanimous consensus between the DoD and the Intelligence Community, CMIC is the recommended target... Because it is basically their flag bearer in the semiconductor sector. Their most prominent, largest semiconductor company, capable of their most advanced technologies..." he emphasized, preemptively answering questions before they were even asked.

"Appropriate target for a punitive operation," the Chairman of the Joint Chiefs of Staff commented approvingly.

"Two: the facility. CMIC has six manufacturing sites throughout the Mainland," the presenter proceeded, "and we feel that the
most suitable target would be the so-called 'SH 300mm Fab' in
Shanghai... Because that is where they have the most advanced
technology node."

"Shanghai is crowded... Opportunity for collateral damage?"
POTUS wondered aloud.

"No sir. None of these facilities are in remote areas, and the
hybrid nature and the limited scope of the operation eliminates
risks of collateral damage," the Director of CIA cooed reassuringly.

"And three: the equipment," the presenter moved on. "CMIC
has two 'Atomic Layer/Reactive Ion' etch model Kiyo 5100 plasma etchers made by PicoWati Research Corporation—in fact, a
US company. Pardon the details: these are machines that are used
to define the critical features in the so-called FinFet devices which
are vitally necessary for manufacturing the most advanced chips..."

POTUS waved him on with an impatient gesture.

The Associate Deputy Director nodded and moved on without skipping a beat. "With this kind of operations there are always three major elements to consider: how to get in, how to
execute the mission, and how to get out." He went on in his
clipped dry manner, clicking through the PowerPoint presentation with few interruptions.

Basically, the plan he proposed was to address the first element—how to get in—by using a very limited cyber weapon to
inject a bogus failure signal into the targeted equipment so that
CMIC would invite the supplier, in this case PicoWati Research,
to send suitable technicians to fix the problem.

"So, the operatives would be there by invitation of the Peoples
Republic?" someone asked with a smirk.

"Yes and no, Sir. This is a part of a layered approach that we
are using with this operation. The entire mission is planned as
a belt-and-suspenders solution, where one vector is focused on
ensuring that it is successful, and a parallel vector is developed to
ensure that should something go off the rails, the damage would
be limited and there would be nothing that could be traced back
to the USA. The primary reason for the use of the simple cyber
weapon was to give us control over timing of the operation. A

'start' button, if you like, sir."

"Like triggering a 'check engine' light in a car to compel the owner to take it in for a service," the Director of CIA explained.

"But, without a doubt," the Associate Deputy Director carried on, "being invited in this way would help the 'technicians' clear the hurdles that have to be crossed to enter into the country—especially convenient these days of heightened tensions between us and China. However, the two American technicians who would be flown in from the headquarters in California, supposedly to fix the problem, would be decoys. They are bound to stick out like sore thumbs and will draw all the attention of their security services. One will even be a female—since women service techs are rare in China, she will automatically draw the attention of random factory personnel. This would give our real operative more latitude to act. He is Chinese and will be introduced as a trainee service technician who was recently hired to provide better local service."

The second element of the plan—carrying out the actual mission—was presented as a low-risk approach because it relied just on a high temperature magnesium-phosphorus incendiary device with a timed trigger.

"So, you propose to plant an IED in their factory?" someone asked for clarification.

"Yes, but a bit more sophisticated than a device made by some jihadist garage shop. This is a high-tech instrument built in our best labs, and guaranteed to work. However, its deployment is simple and does not call for anything fancy, like remote detonation, or triggering by some external event. Just a simple built-in timer..." the presenter explained. "The equipment that has been targeted includes a lot of plumbing that pipes in various gasses and liquids required by the manufacturing process. Some of this plumbing—specifically the lines carrying liquid nitrogen—is naturally protected by wrapping the piping with insulating foam. While performing routine maintenance on the target equipment, the operative will replace this foam with the incendiary material that he will smuggle in as a part of the padding of his vest. It will take him less than fifteen seconds to complete the swap. Everything will be pre-cut precisely to size, the old foam will be refitted into the vest, the new incendiary foam will be installed around the pipes and will be visually indistinguishable from the original. Meanwhile, the American technicians will be busily explaining to their hosts that the source of the problem was a software glitch caused by a mismatch between the new and old program releases, which was there because CMIC did not have the latest rev, because of the restrictions imposed by the current 'trade war', and that they will just write a patch locally, and thereby skirt around US restrictions, and that while they were doing that, they will also supervise the trainee in performing routine maintenance and checks, and... All of which would be true."

"And the getting out part?"

"They will service the equipment and will stay in the area until the customer completes the standard acceptance tests and is satisfied that the machine is fully operational and back to normal. Given the usual pressures to minimize down-time in a manufacturing facility, we expect this to be a day—maybe two at most. After that the two techs will fly home, and the local trainee will go back to his base in Hong Kong. No hurry and no heroics. We will allow a safety margin of an extra day and a half, so the incendiary device will self-ignite 84 hours after installation. It will look like there was simply a random fire in the facility."

"Fire in a high-tech factory? Clean rooms and all? Isn't that somewhat anachronistic, not to mention suspicious?" someone pointed out.

"No, sir. Fires in semiconductor factories are not rare. On average, at least one major fire is reported to occur every year in some chip fabrication facility somewhere in the world. In fact, we estimate that the frequency of fires is at least four times that much, but that the IC companies tend to cover them up in order to avoid loss of customers or panic in the market. In a way, this is not surprising given that semiconductor manufacturing processes use many different spontaneously combustible and highly flammable chemicals. We know that this facility is fitted with the state of the art fire extinguishing installations, and expect that the fire will be put out quickly, and that the incident assessment study that they will no doubt conduct, will confirm that silane—capable of autoignition at temperatures below 54 °C, and hydrogen—highly flammable, were both plumbed into that specific equipment and that there must have been a leak. *Unfortunately*, the high temperature fire will damage the equipment beyond repair, and there will be no usable physical evidence to prove—or disprove—this."

He paused there to allow for questions, and when none came, he proceeded. "They will most likely write off the event as a random occurrence of fire caused by an undetected leak. According to our scenario modeling exercises, there is 94% probability that this is what they would conclude. They will of course conduct forensic analyses, but that will take a few weeks, by which time our operative, the 'trainee technician', will have disappeared. If they suspect that the fire was an act of arson—we estimate less than 14% probability that such a scenario would be proposed—then the American Technicians would be their obvious suspects—80% probability under those circumstances. But no matter how hard they try, they will find no evidence that will connect the Americans to the fire, because in fact there *would have been* nothing. If necessary, we could misdirect them further by hacking into their citizen-tracking databases and injecting a legend that will show links between the trainee technician and Uighur minority. This would lead them to believe that this was a terrorist act—78% probability for that scenario..."

The presentation was completed, and the presenter turned off PowerPoint. There was silence in the room.

"If you approve, Mr. President, we can position all the pieces and be ready to initiate the sequence with forty-eight hours' notice. As stated, this is a low-risk operation that uses a hybrid approach, with inter-departmental cooperation that brought together elements of cyber, commando and covert warfare, all synchronized to maximize the probability of success and minimize risks. The multiple opportunities to misdirect their analyses are built-in, and will preserve total deniability, if you choose, Sir. And then diplomatic or other channels can be used to inform the target...or not. As you decide, Sir."

All eyes focused on the president.

"Very good. Thank you. I appreciate the degree of deniability that you people baked in. Yes, set it up."

"Mr. President, may I suggest," the Chairman of the Joint Chiefs of Staff ventured, "that it may be prudent to ready an element of the 7th Fleet to enter the Straits with a 48-hour notice as well. Just an expeditionary presence, enough to deter but not so much as to provoke. Just in case…"

POTUS looked at mostly nodding heads around the table, thought about it, and responded. "Good idea. That would be the kind of a message that speaks volumes. Yes, set it up. I want the two initiatives locked and loaded and primed to go on my order."

"Yes Sir!"

"And before some of you remind me of the risks," he said quite emphatically, "this is the way I think of it: either it was China or it was not China; in my judgment, it would be worse for our national security if it *was* China and we did *not* react, than if it was *not* China and we did hit them wrongly, and then had to exercise the deniability options."

"Absolutely, Sir."

*"You know where your enemies
stand. This is not always true of friends"*
—Tom Clancy

t-0 + 37 months, Beijing, China

It was an honor to be invited to such a briefing. But it was intimidating too. It was the first time for Houxi to attend this level
of a review. He was one of half a dozen silent aides sitting in the
back of the room, as opposed to the real decision makers who sat
around a conference table. At the head of the table and chairing
the meeting was General Laosheng himself. Houxi's superior officer was there too, along with other senior officers whose roles and
names he did not know.

"We received the USB stick with the virus," one of them said,
"and after the usual procedures to quarantine it and to make sure
that the Americans were not trying to slip something into our systems, we ran our standard software-fingerprint analysis. There are
elements of that code—stylistics, naming conventions, and even
portions of actual subroutines—that we have seen before. Based
on comparisons versus the data base that catalogs known malware, the top hit for most likely author of this particular virus is
an individual named Zhao YouWen, a known hacker from Hong
Kong who is believed to operate under the online pseudonym of
89WangDan. Our standard software assessment and analyses tools
put the confidence level of a match at seventy-eight percent. In
the past he was mostly responsible for spreading unauthorized
material on the internet, and writing bots that brought down a
number of government-approved sites. Online hooligan. So, this
type of a virus is something new for him, but the code is quite

sophisticated. We will alert the Firewall managers."

General Laosheng nodded, muttering, "Seventy-eight percent," and jotted something in his notebook. He then pointed to the man seated next to the one who had just spoken.

"Yes, Zhao YouWen is known to us. Age twenty-nine. A Hong Kong citizen. Illegitimate son of Dr. Daniel Chan, a professor of sociology at the University of Hong Kong, deceased in 2012, and Zhao Charlotte, a journalist with *South China Morning Post*, deceased in 2019. Both were radicals and pro-democracy activists since 1997. YouWen *is* '89WangDan', is known in hacker circles, and is apparently well respected on various netizen forums. We believe that his chosen moniker is a pointed reference to the activist from '89 Tiananmen Square riots and likely reflects his own leanings. He has a prominent and ongoing presence in the anti-China movement, nowadays mostly through his hacking activities. Active in the Hong Kong Umbrella movement in 2014 and the street riots in 2019 and 2020. Already on our list of the top fifty Hong Kong troublemakers. He escaped to Taiwan in June 2020 just before the enactment of the National Security laws, and is currently a resident of Taipei. He seems to be making a living there as a freelance programmer for several commercial clients and by doing some tutoring on the side. We do monitor his online activities quite closely, and keep an eye on his physical activities as much as this is practical in Taipei."

The general nodded and pointed to the next person.

"Lingdao Cliff, male, age sixty-four, resident of apartment 1288, at 164, Fugang Street, Shilin District, Taipei. He is a son of Lingdao Morris, a commercial agent from Guangzhou, who ran to Taipei with Chiang Kai-shek's rebels in 1949. Educated in Minglun Senior High School and then National Tsing Hua University. Holds a degree in Economics from the College of Technology Management. He is the father of two adult children. Publicly, a Senior Permanent Consultant to the Government of the Republic of China—a strange title shared by only seventeen other people. He is currently assigned to the Ministry of Defense, but after graduating from college in 1987, he started at the Ministry of Science and Technology and moved to Defense in 2009. What is *not* public knowledge is that he is also a senior officer believed to hold at least a Commander rank in NSB. We have a complete catalog of various projects, including some dark operations, that have been sponsored and/or conducted by the rogue Taipei government, where Cliff Lingdao has played a role—to be exact, where he is known to have been either the leader or a principal contributor. It is a long list, with, unfortunately, some notable successes. Apparently, he is very well respected by his colleagues and peers..."

And so it went around the table, senior officers from various departments—IT, Internal Security, External Security, North America Operations, Surveillance Operations, and so on—contributing to the discussion and reviewing the highlights of what MSS knew about specific persons of interest: You Wen Zhao, Cliff Lingdao, Enchong Dee, Cedric Dyson, John Lin...

When it was his turn, Houxi's superior officer presented a similar report, summarizing the interactions among the suspects that *All-Seeing-Eyes* and Houxi had observed over the last few years.

General Laosheng listened, nodded knowingly, and jotted things down in his notebook. When all the reports were presented, he thanked everybody and commented, "And so the circle is complete. The computer virus that caused the problem in the Americans' factory... The Filipino assassin paid to prevent its discovery... And Cliff Lingdao seems to be at its center! Is that our collective conclusion?"

All nodded their agreement.

"I need you to compile a full written report based on the materials available from all the departments," he said, pointing at Houxi's superior officer. "On paper. Something that can be shared *outside* the Ministry. I need a report that documents the facts and the sequence of events that took place. With a focus on this Cliff Lingdao and what we know he did and with whom he met. Include the details, the dates, the photographs. No mention should be made of our theories or speculations, or reference to our internal discussions and suppositions. Delete everything that identifies our sources of information. Delete all references to the tools and techniques that we use. And absolutely no mention of *All-Seeing-Eyes*, of our satellites, of our agents in the US or their reports. Just the facts."

"Yes comrade."

"By day after tomorrow, on my desk."

"Yes comrade."

Houxi noted that he should cancel plans for a family get-to-gether because the next day was shaping up to be a long one. Maybe a long night as well...

t-0 + 38 months,
Washington DC – part 2

"Let me see if I understand this," POTUS said. "You are telling me that the saboteur of *our* facility was Taiwan? Our friend Taiwan?"

"Yes Sir," Jane responded. "We have received communications from China, via the professor here, that strings together a credible trail of evidence which points to the possibility that Taiwan was the originator. Mind you, Sir, the evidence *is* circumstantial. By nature of the act, and how it was done, there is no smoking gun, and therefore no incontrovertible proof of their complicity."

"Based on the evidence supplied by the Peoples Republic of China—our prime suspect," the Secretary of Defense commented sarcastically. "Not exactly a credible source, even if we were to believe their protestations that they have no skin in this game."

This was an ad hoc gathering in the Oval Office... Jane called the meeting to review the latest 'proof', furnished by China, via Professor Bartholomew Harriman, mostly based on an analysis of the virus code that she had authorized to be leaked back to them. The President, DNI, Secretaries of Defense and State, Directors of CIA and FBI, Jane and the professor were present.

"Unbelievable!" POTUS exclaimed. "Taiwan? Our friends and allies," he repeated incredulously. "I can't believe it."

"Well, Sir, it is possible—perhaps probable—that it was not the *government* of Taiwan," Jane qualified. "There could be 'rogue elements' there too. Just like we have our Three Percenters or Oath Keepers, they could have extremist groups with misguided agendas. There are certainly well-known groups like that in Japan, and in South Korea, so why not in Taiwan? Some crazy group of fanatics operating in the shadows unbeknownst to the government of Taiwan… Or some version of Deep State?"

The president eyed her suspiciously, and then asked her to again walk him through the chain of evidence.

"Well, there are two threads of evidence. One is the source of the computer virus. It was apparently written by a Chinese dissident hacker…"

"So says the Chinese Ministry of State Security. Their Gestapo," piped in the Director of CIA.

"Yes," Jane retorted. "That is true. But the point they make is credible. NSA had nothing on this hacker, because he has never attacked the US, but he has apparently been quite active in crossing the Great Firewall of China. So, we could not fingerprint the code, but they could."

"And the other?" POTUS pushed.

"The other is that there was an attempt on the life of an American engineer in Phoenix. The attempt was apparently foiled by the Chinese."

"Again, so says the Chinese MSS," added the Director of the FBI.

"True, but matching the evidence provided by our local police," Jane commented. "Evidence that the Chinese could not possibly have unless they were involved. Down to the circumspect details like the fact that the ammo used for the hit happens to match a caliber popular in China, and rare here."

The president waved her on to continue.

"And there are only two things that connect these threads. One is that said computer virus was used in the sabotage of the Arizona facility, and that said American engineer was the man who discovered and explained it. The only common factor between these is the act of sabotage in our facility. The other is that a certain Cliff Lingdao, a high-ranking Taiwanese secret service officer was the only connection that we know of, to both, the author of the virus and the hitman," Jane finished, placing file folders that contained the data—dated photographs with inscribed names of the individuals shown—in front of the president.

"Implying—simply by connecting the dots—that the sabotage was instigated by this Lingdao and therefore by extension, by Taiwan," concluded the president, while he examined the proffered evidence.

"For what it is worth, sir," Bart piped in, "if I may add a…personal judgment."

"Yes, Professor, of course," The president encouraged. He had known Bart while he was still at the State Department and was certainly familiar with his reputation as the 'China whisperer'.

"Mr. President, I am inclined to believe the Chinese because they really do not have a motive for a limited act such as the one that took place. At this stage, hurting the American semiconductor industry would have negative value for them. Especially hobbling a single facility. Makes no sense. The Taiwanese, on the other hand… The manufacturing facilities recently built in the US, and including the one that was attacked, would primarily hurt *their* businesses. If we were not making these chips ourselves, we would be buying them from Taiwan. So, they have a motive to handicap our capabilities. Now, there are two scenarios that one could imagine here. One is that it is all about protecting their business. Dollars and cents. However, in this day and age of chip shortages, I personally do not buy into that scenario. The other is that it is all about keeping us *dependent* on them to the point that we would be ready to go to war to protect our access to their chip manufacturing capabilities. Given that the sabotage that we experienced was very focused on one specific site—which happens to be intended for manufacturing of the kind of chips that are most strategic to us—I find that more credible. But as to *who* did it, I do not know. It may be the government, it may be the so-called Deep State, it may be a rogue group, or it may be some combination of those elements."

The president stared through the window at the Rose Garden for a long time, assimilating what he'd heard, and then swiveled back and scanned the faces of the people in the room…

"Well, then, goddamnit, let's find out. I want us—you," he said pointing to the Director of FBI, "to conduct an investigation to get to the bottom of this. In Taiwan. Or wherever the evidence leads us. No more suppositions and theories; I want facts—cold hard facts."

"Yes Sir."

"And meanwhile, let's put the other thing on hold," the president added, looking pointedly at the Secretary of Defense and Director of the CIA.

"Yes Mr. President!"

Post-Bout Party

t-0 + 40 months, Taiwan

Despite the difficulties that this caused, Jane and the Director of the FBI agreed that they should attend the full review of the investigation in-person, in Taiwan, rather than by phone or video. Following the president shelving the plans for retaliation pending the investigation, and since many of the remaining members of NSC were engaged with other issues, it fell mostly on the two of them to manage the follow-up. The Director of the FBI had to be there since it was essentially his investigation, and Jane, the National Security Adviser, had been tasked with managing the issue since the beginning and now wanted to see it through to the end.

In addition to the usual problems that international travel posed for busy high-level government officials, this particular trip raised some special challenges. It necessarily had to be a low-key affair for two reasons: one was that Mainland China tended to get quite stroppy whenever a high-ranking US government official visited the 'renegade province', to use their terminology, and she did not want to stir things up in a region that was already quite tense. And the other was that given the nature of their business, for once even the government of Taiwan wanted to keep their visit quiet. So, they did not get to stay, or to conduct their meetings, in venues reserved for formal events, such as the Shilin Residence, that would normally be used for hosting visiting dignitaries. Instead, they needed to find a local venue with all the necessary facilities, but that also provided them with a suitable level of discretion. They could not use The American Institute in Taiwan, which was the US Embassy in all but name, because their presence would have been registered by both, the press and the Mainland 'observers'. And the optics of the local dignitaries parading in an out of the facility while the US

Director of the FBI was visiting were bound to start rumors—understandably so. Similarly, they could not use a local hotel, even if it was fully equipped to cater to normal business needs, because these could not provide the level of discretion and security that people of their rank needed.

So, Jane's competent staff found, and rented the entire *Villa-32* facility for the duration of their stay. In addition to the spa, restaurant and suitably luxurious sleeping quarters that this high-end retreat offered, it also included convenient conference rooms and other business amenities that they needed. Furthermore, it was located in the right part of Taipei, with easy access to government ministries. Even with the chaotic Taipei traffic it was just twenty minutes to the Presidential Office Building. Yet, the site was also sufficiently private that potential 'witnesses' could be interviewed discreetly, without raising undue attention. And being a private compound that was surrounded by a seven-foot stone wall, it could be easily secured.

Accompanied by essential staff only, and lamenting the fact that they were not flying on Air Force One, they toughed out the hassles of traveling on commercial airlines and arrived in the evening. They were duly whisked off to the Villa, where they had a quick meal, followed by a few hours of sleep that they squeezed in between the calls and e-mails that had to be tended to.

Jane and the Director agreed that they should approach the session as a working meeting, rather than just a simple final review, so they started the next day quite early, partially due to jet lag, and partially because they wanted to give themselves time to accommodate extra interviews, should the information they gathered call for this.

Their de-facto hosts were the FBI Special Agent-in-Charge (SAC) and the Associate Deputy (AD) who were assigned to the case. These two senior functionaries had been stationed in Taipei since the probe was first launched in November, whereas all the other various specialists and auxiliary staff that were required for the investigation were flown in as needed. The four of them— Jane, the Director, and the two lead investigators—met for a private breakfast at the Villa.

"Madam," the Special Agent in Charge began in response to

Jane's question about the level of cooperation that they were receiving from local government officials, "all have been open and direct. I am sure that this has been helped along by the orders from on-high—the president herself, I believe—to give us full and unlimited cooperation. But frankly, I think that they have been so open and cooperative mostly because they know nothing. None of them have anything to hide."

Yes," the Associate Deputy added in support of his colleague, "the last two months of surgical digging have produced no real evidence of conspiracy. We looked under every rock and there are no traces of a paper trail or even a money trail that a normal government initiative, or even a rogue conspiracy, is bound to leave. No unusual bank activities, unexplained code names, unusual meetings, phone calls to unrecognized numbers, visits to government offices by unusual people... Nothing... Our opinion is that this is not because the local government is hiding something or because it is obfuscating, or because we did not have sufficient resources..."

"So, you don't think that the plot to sabotage our facilities originated here?" the Director of FBI prodded.

"Yes and no, sir. I cannot confirm the source," the Special Agent in Charge reacted, "but I do believe that there was a plot. I think that it was carried out by elements outside the government circles."

"What about Cliff Lingdao?" Jane asked.

"Commander Cliff Lingdao... We have accumulated quite a dossier on him. He has an impressive track record and there is no doubt that he was an agent of the Taiwanese NSB who often operated under cover. Our own spooks knew him well. This has been openly confirmed by our hosts. They have even shared his personal files with us. But there is no evidence that we could find to link him to any operation that was not fully condoned and authorized by his chain of command. No unexplained money, no absences, nothing. We turned his place upside down: nothing suspicious. We crawled through his finances: nothing. We interviewed many of his colleagues and collaborators, and every single interaction was mapped back to some legitimate, approved project. We could find nothing suspicious."

"Other than his death, of course," added the Associate Deputy. "He was unfortunately killed in a hit and run accident about six weeks ago... Just before we could interview him in person."

"Really?" Jane was shocked. "Really?" she repeated incredulously. "That has to be suspicious... Are hit-and-runs common here?"

"Well, hit and run accidents may not be rare here, per se. But the way this one happened *was* unusual. Time of day when there are no witnesses even in teeming Taipei, location where there are no CCTV cameras anywhere near, vehicle that left no traces behind it—not even a chip of paint—it all appears to be more like a well-planned assassination rather than a mere accident. So, his death does indicate that he was involved with something that was inconvenient to someone. What that something was, and who the someone may be, is conjecture... I personally do believe that he was involved in our plot, but I suspect that it will remain just that: a personal belief, not a proven fact," the SAC concluded.

"Okay, but this entire act of sabotage was very sophisticated. It feels like something perpetrated by a group rather than an individual. So, he could not have acted alone. And furthermore, I am told that it was clearly devised by someone who understood both, the semiconductor technology and the manufacturing facilities. Given what I have seen in all the reports, Cliff Lingdao does not fit the description. Any luck finding the *others*?" Jane prodded.

After breakfast and without breaking the thread of their conversation they moved to one of the conference rooms. The Associate Deputy Director hooked up his laptop to the projector and continued. "Excellent point about 'the others'... From one of the photographs that the Mainland Chinese gave us—the one where Lingdao met with the hacker—we traced the identity of the third person. This turned out to be a Dr. Argon Zhi." He projected a photograph of a man with graying hair, glasses, and a friendly smile. "We dug through his past and confirmed that in fact the two of them—Cliff and this Argon—were close friends and went to the same schools all the way up to college. Although back then, his friend's anglicized name was RG, not Argon. That name change was something that we did not immediately pick up, so he appeared in our databases as two separate individuals. After high school they split up: Cliff went to Tsing Hua to study Economics, and RG went to the National Taiwan University and earned a degree in Engineering. Cliff then joined the government here, and RG went to the States and got a PhD in Semiconductor Device Physics at Berkeley. Apparently, that is when RG became 'Argon'. Supposedly, he was tired of Americans confusing him with other Chinese people with a common last name like Zhi, so he picked a first name that was unique and easily distinguishable to Anglo-Saxons: Argon. We interviewed many of his classmates from the time at Berkeley, and the feedback was uniform: nice guy, friendly, intelligent, inquisitive, hard-working, not a party animal but not a recluse either... Graduated in 1992, returned to Taiwan and had a very successful career, mostly with FSMC. Topped out as a Senior Vice President of Strategic Business Development—whatever the hell that means..."

"So, Argon clearly had the background and the capability for that insider knowledge. He could very well be that 'other man'," interjected the Special Agent in Charge. "However, he does not fit any of our standard profiles. We could not find any elements in his past, or for that matter in his character, that would explain him harboring resentment against the US, or against the establishment, or anything like that. In fact, he *was* the establishment. Very successful. And judging from interviews with the people here who knew him, a very nice, thoughtful man. A family man..."

"So, you think that he *could have done* it, but had no reason to do it," observed the Director.

"Yes sir. And get this: he, too, was a victim of a hit and run accident—on the same night and with the same MO as the one that killed Cliff!"

"Really?" Jane exclaimed. "Surely that is more than a coincidence. That must be the proverbial smoking gun..."

"Yes ma'am. But that is it. By virtue of how they died, we do believe that these two men were responsible, or at least complicit, in something that merited such extreme action in someone's eyes. But that is all we have," the SAC concluded. "Again, what that 'something', and who that 'someone' was, is conjecture. We cannot trace either the hit-and-runs, or anyone beyond Cliff Lingdao and Argon Zhi, to a conspiracy to sabotage our facility. And, let us face it, they were implicated solely based on a couple of photographs provided by Mainland China, who, after all, is not an unbiased or a credible witness. Arguably, these two men were able and capable. But, equally arguably, based on the way the plot was executed, it must have involved more than just these two individuals, and we cannot find any traces of those. And we certainly cannot find anything that would link them to a conspiracy by the government of Taiwan."

"What about the third man in one of those pictures? The hacker?" Jane inquired.

"Ah, yes. You Wen Zhao. Born and raised in Hong Kong. Came to Taiwan in 2020 following the troubles there. He also disappeared. Not even a body. Nothing..."

"Really?" Jane questioned. "C'mon!"

"But," the SAC raised his finger and continued, "by all accounts, he was very anti-Mainland China and quite pro-USA, so his background does not fit someone who would knowingly sabotage a US facility. In fact, the local intelligence people believe that his disappearance is most likely the doing of the Mainland secret service. It has their fingerprints all over it. Probably absconded and whisked off to the Mainland. We have seen cases like that. I would not be surprised if he surfaces there in a few months, ready to confess to all sorts of anti-government sins. Or, more likely, he is just 'vanished.'"

"All this sounds too much like a conspiracy not to be one," Jane assessed. "All three of the men who may have been involved, have disappeared?"

"Yes ma'am," SAC confirmed, nodding his agreement with her conclusion. "All three are dead or presumed dead."

"What about the guy from the Philippines. Anything there?" the Director asked.

"Well, sir, as you know, he is also dead. Killed in the US. The report provided by the CIA station in Manilla is still the best source of information on him. Professional soldier with the Philippine army. Completed the full twenty-year stint. Distinguished service. Single. No living close family. Blah blah blah... Evidently, after leaving the army, this Mr. Enchong Dee was a security consultant and a gun for hire, but, supposedly, with links to Mainland China, not Taiwan. Other than that single photograph of Cliff Lingdao and him together—again provided solely by the Peoples Republic—there is nothing that links him to Taiwan, or to a plot that originated in Taiwan. In fact, if anything, there are credible sources that connect him with the Mainland. He is known to have travelled there several times, ostensibly to visit his father's family. Apparently, he has several distant cousins living in Fujian province. In addition, the ground-level rumor mill in the Philippines suggests that he has done some contract work for the Chinese. But again, nothing substantiated, just 'he-said-she-said' gossip among the professionals in the business. Even the money that appeared in his account a few days before he left for the US seems to have originated in the Mainland…" the Associate Deputy responded.

"So… The operative word here is 'dead-end'," Jane summed up. The others nodded in agreement.

And that conclusion was neither affected nor changed by the ensuing meetings and interviews with people who had known and had worked with Cliff Lingdao and Argon Zhi. Both men had been respected members of the community, men who were adored by their families, capable professionals who were by all accounts very good at what they did… Possibly capable of mounting an act of sabotage against a semiconductor facility some seven thousand miles away. With zero proof and no trace of anything that could be used to elevate this theory past the level of 'belief' or 'possibility'. They had even interviewed Jason Wong, the acting Minister of National Defense, who readily admitted that General Chiu Kung-pow, his predecessor, was fired by the president not because there was any evidence of his complicity in a conspiracy, but because 'it'—whatever that may have been—happened *on his watch*. Both FBI men confirmed this.

Shaking her head, Jane lamented, "POTUS will not be pleased."

Epilogue

Formosa English News

INDEPENDENT NEWS IN A FREE AND DEMOCRATIC NATION

<u>Tue, Dec 19</u>

According to the World Health Organization and the World Bank, every year about 20 to 50 million people are injured in road accidents, and as many as 1.2 million people are killed. Every year! That's more than 3,000 people dying daily, most of them kids, the elderly, and cyclists. These figures are set to increase by more than 50 percent over the next 20 years. If nothing changes...

For perspective, globally there are something like 80 shark attacks a year, but fatalities are rare. Iraq led the world in terms of terrorist attacks in 2016, with 9,764 fatalities in that year, nearly twice as many as second-place Afghanistan. There have been as many diagnoses of AIDS in the United States since the epidemic began in the early 1980s as there are road traffic deaths or injuries <u>in a single year</u>.

It looks like the good citizens of Taiwan are doing their share and are contributing to these macabre statistics. Last night alone, we had not one, but two, incidents just in the Northern Province.

The police are investigating a fatal hit and run 'accident' in Hsinchu. They were called to the scene of an incident on Zhongshan Road, Section 3, at around 8:00 pm yesterday, to find a 64-year-old man, later identified as <u>Argon Zhi</u>, with no vital signs. Mr. Zhi was rushed to the nearest hospital, but he did not respond to the resuscitation efforts and was later declared dead. Witnesses said that the victim was just walking on the sidewalk when a black car seemed to swerve out of control, hit the man, and then take off towards the nearby highway exit. The passersby could not identify the make and model of the car, and miraculously, none of the road cameras or other CCTV systems in the area imaged that particular section of the road.

A similar and presumably unrelated incident has taken place less than 100km away, in Shilin District in Taipei, where police are investigating a fatal accident involving a <u>Mr. Cliff Lingdao</u>, aged 65. The circumstances were eerily similar, and, according to a witness, the car just took off. The police are also treating this incident as a hit-and-run event.

We, the editorial staff at Formosa English News are outraged by the thought that there are citizens amongst us who are so cavalier about human life that they seem to think that driving like madmen on city streets is acceptable – presumably to save a few minutes in their, oh so very busy schedules. And worse, when there is an accident, they do not even bother to stop to help the victim and take responsibility. For Shame!

Our sympathies go to the victims' families.

NORTH 被 侯 TIMES

Minister of National Defense Resigns post
Fri, Jan 19th Taipei

General Chiu Kung-pow, the Minister of National Defense, has tended his resignation, effective immediately. The surprise announcement came at 20:00 yesterday evening, and was accompanied with a terse statement that said that 'certain personal issues' have come up that made it impossible for him to continue to serve.

His deputy, Mr. Jason Wang, will assume the responsibilities of the office until President Tsai Ing-wen appoints a successor.

Prior to his appointment as the Minister of National Defense (March 2021) General Chiu Kung-pow was the Director-General of the National Security Bureau. He has also served several governments, first as Minister of the Veterans Affairs and then as a Minister of National Defense for Armaments. Mr. Chiu Kung-pow is a professional soldier who has served the Army of the Republic of China since 1978, rising through a series of ranks all the way up to a 3-star General. He has held the post of the Chief of General Staff from 2008 to 2010.

Chiu graduated from the United States Army War College in 1995 and was inducted into the school's International Fellows Hall of Fame in 2016. He was born in Taipei, Taiwan, 1st April 1956.

El.Int Announces Retirement of Dr. Cedric Dyson

After 47 years in the industry, Dr. Cedric Dyson, El.Int Fellow, and the head of the Physical and Failure analyses Lab at Fab-8, in Chandler, Arizona, has decided to spend more time with his lovely vintage 1964 Jaguar E-Type, and has therefore opted to shut off his Scanning Electron Microscope for good.

Cedric Dyson was born in Salford, in Britain, in 1954 and has earned his first degree at the University of Manchester, UK and his PhD at University of Illinois, Urbana. He has blazed his way through the industry and left his mark on many a company, authoring and/or co-authoring over 100 technical papers and filing 27 patents. It is possible that it is his telltale carrottop and his inimitable accent that he brought from motherland that have earned him the moniker 'Sherlock', or perhaps he has been so dubbed because of the countless cases of bugs and failures that he solved. It would not be an exaggeration to say that there are many IC products that would not have been the successes that they were without his contribution.

Learn More

His presence – the energy and enthusiasm that he brings to everything that he touches – will be missed by all. His staff, his colleagues, and his many friends wish him the best.

Jane Stewart, first female National Security Adviser, Resigns

By <u>Cokie Roberts</u>   June 1st

Jane Stewart, the 28th National Security Adviser to the President of the United States, and the first woman to hold the office, has tended her resignation, effective as of June 10th. She is rumored to be joining the Committee to Elect Amy Krstic and is believed to be slated for a cabinet spot, most likely as the next Secretary of State, should the Democrats' campaign be successful.

The polls indicate that Amy Krstic is all but guaranteed to win, with the GOP fragmented into two warring factions and the diehard Republican voters dispirited by the recent news that as a part of a Nolo Contendere plea to the multiple legal actions against him, Paja Bozos has pled insanity and incontinence, and as such is barred from holding any public office.

But there are still five months to go to the polling day, and as they say, this is a long time in politics.

The Milkweed

Georgetown University Gazette since 1920

June Issue

Professor Bartholomew Harriman, known just as 'Bart' to all who were lucky enough to know him, has announced that he is hanging up his professorial robes for good, and that this was the very last semester that he would be teaching. He has been with the University only since 2016, but his profound and intimate knowledge of the world and the history of international relations that he has honed through a four-decade career with the State Department, has been an asset to the University and to all of his students.

His insights, his humor, his wisdom, and his care for the individuals he interacted with will be missed.

We look forward to the book that he will be undoubtedly writing, and we are sure that it will not only be part of the curriculum here as soon as it is published, but will also be 'required reading' for any aspiring diplomat.

Suggested title: *The Memoirs of a China Whisperer* ...

Author's Notes

Ch 1: t-0 = November of an Election Year, Washington DC

1. National Security Adviser: A senior official who serves as the principal advisor to the President of the United States on all national security issues. National Security Advisor is appointed by the President, does not require confirmation by the United States Senate, and usually participates (and often chairs) the National Security Council and Homeland Security Council meetings.

2. First woman National Security Advisor: Condoleezza Rice served as the 20th National Security Adviser (2001 to 2005), and as the 66th United States secretary of state (2005 to 2009), both during G.W. Bush administrations.

3. Foggy Bottom: One of the oldest neighborhoods in Washington, D.C., and, home to, and an informal name for the United States Department of State, since the late 1940's when it moved its headquarters to the area.

4. Containment Policy: A geopolitical strategic foreign policy, adopted by the United States and its allies, to prevent the spread of communism. Following WW2 the tensions with Soviet Union ramped up (Cold war), mostly due to ideological differences, but also due to Soviet takeover of much of Eastern Europe and the perceived threat of expansion. The concerns were amplified after the Russians demonstrated their A-Bomb (1949). The US explored and debated three broad strategic options (Isolationism, Détente and Rollback) and ended up selecting 'containment' which

was a middle-ground position between detente and rollback and relied on use of proxy wars (Korea, Vietnam, Afghanistan-1..). Containment policy predicted that without an existential threat, the Soviet Union would eventually implode.

5. The "X Article": An article published in 1947 in *Foreign Affairs* magazine, that was formally titled "The Sources of Soviet Conduct", written by George Kennan, but under the pseudonym "X". The article proposed a strategy for avoiding direct military confrontation with the Soviet Union, and was the foundation of the 'containment' policy, which was followed by the US, in one form or another, until the fall of USSR in 1989.

6. Wise Men: The containment policy was embraced in various forms by multiple presidencies through the ensuing 4 decades. It was nurtured and shepherded by influential East Coast foreign policy establishment, consisting of a group of five historic individuals, referred to as 'the Wise Men' (after an eponymous book).

7. Averell Harriman (1891 – 1986): An American Democratic politician, businessman, and a diplomat. The son of railroad baron, he held various positions in FDR, Truman and Kennedy administrations, and was a core member of the group of foreign policy elders known as "The Wise Men". He was also a candidate for the Democratic presidential nomination in 1952 and 1956.

8. Open-Door Policy: A term broadly used to describe the policy that transformed China from a poor 3rd world country of Mao's era, to its current status as a major economic power. Following the end of Chinese Civil War (1949), and especially after the Korean War (1952), the US pursued a policy of total isolation towards Mao's Communist China. But, motivated by desire to gain more leverage in relations with the Soviet Union – which was perceived as the primary threat – the US embraced a strategic policy shift which culminated with President Richard Nixon's visit to the People's Republic of China In 1972. After Mao Zedong's death

in 1976, Deng Xiaoping, became the paramount leader of the People's Republic of China (PRC), serving from 1978 to 1989. He believed that in order to modernize its economy after the massive failures of Maoist industrial policies, China needed foreign direct investment. Hence, in 1980 Special Economic Zones (SEZ) were set up to attract foreign capital – first in Guangdong and Fujan Provinces, and then (1984) in another 14 coastal cities. As of 1988 most of Mainland China has invited outside investments, resulting in its becoming 'The World's Factory'. China became a full member of the World Trade Organization (WTO) in 2001, pretty much normalizing its economic relationship with the rest of the world.

9. Export Compliance: The US was supportive of the Open-Door policy and encouraged investment in China, choosing to control the trade through existing Export Laws (dating back to 1940's) which restricted access to controlled information, goods, and technology for reasons of national security or protection of trade secrets. A number of countries have been placed (and/or removed) on the so-called List of Countries of Concern, including Afghanistan, Belarus, Burma (Myanmar), China, Congo, Cuba, Cyprus, Eritrea, Fiji, Haiti, Iran, Iraq, Ivory Coast, Lebanon, Liberia, Libya, North Korea, Palestinian Authority / Hamas, Somalia, Sri Lanka, Sudan, Syria, Vietnam, Venezuela, Yemen, and Zimbabwe.

10. CPC (Communist Party of China): The founding and sole governing political party of the People's Republic of China

11. SOE (State Owned Enterprise): A company created by, and wholly or partially owned by a government, in order to pursue specific commercial activities of a country. SOE's account for about 30% of GDP, and approximately 40% of net profits of Chinese economy

12. Han Chinese: An East Asian ethnic group commonly referred to just as 'Chinese'. They speak seven different dialects (Mandarin, Wu, Xiang, Gan, Min, Cantonese, Hakka) that are not necessarily mutually understandable, but share

a common alphabet. Historically, they were native to the Yellow River Basin region, and now constitute about 92% of the population of People's Republic of China, about 97% of the Taiwanese, 75% of Singaporean, and an average of around 5% of Southeast Asian populations.

13. Guns before Butter: A shorthand term used to describe a government's dilemma over how to allocate funds, referring to an ongoing debate over whether resources should be used to build up the military, or should they be spent on domestic programs.

14. Hong Kong Democracy Movement and Crackdown: In 1997, Britain handed Hong Kong back to China with an agreement that allowed the region considerable political autonomy under a framework known as "one country, two systems." In recent years, Beijing has cracked down on Hong Kong's freedoms, and in the wake of massive street protests it imposed a national security law that gave it broad powers to silence dissenters, thereby violating the agreement and making Hong Kong more like the rest of Mainland China.

15. South China Sea conflicts: People's Republic of China claims a major part of the South China Sea, as defined by their so called 'nine-dash-line' map. Vietnam, Philippines, Indonesia, Malaysia and Taiwan have many competing claims in the area. The United Nations Convention on the Law of the Sea (UNCLOS) has ruled that the Chinese claim is unlawful but low-level run-ins continue and China persists in building fortified islands in the region.

16. The Ugly American: A 1958 political novel by Eugene Burdick and William Lederer that depicts the failures of the U.S. diplomatic corps in Southeast Asia. It has become a term to describe the arrogant American attitudes that are insensitive to the local culture in foreign countries

17. US dependence on Taiwan: Taiwan has been extremely successful in first championing, and then dominating, several critical portions of the semiconductor supply chain, so that

currently modern US digital economy would be entirely impossible without Taiwan. Taiwanese 'pure play foundries' control about 70% of the global capacity for this kind of semiconductor manufacturing services (this excludes manufacturing capacity for memory chips and standard products like CPU's) . Contract Manufacturing Services (i.e. foundry services) are used by all producers of 'application specific' electronic systems, including Apple, Facebook, Google, Microsoft, etc., as well as by many of the US 'fabless' chip manufacturers, including Qualcomm, nVidia, AMD, etc.

18. 7th Fleet: The largest of the U.S. Navy's fleets, including roughly 60-70 ships and submarines, 300 aircraft, and approximately 40,000 Sailors. As such, it in itself, is a regional power that operates in Indo-Pacific region that includes four largest foreign militaries (China, Russia, India, North Korea) and five regional allies (Philippines, Australia, South Korea, Japan, Thailand).

19. Semiconductor: A class of materials, such as Silicon, Germanium or Gallium Arsenide, characterized by electrical properties that fall between insulators (e.g. glass or ceramic) and conductors (e.g. metals) and that make it suitable for manufacturing Integrated Circuits, solar cells and any other modern electronic device. Some key terms and definitions:

- **Silicon:** A semiconductor element with the symbol Si and atomic number 14.

- **Silicon Wafer** (also a slice or substrate): a thin slice of pure crystalline silicon (Si), used as the substrate for fabrication of integrated circuits.

- **Transistor**: A device composed of semiconductor material usually with three terminals for connection to an external circuit. A transistor can be used to amplify an analog signal or as a binary switch to represent the 0 or 1 value in digital circuits.

- **Integrated Circuit** (IC): A set of electronic circuits, that typically interconnects millions or even billions of transistors, on one small flat piece of semiconductor material – normally called a 'chip' or a 'die'.

- **Fab** (or Foundry): A semiconductor fabrication plant, i.e. a factory where integrated circuits are manufactured.

- **Photomask**: An opaque glass plate with transparent regions that allow light to shine through to transfer a defined pattern onto the Si wafer in a process called photolithography – a key step in the production of ICs

- **System (or Chip) Architecture**: Definition of the fundamental structure, goals, and principles of an electronic product, addressing the key value propositions and taking in account most high-level tradeoffs.

- **IC Design**: A procedure involving many hierarchical steps that translate the product Architecture into a specific IC layout. Note that modern ICs are enormously complicated – e.g. an average laptop or smartphone processor chip has well over 10 billion transistors. Hence automated CAD design tools have to be used.

- **IC Packaging**: final stage of semiconductor device fabrication, in which a silicon chip is encapsulated in a supporting case that prevents physical damage. The case, known as a "package", also supports the electrical contacts which connect the device to a circuit board.

- **OSAT** (Outsourced Semiconductor Assembly and Test): Companies that offer third-party IC-packaging and test services. Like foundries but for assembly services rather than for Si wafer manufacturing services.

Ch 2: t-0 + 7 months, Washington DC

1. US Government funding for semiconductors: Following a concerted push by the Biden Administration, US Senate approved $52B for Semiconductor Chip R&D in 2021. This allocation was intended to be a part of a larger ($280B) package of support for US industry and the 'Creating Helpful

Incentives to Produce Semiconductors for America Act (the CHIPS Act) was finally passed by both the House and Senate with bipartisan support. President Joe Biden signed the bill into law on August 2022.

2. Other governments funding for Semiconductors: Korea, Peoples Republic of China, European Union, etc. have also pumped billions of dollars in subsidies and incentives for semiconductor technology and manufacturing capacity through 2021 and 2022.

3. JD (Juris Doctor) degree: A graduate-entry professional degree in law. Although, strictly speaking it is a graduate degree, in the United States J.D. is the standard minimum degree obtained to practice law.

4. Iron-Bru (iron brew): A Scottish carbonated soft drink, often described as 'Scotland's other national drink' (after whisky). The bright orange drink, with its unique flavor ascribed to ammonium ferric citrate, sugar, 32 added agents including caffeine and quinine and two synthetic food dyes, was first introduced in 1901 in Glasgow, Scotland. It has since become quite popular in Britain and many places around the world with sizable Scottish communities. Its marketing tagline used in adverts is: 'Made in Scotland from girders'

Ch 3: t-0 + 8 months, Hsinchu, Taiwan

1. Taiwan: An island nation of about 24million people, situated in the Pacific between Japan and Philippines, just east of Mainland China. An outline of the history of the island:

   - Pre 1544: Isolated islands populated by aboriginal tribes and iterant settlers from mainland China

   - 1544 – 1683: Partially colonized by various European interests (Portuguese, Dutch, Spanish) who all maintained outposts through to 19th century. Known as Formosa (means 'beautiful' island in Portuguese).

   - 1683 – 1895: Officially a part of Imperial China but

mostly peripheral to the country's attention span

- 1895 – 1945: Colonized and occupied by Japan

- 1949 – 1986: Republic of China, ruled by Chiang Kai-shek until his death in 1975, and his Kuomintang party exiled to Taiwan on losing the civil war to Mao Ze-dong's Communists.

- Post 1986: Taiwan has become a vibrant open multi-party democracy. The question of independence from Mainland China remains a contentious and an ongoing issue both internally and globally. The US has officially recognized Peoples Republic of China (Mainland) since 1979, but maintains very close political, economic and military relationships with Republic of China (Taiwan) and remains its protector.

2. Zhi: A common Chinese surname derived from the term for 'Wisdom', and one of the four virtues named in the traditional works. It stands for the ability to distinguish right from wrong in the actions of other people.

3. Lingdao: A Chinese surname derived from the term for 'Leader', often used in Chinese for an executive, a boss, or anyone's direct superior.

4. Fukuda: A well-known brand of Japanese custom handmade shoes by Yohei Fukuda. Pricing: $2,700 – $3,840

5. Akemi: Chinese girl's name meaning Bright or Beauty

6. Tai-tai: A Chinese colloquial term for a wealthy married woman. It is the same as the Cantonese title for a married woman and has similar euphemistic value as "lady" in English: sometimes flattery, sometimes subtle insult. Derived from word 'tai' meaning 'very' or 'main'...

7. ITRI (Industrial Technology Research Institute): A technology research and development institution headquartered in Hsinchu, Taiwan. Founded in 1973, ITRI has played a vital role in transforming Taiwan's industries into

innovation-driven behemoths. Its open lab and incubator policies have fostered emerging industries and startups including well-known names such as ASU, UMC and TSMC.

8. Siloviki: Literally translated as "people of force" or "strongmen" is a colloquial term for Russian politicians surrounding Vladimir Putin, who often were ex-officers of the former KGB, GRU, FSB, or other armed services. They are typically believed to be corrupt and people with a natural preference for the reemergence of a strong Russian state.

9. Degrees of Separation: A measure of social distance between people. You are one degree of separation away from everyone you know, two degrees away from everyone that they, in turn, know, and so on. Statistically there are only up to six degrees of separation between any two individuals on this planet.

10. Chiang Kai-shek (1887 – 1975): A Chinese Nationalist politician, revolutionary and military commander who served as the leader of the Republic of China between 1928 and 1975, first in Mainland China and then in Taiwan. Following WW2 and the Chinese Civil War, the US recognized him as the official leader of the legitimate post-imperial-Chinese government (Republic of China), which has been in exile in Taiwan since 1949. After his death, the US normalized the diplomatic relationships with Peoples Republic of China, and Taiwan adopted an open multi-party democratic system.

11. Foxconn, Asus, ASE, Mediatech: a set of the prestigious Taiwanese public companies in Electronics and Semiconductor industries

12. Fab (alt: wafer fab, silicon fab, foundry): Semiconductor manufacturing facility which turns bare wafers into 'chips' through a series of complex steps (usually referred to as 'the process') to define conductors, transistors, resistors, and other electronic components that comprise Integrated Circuits (IC).

13. Taiwan Arms Spending: The US has been a strong supporter of Taiwan even after normalization of relations with the

Peoples Republic of China. For example, just between FY17 and FY21, the U.S. government has approved 20 Foreign Military Sales cases for Taiwan, potentially worth an estimated $18.3 billion. While that includes packages of both F-16 aircraft and Abrams tanks, the majority of the cases have involved missiles, rocket launchers, sensors and artillery.

Ch 4: t-0 + 8 months, Hsinchu, Taiwan

1. NSB (National Security Bureau): The principal intelligence (including military intelligence) agency of the Republic of China (Taiwan).

2. Greater Green Snake (Ptyas Major): A type of a non-venomous snake that lives in humid forests and farmlands in Central/South China, Taiwan, North Vietnam, Laos and Bangladesh. When encountered, they are mild-mannered and rarely bite. They are bright green with greenish-yellow ventral scales, normally feed on earthworms, insect larvae, and other soft-bodied invertebrates and grow to about 1 meter in length.

Ch 5: t-0 + 13 months, Austin, TX

1. Dalit: People belonging to the lowest caste in India, sometimes characterized as "untouchables".

2. Coronation Street: A British soap opera shown since December 1960. The program centers around the residents of *Coronation Street*: a cobbled, terraced street in inner-city Salford (Manchester) and is noted for its kitchen sink realism, depicting down-to-earth, working-class community, combined with light-hearted humor and strong characters.

3. Poofter: A British term for a gay man—used as a term of abuse and disparagement. Offensive.

4. Navvy: A term, typically used in North England, to describe a manual laborer. The term was coined in the late 18th century in Great Britain, when numerous canals—sometimes known as "navigations"—were built, and has evolved firstly

to describe workers on large civil engineering projects, and subsequently any manual laborer. Slightly derogatory.

5. Woodbine: A British brand of cigarettes noted for its strong unfiltered taste and for being cheap. The brand was popular in the early 20th century with the working-class, as well as with army men during the First and Second World Wars

6. Chip butty: A buttered bread sandwich filled with French fries, optionally doused in brown sauce, ketchup, mayonnaise, or malt vinegar. The chip butty can be found in pubs in Britain and Ireland and is especially popular in Northern England.

7. Dallas, Dynasty, Knots Landing: American TV soap-opera-like dramas shown in Britain in late 1970s and 1980s.

8. FA: Failure Analyses – an engineering discipline and practice to determine cause of a failures of products or installations.

9. Mega-Fab: In common parlance the term means a very large semiconductor fabrication facility. Note that the term giga-fab, implying something much larger, has been trade-marked but with narrower definition.

Ch 6: t-0 + 9 months, Beipu, Taiwan

1. Chinese use of Western Names: People in China often have an English name (more so than in Japan or Korea). Western names are usually assigned at random, by for example, an English teacher in school, or are based on the meaning or the sound of a Chinese name or are even based on the name of favorite celebrity.

2. Straight-Line-Walk: One of President Teddy Roosevelt's pastimes was point-to-point cross-country hikes – whereby he would proceed in a straight line in a selected direction and go "over, under or through – but never around" all obstacles.

3. Guqin, Se, Zheng: Names of traditional Chinese zithers with 7, 25 and 16–26 strings, respectively, with movable bridges.

4. Laoshi: Term of respect for a teacher or an old master.

5. Nítuǐ: Peasant, yokel (literally: mud legs)

6. Semiconductor Manufacturing Facilities (Fabs): Modern ICs are manufactured in extremely large and complex factories. Note that building a fabrication facility capable of competitive manufacturing of leading-edge chips requires an investment of between $10B and $20B, and typically takes somewhere between 2 and 3 years to come on line. Such a facility is typically capable of producing between 30,000 and 50,000 wafers (300mm diameter) per month. These sites are a typically giant three floor constructions, with the fab itself (clean rooms and production machines) occupies the middle level, and the levels above and below it are there to furnish the necessary infrastructure. Some of the key utility requirements are:

   - **Water :** All fabs consume something of the order of <u>5 million liters of water per day</u> (equal to the daily requirements of ~30,000 people). The conversion of raw water to ultrahigh purity water, and its distribution throughout the fab, is very expensive and requires all sorts of specialized filtration to remove particulate, ionic, gaseous and bacterial contaminants.

   - **Gases**: A variety of gases – typically at least 99.999% pure—are used by a fab. This includes specialty gases (ammonia, methane, silane, dichlorosilane, silicon tetrachloride, phosphine, arsine…), corrosive gases (chlorine, fluorine, halocarbons, nitrogen trifluoride…) and atmospheric gasses (oxygen, hydrogen, nitrogen, helium…). Atmospheric gases are stored in cryogenic liquid storage tanks and are piped through the fab. Hazardous and specialty gases are usually stored in highly ventilated high-pressure cylinders close to the point of use.

   - **Exhaust Treatment:** The waste gasses produced in a fab contain many corrosive and/or toxic compounds that must be removed from the exhaust prior to release to the atmosphere. Specialized chemical scrubbing equipment, dedicated piping, and unique control valves are required.

- **Cleanroom Air**: Fab environments require ultra-clean conditions to ensure low particulate count (for Class 1 room: <1 particle that is <1um in size per cubic foot of air). To meet this requirement ultra-clean air is produced using advanced filters, and the air circulation is carefully managed (laminar flow from top, elevated flooring...)

- **Power**: Typical semiconductor fab uses about 300–400 kWh/day – as much power as about ~50,000 homes. This requires dedicated power delivery and suitable conditioning of power, plus sufficient back-up power sources.

- **Others**: Semiconductor fabs often include specialized features to dampen or even to isolate entire portions of the floorplan – not just specific equipment – from external vibrations, caused by people (trains, traffic...) or natural activities (water waves, earthquakes).

7. Pure Play Foundry: A business model popular in the microelectronics industry, where one company invests in a semiconductor manufacturing facility, develops the manufacturing technologies, and then sells semiconductor wafer manufacturing services to other companies. Pure Play Foundries do not have an IC product of their own.

8. IDM (Integrated Device Manufacturer): A type of a semiconductor company that manufactures its own IC products and has its own internal fabs that run its own proprietary manufacturing process (vs. pure-play-foundry: fabless multi company arrangement). Examples of IDMs: Intel, Samsung, Texas Instruments...

9. Chip Yield: Ratio of number of good product units coming out of a manufacturing line to the number of units started, and a key metric of fab efficiency. For IC's, Yield is measured at several key junctures in the manufacturing flow.

- **Wafer Yield:** Number of whole wafers coming out of the fab relative to the number of wafer-starts. Loss could be due to 'in-line scrap' (wafer breakage or chipping, misprocessing, physical damage, etc.), or 'end-of-line scrap' (unacceptable parametric characteristics (resistance, conductance, capacitance...) measured on special test structures placed in the scribe lanes between the die). In a fab line that is well controlled and running a stable process, this is typically in the ninetieth percentiles.

- **Die Yield (alt. SORT or PROBE or MAP Yield):** Number of good die per wafer relative to the gross die per wafer, measured by testing basic electrical characteristics on each product die. This is done by lowering tiny probes to connect with the pads on an IC and running a selected set of tests to identify the bad die. For a mature product this is of the order of 80% (function of die size), but it may vary and go down to ~0%. It is almost never 100%. This can be expressed as an average for a wafer, or a wafer lot, or the entire fab line.

- **Assembly Yield (alt Packaging Yield):** Number of good packages coming out of the assembly line. Loss could be due to 'in-line scrap' due to mechanical or cosmetic issues detected in line—such as missing balls, bent pins, incomplete plating, etc. This is typically in the high ninetieth percentiles.

- **Final Test Yield (alt. Product Yield) :** All IC's are tested prior to shipping to verify that each unit meets specifications. Final Test is a complex and comprehensive—albeit indirect—electrical evaluation. 'Digital' yield is assessed by verifying that all transistors on a die wiggle between 1 and 0 as expected. 'Parametric' yield is assessed by verifying that a selected subset of transistors meet the frequency, leakage current (current in OFF state) and drive current (Current in ON state) specifications. For a fully de-bugged product FT yield should be in the high ninetieth percentiles, but various

230

interactions can cause this to fluctuate.

10. Yield Learning Curve: A well-known concept where yield over time follows an S-Curve, with low yields in the beginning of a technology life, a period of rapidly rising yields as engineering learns from actual data, followed by stable high yields typical of a mature technology.

11. Moore's law: An empirical observation of a trend that the number of transistors in an integrated circuit (IC) doubles about every two years. Traditionally this was achieved through 'scaling' where in every generation of technology the linear dimensions of features are reduced by about 70%. Since smaller devices are also cheaper to manufacture (larger number of features can be packed per unit area), and have better power-performance characteristics (electrons don't have to travel as far), this scaling results in the exponential improvement in chip <u>cost-performance</u>, that has been experienced over the last 50 years (mid 1970's to now)

- Number of transistors per chip have gone up by 9 orders of magnitude (billion times)

- Frequency of operation has gone up by 3 orders of magnitude (thousand times faster)

- Cost per operation has gone down by 4 orders of magnitude (ten thousand times)

- Production has moved from 1" wafers to 12" wafers (hundred times larger)

12. Process (or Technology) Node: A term used to characterize a generation of a manufacturing technology. Historically, the process node name referred to the minimum critical dimensions allowed, but each generation of technology also included many other new features – such as the number of layers of interconnect or the operating voltage, etc. Moore's Law trend is often expressed in terms of a cadence of introduction of these new technology 'nodes'.

13. Sishen soup: A traditional Taiwanese dish prepared with a

mixture of herbs, pig stomach, and lean pork or pork spare-ribs that are simmered together in water or pork stock.

14. NT (New Taiwan dollar, symbol: NT$): The official currency of Taiwan, with an exchange rate of about 30 NT$ to one USD

Ch 7: t-0 + 13 months, Taipei, Taiwan

1. Snake Alley (also known as Huaxi Street Night Market): A market in Taipei that used to house snake-meat restaurants, which would get attention by putting on performances where handlers would kill and skin live snakes and sell specialty drinks (snake bile mixed with rice wine was considered to be an invigorating beverage, and snake blood was thought to be an aphrodisiac). The practice has been outlawed and the last live snake restaurant closed in 2018. The market now includes food stands that serve local snacks and traditional dishes.

2. The Great Firewall of China (aka Golden Shield Project): A combination of legislative actions, technologies and human censors that control domestic use of the Internet throughout Mainland China, as dictated by CPC regulators. It monitors the internet traffic and ensures that undesirable content is censored, and is respected as the most advanced and success-ful content-filtering Internet policy in the world

3. Digital Certificate: A digital signature that has been approved by a certification authority such as the makers of operating systems, web browsers, and major software (e.g. Microsoft, Adobe, Mac, Mozilla, Google, etc.). This means that the pro-vider has been verified to be a bona-fide supplier of software that can be downloaded safely.

4. Stuxnet: A name of a notorious computer virus. Stuxnet was the first instance of a cyberweapon that operated in the physical domain, i.e. doing more than just stealing data or harming host computers. First uncovered in 2010, it is wide-ly believed to have been built by the United States and Israel, to handicap Iran's nuclear ambitions. It was initially inject-ed onto internet via a USB stick, and then piggybacked on

Windows software to spread all over the world. It remained entirely <u>harmless</u> until it found itself in a network that was running a specific kind of software control system manufactured by specific vendor. When this target software was used to control electrical motors made by a specific company, the worm concluded that it was in Iran's Natanz facility which used high speed centrifuges to enrich Uranium, as required to make nuclear weapons. The worm then seized control of the system and in a delicate operation it desynchronized the centrifuges, causing nearly a thousand of them to seize up and self-destruct. The Natanz facility was subsequently shut down for a period of time, and Iran's attempt to build a nuclear weapon was delayed by what experts estimate to have been months or even years. Stuxnet has been programed to self-destruct by June 2012.

5. Duqu: A collection of computer malware thought to be related to the Stuxnet worm. Budapest University of Technology and Economics discovered the threat and gave it its name.

6. Mass Flow Controller (MFC): A device used to measure and control the flow of liquids and gases. MFC is typically a box that is about 5" x 3" x 1". All mass flow controllers have an inlet port, an outlet port, a mass flow sensor and a proportional control valve. There are literally thousands of MFC's in a semiconductor fab – both to manage the utilities (house gasses like O_2 or N_2, ultra-pure water, etc.), as well as for management of specialty gasses (NH_3, CH_4, SiH_4, GeH_4, SiH_2Cl_2, $SiCl_4$, PH_3, Cl, F, NF_3...) associated with specific pieces of equipment.

7. Quantum Dots (QDs): Semiconductor particles a few nanometers in size, that have unique optical and electronic properties that differ from bulk crystals.

Ch 8: t-0 + 13 months, Beijing, China

1. Apparatchik: A blindly devoted official or a devoted member of the Communist organization (from Russian 'apparat' meaning 'party machine')

2. MSS (Ministry of State Security): Civilian intelligence, security and secret police agency of the People's Republic of China, responsible for counterintelligence, foreign intelligence and political security – like a combination of CIA and FBI.

3. Hokkien: A southern Han language spoken widely in Taiwan and by the Chinese diaspora in Malaysia, Singapore, Indonesia, the Philippines and other parts of Southeast Asia.

4. 996 Work Culture: A work schedule practiced by some companies in the People's Republic of China. It derives its name from its requirement that employees work from 9:00 am to 9:00 pm, 6 days per week.

5. Hukou: A system of household registration used in Mainland China. Its connection to the social programs provided by the government – education, health care, pension and housing—creates a kind of a two-class system in industrial cities, where even after years, and even generations, of residence, millions of rural migrant workers are denied equal access to services available to the native urban population.

6. Sharp Eyes AI: Name of a Chinese population monitoring system, related to the mass surveillance systems Skynet, which combines powerful facial recognition and big data with Artificial Intelligence. China is believed to have a significant technological lead with AI Technology in general, and this type of AI, in particular.

7. Social Credit System: A system under development in China, intended to include data such as for example paying taxes and bills on time, as an extension of the financial credit rating system. The goal is to monitor and rate citizens' (and businesses') "trustworthiness", and to eventually track social behavior of the people

Ch 9: t-0 + 13 months, Chandler, AZ

1. Hong Kong LegCo (Legislative Council): The legislature of the Hong Kong. It was first established as an advisory council to the colonial Governor, but as of 1997 it has become

the principal and only democratically elected body that was intended to ensure Hong Kong's special status within PRC.

2. Hong Kong National Security Law: A piece of legislation passed in 2020 by the Mainland government in the wake of intense street protests in Hong Kong. The law is seen as ending the democratic traditions of Hong Kong, as it entitles Mainland authorities to detain people suspected of acts of collusion with foreign organizations, and to require publishers to remove content.

3. IC Test: A procedure performed on every IC to separate the 'good' from the 'bad' chips. Typically, test is implemented first at wafer level (also called die sort or probe test), using a special 'prober' to make electrical connections to contact pads on the die, and then at package level (also called final test) using a special socket to connect to the pins of the package (which are connected internally to the pads on the die).

4. ATE (Automatic Test Equipment): A specialized system of computer-controlled instruments that is capable of: (a) providing the right stimulus on the input pins of an IC in order to put a given Device Under Test (DUT) through a series of predetermined states, and (b) of measuring the values observed on the output pins. Comparing the measured output to expected values then determines if a DUT is 'good' or 'bad'. Note that testing advanced ICs requires many millions of these 'predetermined states' (called 'vectors'), and that the corresponding high end ATE machines are expensive – of the order of several $M's each.

5. Test Center: A specialized facility, and often a separate company, that specializes in testing of IC's. In effect it is in business of acquiring a number of ATE machines and then renting them out. ATE machines are programable and so can be set up to test any given IC. Note that test time per single DUT can be of the order of minutes, so that testing of a million units (not an unusual volume for an IC) would literally take years on a single ATE machine.

6. Arizona Earthquake Activity: During 2020, Arizona experienced: 1 quake of magnitude 5.5, 19 quakes between 4.0 and 5.0, 256 quakes between 3.0 and 4.0, and 626 quakes between 2.0 and 3.0. There were also 2000 quakes below magnitude 2.0 which people don't normally feel.

7. Solindra: A US manufacturer of special thin film solar cells which was promoted as a leader in the Clean Energy sector, and which received $535 million in government loans under Obama's economic stimulus program. However, unable to compete with the conventional silicon solar cells the company filed for bankruptcy in 2011

Ch 10: t-0 + 16 months, Scottsdale, AZ

1. Taliesin West: Architect Frank Lloyd Wright's winter home and school in the desert that he used from 1937 until his death in 1959. Today it is the headquarters of the Frank Lloyd Wright Foundation.

Ch 11: t-0 + 15 months, Tainan, Taiwan

1. Micro solenoid valve: a miniature electrically controlled valve that uses a solenoid (an electric coil with a movable ferromagnetic plunger) to open/close a small orifice to control the flow of a given gas or liquid. These devices are ubiquitously used in various precision instruments, medical devices and all sorts of other applications.

2. PCB (Printed Circuit Board): A laminated sandwich structure of conductive and insulating layers – usually referred to as motherboards in the PC world – that are used to hold and interconnect electronic components and IC's.

Ch 12: t-0 + 16 months, Taipei, Taiwan

1. Dead Drop: A method used in espionage where a source leaves a physical object in a pre-agreed secret hiding spot and the recipient picks it up some time later, thereby avoiding a direct meeting between the source and the recipient.

2. National Tsing Hua University (NTHU): A research university in Taiwan. National Tsing Hua University was initially founded in Beijing in 1911, but during the Chinese Civil War many academics fled with the retreating Nationalist government to Taiwan, and in 1956 they (re)established National Tsing Hua University in Hsinchu, Taiwan. This institution is independent and distinct from the Tsinghua University in Beijing, which continued to operate in Mainland China and is now ranked as the 15th best university in the world.

3. Fire-and-Forget: A type of missile guidance system which does not require any control after launching. In general, this guidance approach relies on information about the target that is programmed into the missile just prior to launching.

4. Command guidance: A type of active missile guidance system in which a ground station or aircraft interactively steer the projectile to its target by radio control or even through a wire.

5. Xerox PARC (Palo Alto Research Center): A research and development institution set up in 1969 by Xerox as a separate company that was tasked with creating computer technology-related products. It has been profoundly successful and was credited to be at the heart of numerous revolutionary developments, including laser printing, Ethernet, the modern personal computer, graphical user interface, object-oriented programming, ubiquitous computing, electronic paper, amorphous silicon… and the computer mouse. Apple's Steven Jobs was inspired by things he saw at Xerox PARC and used many of its concepts in the design of Apple products.

Ch 15: t-0 + 20 months, Chandler, AZ

1. Cleanroom: An area in a semiconductor fab where the environmental conditions, including particulate contamination (dust, airborne organisms, vaporized particles…), are highly controlled. The standard of cleanliness is characterized in terms of the number of particles of a given size range per cubic foot (or cubic meter) of air. Class 1, corresponding to one particle >=0.5 um per cubic foot of air, is the current

standard requirement for semiconductor fabs.

2. Bunny Suit: A type of overalls worn on top of normal clothes in Cleanrooms to prevent contamination of the local environment. Normally the suit also incorporates gloves, boots, a hood, and face covers, and it looks a bit like a space suit. Note that putting on a bunny suit also involves various associated cleansing procedures, such as walking on a tacky floor, air showers, mouth rinses, etc. and typically takes around 15 minutes. A semiconductor grade bunny suit is dry cleaned after every single use and costs around $100 a pop.

3. Peace of Westphalia (1648): Treaties that ended the Thirty Years' War and the Eighty Years' War, and brought peace to the Holy Roman Empire, closing a calamitous period of European history that killed approximately eight million people.

4. Congress of Vienna (1815): A treaty signed at the end of the Napoleonic Wars (1803–1815), which were collectively responsible for between 3.5 and 6.5 million military and civilian deaths. This treaty shaped modern Europe and much of its history for the following century.

Ch 16: t-0 + 25 months, Chandler, AZ

1. IC Failure Analyses Techniques: Methods and tools necessary to image features as small as few nanometers, and to fingerprint traces of materials as minute as parts per billion, as required to determine the root cause of failures in modern IC's. Most common of these are:

   - **SEM (Scanning Electron Microscopy):** A type of microscope that scans a sample with a focused beam of electrons and collects the scattered electrons to produce a detailed image of the surface. Resolution >1 nm.

   - **EDX (Energy Dispersive X-ray Spectroscopy):** An analytical technique used for chemical characterization of a sample. It relies on an electron beam (as from a SEM) to excite the atoms, which then produce X-rays whose energy spectrum is characteristic for each and every element.

- **AES (Auger Electron Spectroscopy)** : A technique that utilizes a high-energy electron beam (a la SEM) to scan an area of a sample, and then analyses the energy of "Auger" electrons that are emitted from the top 3-10 nm of the sample surface (vs. EDX which interacts with sample atoms as deep as ~5000 nm from the surface).

- **TEM (Transmission Electron Microscopy):** A technique in which a beam of electrons is transmitted through an ultrathin section (less than 100 nm) of a specimen to form an image. The resolution is higher than that of an SEM, enabling the instrument to capture detail as small as a single column of atoms.

- **SIMS (Secondary Ion Mass Spectroscopy):** A technique used to analyze the composition of a surface (to depth of 1 or 2 nm) by bombarding a sample with a focused ion beam and analyzing mass-to-charge ratio of the ejected secondary ions which are characteristic for elemental, isotopic, or molecular compositions. SIMS is the most sensitive material analysis technique, with elemental detection limits ranging from parts per million to parts per billion.

- **FIB (Focused Ion Beam):** A technique used for imaging, analysis, deposition, and/or ablation of materials using a focused beam of ions (vs electrons). Ions are heavier than electrons and can be used to knock out atoms from the sample surface, either for analyses (as in SIMS) or for ablation of the sample (a la sand blaster)

- **AFM (Atomic Force Microscopy):** A type of scanning probe microscope, where the electrostatic and atomic interactions between a stylus and the surface of a sample is measured. The technique has a resolution on the order of fractions of a nanometer and can image the shape of a single atom

- **FTIR (Fourier Transformed Infrared Spectroscopy)** : A technique used to obtain the spectrum of absorption or emission of Infrared light by a test sample – which is characteristic for certain materials. The technique has both a high spatial resolution (the stimulating IR beam can be focused on a small area) and good spectral resolution (able to detect trace amounts of certain type of materials). Good for samples with large molecules.

- **SAM (Scanning Acoustic Microscopy):** A technique that analyzes the scattered, absorbed, reflected or transmitted portion of a sound 'beam' that is directed at a sample, to infer density and other mechanical characteristics (like a microscopic sonar). By scanning a sample the technique can be used to image sub-surface cracks and/or voids in the material, with spatial resolution of the order of 1 to 10 micrometers.

- **CT (X-ray Computed Tomography):** A technique that uses a rotating x-ray tube and a row of detectors to measure X-Ray absorption and to produce 3D cross-sectional images of the bulk of a sample with a spatial resolution of the order of micrometers. Like dental or chest X-Rays but in 3D

- **PEM (Photon Emission Microscopy):** A technique that detects photons emitted by transistors that are turned on and operating. The tool can map this signal and superimpose it on a picture of a sample. Resolution is limited to micrometers.

- **Deprocessing** (alt. delayering): Failure Analyses of an IC calls for successive removal of thin layers of material – like peeling an onion – to be able to see and access the areas below the surface of a chip. This is necessary to identify a defect that may be at any one of the ~50 layers that comprise an IC. In general, this is done by controlled etching of a sample using either 'wet' (chemicals) or 'dry' (plasma) techniques.

- **Ablation:** A tool like FIB can be used to ablate material in a very specific area – by sputtering material away (like microscopic sand blasting). This allows opening of 'peep holes' in one layer to enable seeing things on the underlying layer, while leaving everything else intact, so that the IC could still be operational.

2. Wafer Lot: Usually 20 or 25 silicon wafers are grouped into a 'lot' that moves through a fab line as a single manufacturing batch. Even though nowadays most of the process steps are performed one wafer at a time, and few of the ~1000 steps in the manufacturing flow are performed on the entire batch, maintaining 'lot' identity is an essential practice for moving and tracking wafers through the manufacturing line.

3. Failure Mode vs. Failure Mechanism: 'Mode' describes the behavior of a particular failure – usually in the electrical domain (open/short, functional fail, timing fail, etc…), while 'Mechanism' describes the physical cause of the failure (a metal bridge, a foreign particle, a misprocessing…)

4. FMEA (Failure Modes and Effects Analysis): A structured step-by-step methodology for identifying all possible failures in a design or in a manufacturing process, and then predicting the resultant failure modes. Originally begun in the 1940s by the U.S. military, it is an engineering practice for assessing the robustness of a product or a manufacturing process.

5. Buckingham Palace: The London residence and administrative headquarters of the monarch of the United Kingdom, has 775 rooms, including 19 State rooms, 52 Royal and guest bedrooms, 188 staff bedrooms, 92 offices and 78 bathrooms.

6. Qualcomm: A fabless American multinational corporation headquartered in San Diego, California that creates semiconductor chips, along with associated software and services, related to wireless technology found in every mobile phone.

Ch 17: t-0 + 28 months, Scottsdale, AZ – Part 1

1. FEOL: Front End of Line—a portion of the IC manufacturing process where transistors are defined – as opposed

to the Back End of the Line (BEOL) that is responsible for defining the metal interconnect. Altogether there are ~ 1000 process steps used in manufacturing of semiconductor wafers, which result in between 20 and 50 discrete layers that comprise an IC. FEOL process steps include a sequence of high temperature (~800C) steps required to form regions in the bulk of the semiconductor with very specific material properties. BEOL process steps include a sequence of depositions and etches required to define metal wires in order to connect individual transistors. Note that modern ICs typically require a stack of about 10 to 15 metal layers.

2. CMOS (Complementary Metal–Oxide–Semiconductor): A type of transistor design methodology, and a corresponding fabrication process that is commonly used in digital IC's such as microprocessors, microcontrollers, memory chips, etc..

3. nVidia: A fabless American multinational technology company that designs and markets graphics processing units (GPUs) for the gaming and professional markets, as well as system-on-a-chip units (SoCs) for the computing and automotive markets.

4. Git: A foolish or worthless person (mainly British)

5. Spectrometry: Any measurement method for analyzing a spectrum, i.e. a range of light waves, of radio waves, of energies, etc... (vs. Spectroscopy which is the general study of the spectrum)

6. SIMS: Secondary Ion Mass Spectrometry. a technique used to analyze the composition of solid surfaces & thin films by bombarding the surface with a focused beam of 'primary ions' and collecting and analyzing the ejected 'secondary ions'. The analyses uses Mass Spectrometry where an electric and a magnetic field is applied to modulate the flight path of the ions ejected from the sample surface. The flight arc of secondary ions is characteristic for a given ion mass/charge ratio, which in turn is characteristic for specific atomic and molecular species. Thus, SIMS can fingerprint the sample

under analysis. Note that the secondary ions come from the top 1 to 2 nm of the surface under analyses. If the bombardment with primary ions is continued, the surface of the sample under analyses is ablated, and the secondary ions come from the bottom of a microscopic crater. Thus, continued process can also produce a depth profile of the distribution of the constituent atomic species. Both the stimulation and the analyses portions of the technique are complex, so that SIMS instrument including the vacuum pumps, the primary ion gun, the electric and magnetic lenses, the detector, and the computer system used to control the entire process is a roomful of equipment that can easily cost > $1 million.

7. Ion Milling: A physical etching technique whereby ions are used to bombard a surface of a substrate to remove (or ablate) material—typically up to some desired depth.

8. Sputtering: A phenomenon in which microscopic particles of a solid material are ejected from a surface when this material is bombarded by high energetic particles—such as plasma or ion bombardment. It is a controlled version of Ion Milling.

9. Scratch and sniff: An encapsulation technology where a given aromatic chemical is surrounded by micro–encapsulated bubbles which can be rubbed off to release an aroma. It generally refers to stickers that have been treated with a fragrant coating such that when scratched, the coating releases an odor.

10. Heavy Metals: A fuzzy term for classification of certain metals, loosely based on their density (density of more than 5 g/cm3 is quoted as a criterion). Most lists classify these 23 metals as 'heavy metals': antimony, arsenic, bismuth, cadmium, cerium, chromium, cobalt, copper, gallium, gold, iron, lead, manganese, mercury, nickel, platinum, silver, tellurium, thallium, tin, uranium, vanadium, and zinc. However other lists include different groupings, i.e. it is not an exact term.

11. Carrier Lifetime: In semiconductors, electricity is conducted by electrons that have been excited out of their nominal energy state. Carrier lifetime is the average time it takes for these

excited electrons to fall back into their relaxed energy state (ranging typically between milliseconds and nanoseconds), and is a parameter that affects many semiconductor material properties and some device switching characteristics.

12. PTFE (Polytetrafluoroethylene): A synthetic fluoropolymer of tetrafluoroethylene, commonly known by its brand name 'Teflon', used for handling highly corrosive agents such as Hydrofluoric Acid (HF), which is known to attack normal glassware.

Ch 18: t-0 + 28 months, Scottsdale, AZ, – part 2

1. Wavelength of visible light: red ~ 0.65um, green ~ 0.55um, blue ~ 0.45um corresponding roughly to the minimum feature size in leading silicon technologies back in 1990.

2. Cerebral cortex: The outer layer of neural tissue of the cerebrum of the brain that is known to play a key role in attention, perception, awareness, thought, memory, language, and consciousness.

3. n-type & p-type semiconductor: Terms used to describe semiconductor material that has been intentionally 'doped' with impurities which result in an excess (n-type) or in a shortage (p-type) of electrons relatively to pure undoped material (sometimes referred to as 'intrinsic' material)

4. Grade 316 Stainless Steel: A high-grade type of stainless steel normally used for medical and scientific instrumentation.

5. Nickel-Cadmium batteries: A type of *rechargeable* batteries in common use before Metal Hydride and Lithium-Ion batteries became popular. They are still used in many heavy-duty applications that require low cost, reliable, high-power output with ability for rapid recharge with no risks of fire. They are made of thin plates of nickel oxy-hydroxide (anode) and cadmium (cathode) separated by a membrane containing the electrolyte (potassium-hydroxide) all rolled into a cylindrical shape.

6. Cadmium: A chemical element with the symbol Cd and atomic number 48. It is chemically similar to the other metals in group 12 (zinc, mercury) and occurs as a minor component in most zinc ores. For a long time, Cadmium was used as a corrosion-resistant plating on steel, and cadmium compounds are used as pigments, to color glass, to stabilize plastics, in some specialty solar cells, and in Ni-Cd batterie...

7. EDX (Energy Dispersive X-ray Spectroscopy): An analytical technique used for the elemental analysis of a sample. It relies on an electron beam to excite the atoms in the sample, which then emit X-rays whose energy is characteristic for each and every element.

8. Shite: Originally a Scottish & Irish word, now used in all of Britain in place of "shit", especially when suitable emphases is called for.

9. Dead Chuffed: A British term which means to feel very pleased or delighted about something

Ch 19: t-0 + 29 months, Chandler, AZ

1. Thermal Oxidation Furnace: A piece of equipment used in semiconductor manufacturing to grow a very fine layer of dielectric material, by oxidizing silicon wafer surface at high temperature and in a controlled environment. This is a large (12' tall) sophisticated piece of equipment that involves much more than a heater. Note that wafers are transported in a fab using robots and FOUP pods (Front Opening Universal Pod) which are special boxes that holds silicon wafers in a controlled environment and that enables easy robotic loading and unloading. The thermal oxidation process sequence typically involves the following steps.

   • The FOUP is loaded into a 'Wafer Handler Chamber' of the furnace and wafers are transferred by a robotic arm from FOUP to a quartz holder, commonly called a 'boat', that maintains a precise distance between the wafers.

   • In order to eliminate any potential for uncontrolled

oxide growth, the wafer handling compartment, the process tube and the FOUP are all filled with an inert gas (usually Ar).

- The quartz boat is then mounted on a mechanical elevator which lifts the load into a sealed quartz process tube. The tube is usually hot during the load step, but at some lower temperature (few 100s C).

- The temperature is then raised to process temperature, typically between 950 and 1250°C. Temperatures and temperature profiles within the furnace are precisely controlled, usually to within ±0.5°C from setpoint.

- Once the system has stabilized at the desired process temperature, the oxidant gas is introduced, and a dielectric layer is grown. For Silicon Dioxide dielectric the oxidant gas is usually high purity oxygen but a mixture of steam + oxygen can be used sometimes. For more advanced devices, complex sequence of materials may be introduced into the process...

- After a prescribed time, the, oxidant gas flow is shut off, the tube is purged with inert gas and the temperature of the system is lowered to the unload setpoint.

- The elevator then unloads the system by lowering the boat containing the wafers into the inert gas-filled wafer handling compartment. The load is allowed to cool to ambient temperature and the robotics transfer the processed wafers to the waiting FOUP pods.

2. Dimethylcadmium: A colorless liquid organometallic compound of cadmium with the formula $Cd(CH_3)_2$.

Ch 20: t-0 + 29 months, Chandler AZ and Washington DC

1. "This was their finest hour" was a speech delivered by Winston Churchill to the House of Commons of the United Kingdom in June 1940, intended to rally the national spirits in the wake of the fall of France and the Dunkirk evacuation.

2. Bletchley Park: Name of a place in Britain that housed a team of code breakers who cracked the code for the German 'Enigma' machine during WW2. The effort, and the team, have been glorified by the modern lore, but according to the official historians, the intelligence produced at Bletchley Park did shorten the war by two to four years.

3. The Enigma machine: A cipher device based on electromechanical rotors which scrambled the letters of the alphabet according to a specific code. It was in general use before WW2 to protect commercial and diplomatic communications. However, Nazi Germany also used it extensively for communication of military information during WW 2 and specifically, they used it to communicate plans for U-Boat attacks on allied shipping in the North Atlantic. In order to prevent the Germans from suspecting that the Enigma has been compromised, and hence to stop them from altering the system, great care was taken by the Allies over use of the Intelligence derived from breaking the Enigma code. The policy was that none of the Allies would base any action solely on a decrypt – unless there was also another source of the relevant Intelligence. The care with which Enigma-derived Intelligence was handled, together with Germany's unjustified faith in the machine's power, ensured that the breaking of the Enigma code remained a secret throughout the war.

Ch 21: t-0 + 29 months, Hsinchu, Taiwan

1. Actinic Patterned Mask Inspection system: A tool used to inspect advanced EUV masks for defects. It is special because it operates at the same wavelength (13.5nm) as the light used in the lithography process itself, such that it can detect defects that are important. The first equipment of this kind was made by Lasertec Corporation of Japan.

Ch 22: t-0 + 30 months, Scottsdale, AZ

1. T-CAD (Technology-Computer Aided Design): A specialized kind of electronic design automation tool that models

and simulates semiconductor device operation from the first principles. It models the movement of dopant atoms in silicon through manufacturing flow (such as diffusion and ion implantation) and/or exact profiles of features formed through plasma etching, etc. As such TCAD tools are capable of modelling the behavior of electrical devices based on fundamental physics. However, TCAD techniques can normally be applied to a few transistors at a time, and it is utterly impossible to model an entire IC with TCAD tools.

2. Charles Evans & Associates: A premiere independent commercial analytical service laboratory that specialized in SIMS analyses. It has been morphed through many mergers and acquisitions but is still a center of excellence.

Ch 23: t-0 + 31 months, Singapore and Taiwan

1. IPFA (IEEE International Symposium on the Physical and Failure Analysis of Integrated Circuits): A premier Asian conference focused on the fundamental understanding of failure mechanisms in conventional and new CMOS devices.

2. NDF (No Defect Found): A measure of FA lab solution rate (similar to police 'open' vs. 'solved' case rate). Since many failures in modern IC's are caused by some parametric effect (vs. a 'smoking-hole' that can be imaged), frequency of instances where no visible defect has been found is normally quite high.

3. Hawker Centre: A kind of an open-air food court popular in Singapore and Southeast Asia. They were originally built to provide a more sanitary alternative to mobile 'hawker carts' but have become something of a local cultural tradition. They typically contain many stalls that sell different varieties of affordable meals and provide areas with dedicated tables and chairs for diners.

4. Madam Secretary: An American political drama television series that ran on CBS for six seasons.

5. Left-Handers in China: According to the available statistics

the incidence of left-handedness in China is much lower than in the rest of the world: of the order of ~1% to 3% vs. what is accepted to be the norm in the world of about 10% of the population. It is believed that the reason for this is that a large part of early schooling in China is about learning how to write Chinese characters properly – and this involves following a prescribed order for brushstrokes: right to left, and top to bottom. Consequently, it was difficult to have an educated left hander. Thus, while the West has a long list of successful lefties like Leonardo Da Vinci and Bill Gates, China has none. Note that Chinese society isn't alone when it comes to forcing lefties to change. In parts of the Middle East, Africa and India, the left hand is considered unclean and cannot be used for handshaking, eating or accepting money.

Ch 24: t-0 + 32 months, Hsinchu, Taiwan

1. Premiere Conferences: There are many conferences and meetings that involve chip designers and semiconductor technologists, ranging from some local meeting of a few IEEE members to international events that involve 1000's of attendees. The most prominent events include:

   IRPS: International Reliability Physics Symposium – focused on IC reliability and physics of failure mechanisms.

   DAC: Design Automation Conference—focused on CAD tools and design techniques,

   VLSI: Symposium on VLSI Circuits—focused on process technology and design

   IEDM: International Electronic Device Meeting—focused on Device Physics and process technology.

2. Taoism: A Chinese 'wisdom' that is both a philosophy and a religion. It emphasizes doing what is natural and "going with the flow" in accordance with the Tao – a cosmic force which flows through all things and binds and releases them. The concept of the importance of a harmonious existence of balance fit well with the philosophy of Confucianism. Taoism

and Confucianism are aligned in their view of the innate goodness of human beings but differ in how to bring that goodness to the surface. Whereas Taoism encourages people to live with detachment and calm, resting in non-action and accepting the realities of the world, in practice it also teaches the same sorts of moral behavior as other religions, and the philosophy covers both ethics, (i.e., the personal values of an individual), and morality (i.e., the communal norms and social values). Taoism is a way of life practiced by many Chinese and Taiwanese people.

3. Tao Te Ching: Meaning "The Classic Way of Virtue", is a collection of poems and sayings about the true way to life of harmony and peace. It is attributed to Lao Tzu (c. 500 BCE) and serves as the basis of Taoism, which became an official religion in China as of Tang Dynasty circa 500 BCE.

Ch 25: t-0 + 33 months, Beijing, China

1. CIA Covert Ops: During the Cold War, CIA has been involved in a number of operations that were intended to affect political change in some foreign country. This ranged from simple funding of friendly political parties to covert operations with an aim to change a (unfriendly) regime. In such operations CIA had often partnered with local groups or militias. The most notable cases include,

   • Congo Coup d'Etat: After independence from Belgium in 1960 Congo was led by an elected government of Patrice Lumumba, who the CIA described as a 'classic communist'. The CIA encouraged and funded various mercenary groups and a rebellion by the army, which ousted and eventually executed Lumumba.

   • The Bay of Pigs: a failed landing operation on the southwestern coast of Cuba in 1961 by Cuban exiles who opposed Fidel Castro's Revolution. Covertly financed and directed by the CIA, the operation took place at the height of the Cold War and led to major shifts in international relations between Cuba, the US, and USSR.

- Iran–Contra affair: a scandal in the US where senior administration officials secretly facilitated the sale of arms to the government of the Islamic Republic of Iran, which was subject of an arms embargo. The administration hoped to use the proceeds of the arms sale to fund the 'Contras' – U.S.-backed and funded rebel groups that were opposed to the Marxist Sandinistas who came to power in Nicaragua in 1979.

2. Chinoy: A modern term currently used in Philippine English and Tagalog and other Philippines languages to refer to a person of Chinese descent born in the Philippines.

3. Fujian (alternately Fukien or Hokkien): a province on the southeastern coast of China.

4. G. Gordon Liddy: An ex-FBI agent who was the chief of the 'White House Plumbers' and who masterminded the 1972 burglary of the Democratic National Committee headquarters, which led to the Watergate scandal and the ultimate resignation of President Nixon. He steadfastly refused to testify and was convicted of conspiracy, burglary, and illegal wiretapping. After serving fifty-two months in federal prison he became notorious as an unrepentant operative involved with various bizarre cloak-and-dagger ops, a talk show host, and a name on the speakers circuit.

Ch 26: t-0 + 33 months, Scottsdale, AZ

1. Swagelok: A privately held international company, focusing on the manufacture of gas and fluid systems components, and best known for creating the Swagelok compression tube fitting commonly used for the connection of stainless-steel metal tubing used in semiconductor fabs for piping ultra-pure gasses and liquids.

Ch 27: t-0 + 33 months, Washington DC

1. DNI (Director of National Intelligence): A cabinet-level United States government official who serves as head of the

United States Intelligence Community and oversees the National Intelligence Programs. CIA, FBI and NSA are 'dotted
line' reports of the office of DNI

2. Mossad: The national intelligence agency of Israel responsible for intelligence collection, covert operations, and coun-
terterrorism. Its director answers directly and only to the
Prime Minister and its purpose, objectives, roles, missions,
powers or budget have not been defined in any law.

3. The National Intelligence Service (NIS), aka Korean Central
Intelligence Agency (KCIA): The chief intelligence agency
of South Korea.

4. Superior Orders: A plea in a court of law that a person should
not be considered guilty of committing actions that were ordered by a superior officer, in military or law enforcement
organizations. One of the most noted uses of this plea was
by the accused in the Nuremberg trials, such that it is often
also called the "Nuremberg defense". Historically, the plea of
superior orders has been met with inconsistent rulings.

5. National Security Council: A forum for informing and ad-
vising the president of the United States on issues pertaining
to national security and foreign policy decisions. NSC was
first formed under Harry S. Truman to manage the Cold War
tensions and to ensure coordination and concurrence among
the Army, Marine Corps, Navy, Air Force and other instruments of national security such as the CIA. In response to the
9/11 terrorist attack NSC structure was amended, and a cabinet-level position of Director of National Intelligence (DNI)
was created to oversee and coordinate the activities of the entire Intelligence Community including the CIA, FBI, NSA,
Homeland Security and all the other security organizations.

Ch 28: t-0 + 34 months, Kotor, Montenegro

1. Bareboat charter: An arrangement for hiring a boat that includes no crew or provisions.

2. Flag Q: A yellow flag flown when entering foreign ports

that signals to customs and immigration officials that you request clearance, according to the International Code. Ironically, the "Yellow Jack" signal flag was used to signify a vessel might be harboring a dangerous disease and needed to be quarantined (hence the "Q").

3. Wolf Warrior diplomacy: A name used in the western press to describe the aggressive style adopted by China under Xi Jinping's administration. The term was coined from a Rambo-style Chinese action film, Wolf Warrior 2, and contrasts to the 'keep a low profile' style used since Deng Xiaoping's administration.

Ch 29: t-0 + 34 months, Taipei, Taiwan

1. The Sinaloa Cartel: A large international drug trafficking and organized crime syndicate established in Mexico during the late 1980s. It is based in the city of Culiacán in Sinaloa state, with a notable presence in a number of regions across Latin America, as well as in cities across the U.S.

Ch 30: t-0 + 35 months, Beijing, China

1. UNOOSA (United Nations Office of Outer Space Affairs): Organ of the UN that manages the Outer Space Treaty, which defines the principles that govern the activities of states in the exploration and use of outer space, including the Moon and Other Celestial Bodies. It was enacted in 1967 and signed by 111 countries.

2. UNROLOS (United Nations Register of Objects Launched into Outer Space): A UN convention that requires countries to furnish the details about the orbit of each of their space objects. Convention on Registration of Objects Launched into Outer Space was adopted in 1974 and ratified by 71 states.

3. Genting Awards Alliance: An awards program for patrons of Genting Group casinos and integrated resorts, including their properties in the Americas, Australia, Malaysia, the Philippines, Singapore and the United Kingdom.

4. Macau: A city and a special administrative region of the People's Republic of China, often referred to as the "Las Vegas of the East". It is a major resort city and a top destination for gambling tourism with a gambling industry that is seven times larger than that of Las Vegas.

Ch 31: t-0 + 35 months, Washington DC

1. Entebbe: A counter-terrorist hostage-rescue mission carried out by commandos of the Israel Defense Forces (IDF) at Entebbe Airport in Uganda in 1976. An Air France airliner flying from Tel Aviv to Paris with 248 passengers had been hijacked and diverted to Uganda – which was, under Idi Amin's rule, favorably disposed towards Palestinian cause. The terrorists threatened that all (106) Israelis and non-Israeli Jews would be killed if 53 Palestinian and affiliated militants imprisoned in Israel were not freed. In response, the IDF flew four transport aircraft with 100 commandos over 2500 miles to Uganda, landed, stormed the airport hangar where the hostages were held, freed them and flew back to Israel (via Nairobi, Kenya). Of the 106 hostages, 102 were rescued and 3 were killed. 5 Israeli commandos were wounded, and 1 was killed. All the hijackers (7) and 45 Ugandan soldiers were killed, and 11 fighter jets (a quarter of Ugandan Air Force) were destroyed to prevent pursuit.

2. Rescue of hostages in Iran (Operation Eagle Claw): A United States Armed Forces operation ordered by U.S. President Jimmy Carter to attempt to rescue 52 staff held captive at the Embassy of the United States in Tehran in 1980. The operation, one of Delta Force's first, encountered many obstacles and failures and was subsequently aborted. The mission failed, with 8 US servicemen killed, 4 injured, 1 helicopter and 1 transport aircraft destroyed and five helicopters captured.

Ch 32: t-0 + 36 months, Washington DC

1. VCDR (Vienna Convention on Diplomatic Relations): An international treaty that defines a framework for diplomatic

relations between independent countries and codifies the longstanding custom of diplomatic immunity, including protection of privacy of communications – usually referred to as 'diplomatic pouch'

2. FN57: A semi-automatic pistol designed and manufactured by FN Herstal of Belgium, currently in service with military and police forces in over 40 nations and also apparently very popular with the Mexican cartels. It is known as a 'cop killer' because it can penetrate protective vests.

3. QBU-88: A Chinese marksman rifle developed by Norinco for the People's Liberation Army. It uses a 5.8×42 mm rimless bottlenecked cartridges. A '*bullpup,* version with a firing grip located <u>in front</u> of the breech, instead of behind it, allows for a lighter and shorter weapon that is more easily concealed.

Ch 33: t-0 + 37 months, Washington DC – part 1

1. National Intelligence Community: A collective name for 18 separate government organizations that are involved in intelligence work. A primary responsibility of DNI is to coordinate these diverse groups. The U.S. Intelligence Community is composed of the following 18 organizations,

Two independent agencies

- Office of the Director of National Intelligence (ODNI)

- **Central Intelligence Agency (CIA)**

Nine Department of Defense elements

- Defense Intelligence Agency (DIA),

- **National Security Agency (NSA),**

- National Geospatial Intelligence Agency (NGA),

- National Reconnaissance Office (NRO),

- U.S. Army Intelligence (G-2)

- U.S. Naval Intelligence

- U.S. Marine Corps Intelligence

- U.S. Air Force Intelligence,

- U.S. Space Force (USSF) Intelligence

Seven elements of other departments and agencies

- Department of Energy's Office of Intelligence

- Department of Homeland Security Intelligence

- U.S. Coast Guard Intelligence

- Department of Justice's **Federal Bureau of Investigation** (FBI)

- Drug Enforcement Agency (DEA) Office of Intelligence

- Department of State's Bureau of Intelligence and Research

- Department of the Treasury's Office of Intelligence and Analysis

2. FinFET: A type of non-planar, or "3D" transistor. It is the basis for modern nanoelectronic semiconductor devices and has been the dominant transistor architecture since 14 nm process node, introduced circa 2014.

3. IED (Improvised Explosive Device): A bomb constructed and deployed in ways other than in conventional military action.

4. Fab Fires: Fires in semiconductor fabs are not unusual, and modern fab infrastructure includes extensive state of the art fire-fighting mechanisms, which include not only water sprinklers but also systems for flushing rooms with inert gasses in order to avoid water damage of expensive equipment, etc. Notable recent instances:

- Renesas Electronics Corporation (Mar 2021) in the N3 Building of the Naka Factory. The fire was extinguished on the same day...

- Asahi Kasei Microdevices AKM (Oct 2020): reported

a massive fire factory based in Nobeoka City, Miyazaki Prefecture, that burned for three days

- Samsung (Mar 2020): reported a fire in Hwaseong plant situated to the south of Seoul, but the production was not affected.

- "Kioxia (nee Toshiba Memory) (Jan 2020): reported a fire in a fab that makes 3-4% of world's NAND memory. Cause of fire and the impact to production is "under review".

5. Silane: A collective name for chemicals based on a molecule of one central silicon atom with four attachments of any of a series of covalently bonded compounds containing silicon and hydrogen. Silane is a pyrophoric gas (capable of autoignition at temperatures below 54 °C /130 °F).

Ch 34: t-0 + 37 months, Beijing, China

1. Wang Dan: One of the most visible student leaders in the Tiananmen Square protests of 1989. He was sentenced to four years imprisonment, released on parole, and re-sentenced for repeat offences. He was eventually exiled to the United States. He holds a PhD in history from Harvard University and is still active in movements that promote freedom and democracy in China.

2. The Umbrella Movement: A political movement that emerged during the Hong Kong democracy protests of 2014. Its name arose from the use of umbrellas as a tool for passive resistance to the Hong Kong Police's use of pepper spray.

Ch 35: t-0 + 38 months, Washington DC – part 2

1. The Three Percenters: An American and Canadian far-right anti-government militia that advocates gun ownership rights and resistance to the U.S. federal government.

2. Oath Keepers: An American far-right anti-government militia whose members claim to be defending the Constitution of the United States. Most research estimates their membership

at approximately 5,000 people, with about two thirds being current or former military or law enforcement personnel.

3. Deep State: A clandestine network of actors in government, in high-level banking and in industry, that operates as a hidden power which exists in parallel with, or within, the legitimate government. Claims that such "deep state" exists are typically conspiracy theories.

Ch 36: February 2024, Taiwan

1. Shilin Official Residence: The former residence of late Republic of China President Chiang Kai-shek located in Taipei. It is used to host famous guests and foreign dignitaries.

2. American Institute in Taiwan: The de facto Embassy of the United States of America in Taiwan. The establishment of diplomatic relations with the People's Republic of China (PRC) in 1979 required acknowledgment of the "one-China policy" and subsequent termination of formal diplomatic relations with Taiwan. Since then, the AIT, a wholly owned subsidiary of the federal government of the United States, provides all the services normally performed by diplomatic missions. It is staffed by employees of the Department of State and receives full protection from the United States Marine Corps. AIT also has a consular branch in Kaohsiung.

3. Villa 32: A high-end luxury boutique hotel and spa located in Taipei.